Praise for
TEXAS BLUE

THE LONE TEXAN

continued . . .

"The Queen of Texas romance does it again, sweeping readers back to Whispering Mountain for another tale rife with drama, action, and passion. No one makes Texas seem more exciting, romantic, and alive than Thomas. Here's a surefire hit for Western fans to savor." —*Romantic Times* (★ ★ ★ ★ ↗)

TALL, DARK, AND TEXAN

"A gripping, emotional read . . . [I] was left wondering why I haven't read more historical romances set in the American West." —*All About Romance*

"Wonderfully written, romantic, and delightful."
—*The Romance Reader*

"An enjoyable read from start to finish. I read the book over the holidays and found myself stealing away at odd moments from the family in order to sneak in a chapter or two."
—*Reading Romance Books*

"I loved these characters. I cared about them throughout their hardships, and cheered for them when they found their happiness. Her descriptive passages are silky smooth, her dialogue is believable, and she puts the reader right in the middle of the open plains of Texas so you can almost hear the grass rustle in the wind." —*Ezine Articles*

WILD TEXAS ROSE

JODI THOMAS

BERKLEY BOOKS, NEW YORK

THE BERKLEY PUBLISHING GROUP
Published by the Penguin Group
Penguin Group (USA) Inc.
375 Hudson Street, New York, New York 10014, USA
Penguin Group (Canada), 90 Eglinton Avenue East, Suite 700, Toronto, Ontario M4P 2Y3, Canada
(a division of Pearson Penguin Canada Inc.) • Penguin Books Ltd., 80 Strand, London WC2R 0RL,
England • Penguin Group Ireland, 25 St. Stephen's Green, Dublin 2, Ireland (a division of Penguin
Books Ltd.) • Penguin Group (Australia), 250 Camberwell Road, Camberwell, Victoria 3124, Australia
(a division of Pearson Australia Group Pty. Ltd.) • Penguin Books India Pvt. Ltd., 11 Community
Centre, Panchsheel Park, New Delhi—110 017, India • Penguin Group (NZ), 67 Apollo Drive,
Rosedale, Auckland 0632, New Zealand (a division of Pearson New Zealand Ltd.) • Penguin Books
(South Africa) (Pty.) Ltd., 24 Sturdee Avenue, Rosebank, Johannesburg 2196, South Africa

Penguin Books Ltd., Registered Offices: 80 Strand, London WC2R 0RL, England

This is a work of fiction. Names, characters, places, and incidents either are the product of the author's
imagination or are used fictitiously, and any resemblance to actual persons, living or dead, business
establishments, events, or locales is entirely coincidental. The publisher does not have any control over
and does not assume any responsibility for author or third-party websites or their content.

WILD TEXAS ROSE

A Berkley Book / published by arrangement with the author

ISBN: 978-1-62090-285-1

BERKLEY®
Berkley Books are published by The Berkley Publishing Group,
a division of Penguin Group (USA) Inc.,
375 Hudson Street, New York, New York 10014.
BERKLEY® is a registered trademark of Penguin Group (USA) Inc.
The "B" design is a trademark of Penguin Group (USA) Inc.

PRINTED IN THE UNITED STATES OF AMERICA

PROLOGUE

1876
Texas

As the train pulled away from Anderson Glen Station and headed toward Fort Worth, Rose McMurray folded her gloved hands in her lap and tried to remain perfectly still. She knew she looked the part of a proper young woman, all starched and pressed from her navy traveling suit to her polished boots. No one saw inside her where fears threatened to choke even the shallow breaths she took.

I could do this. I could leave Whispering Mountain Ranch. I could go alone.

Cold January rain tapped on the coach windows drawing her attention, demanding she look out into the moonless night. No lights beyond offered even one last memory of all she knew and loved. The wheels of the train picked up speed, whispering "Beware" in rapid heartbeats.

Smoke rolled past her just beyond the glass, pulling a memory with the same sounds and smells of a nightmare that had haunted her since she'd left Chicago with her mother almost twenty years ago.

Rose couldn't remember why her mother had packed her and her two sisters up and run for the train that cold night, but even at five years old she'd known they were running for their lives. Something frightening followed them. Something far worse than the unknown they rushed toward.

"Emily, hold Rose's hand," their mother had ordered as she carried the baby on her back and a carpetbag atop a small trunk in her arms. "Hold tight, girls, until we're on the train. Then we'll be safe. We'll be away."

They moved into a river of people at the station. Everyone seemed to be yelling, running, pushing.

Smoke billowed across the platform as Rose saw her mother step onto the train and vanish. She heard Emily scream. Someone shoved them, scattering them as if the girls were no more than dust mites whirling in the frozen air.

Then her big sister let go of her hand and Rose was alone.

In one horrifying moment something shattered inside her, forever scarring across her heart like a razor sharp blade. She screamed and screamed until she felt like her ears were bleeding.

Even when she was safe back in her mother's arms, Rose couldn't be comforted. Fear still rocked her thin body.

Now, twenty years later, the memory returned full force like a north wind that had just been waiting around the corner. . . . waiting for a chance to catch her alone once more . . . waiting to frighten her to death.

She'd told herself she was an adult. She could travel through the night to help a friend in need. Only as her home and all those she loved grew farther and farther away, Rose wasn't sure.

What if she lost control of her world again and this time when fear claimed her, it wouldn't let go? Would the terror of the night kill her, or was there something more in the darkness waiting to do the job? Waiting unseen to cross out of her dreams.

She sat stone still, her hands clasped tightly in her lap, and counted the seconds until dawn.

CHAPTER 1

Friday, January 1876
Main Street, Fort Worth

SNOW WHIRLED IN THE COLD DAWN AIR AS THE TOWN
seemed to come alive like a sleeping giant who'd given up
bathing for the winter. Cook fires and coal smoke blended
amid the smell of garbage and too many people crammed
together. A good three-day rain wouldn't whitewash this
place enough to make it presentable, Rose McMurray
thought as she stepped from the rented carriage and fought
to keep from covering her mouth. She noticed shadows of
people scurrying like rats down the walks and wagons
fighting their way through the traffic. The movements of
horses and carts didn't frighten her; she'd survived the train
and the night.

"This is it, miss. The best hotel in town. The Grand," the
driver yelled, but didn't move to help her down. "Point the
doorman in my direction and I'll see he gets your luggage."

"Thank you," Rose managed to say, although she wasn't
sure for what. The ride was barely tolerable and she had no

doubt she could have handled the team with far more skill; after all, her family owned a horse ranch.

Reaching into her glove, she pulled out the amount they'd agreed on for the fare plus two bits for a tip.

When the driver took the money, he lost his grip on the horses, and the carriage jolted forward a few feet.

Rose tumbled off the step almost falling in the mud as she fought to keep her balance with a bag in one hand and her hat in the other. Her skirts snagged on the rough board of a carriage step, catching the lace of her petticoat between splinters and nails.

The driver held the team but offered no help.

Rose tugged on the lace as people swirled around her. Fear threatened to consume her as it had in the night.

Five, maybe six, steps and she could be inside the hotel. She'd be safe. She moved the bothersome hat to join her carpetbag, not daring to set either down in the street, but even with one free hand, the lace wouldn't give.

She hated traveling. No matter how well she planned, there was always the unexpected. Big towns like Fort Worth reminded her of her childhood years in Chicago. She remembered swearing she'd never go anywhere by herself, and with her huge family she'd thought she'd be able to keep that promise . . . until now.

She'd come alone, on a mission that made no sense. Yet she'd come, fighting down reason and fear because her friend had sent word that she needed Rose. After weighing the risk, an overnight train ride, and a dawn carriage ride to the hotel, she'd come to help.

Only she hadn't planned to be tethered to a carriage step in the middle of Main Street.

Glancing at the hotel door, she tugged again. She took a deep breath, reminding herself that this was in the middle of town and she was not facing down gunfighters or being lost in a stampede. The people almost bumping into her as they passed weren't even noticing her; they were only rushing to work.

The driver yelled, "Hurry up, lady, I ain't got all day."

Rose froze as several people turned her direction. Strangers were staring, some smiling, some laughing, a few looking as if they were sorry they didn't have time to stop and help. She felt like she'd been tossed in a river and was about to drown if she didn't act fast.

"May I be of assistance, miss?" a tall stranger in black asked in a tone that seemed more bothered than willing.

Rose detested even the thought that she might be in need of help. She was always the one people turned to on the ranch. "No thank you, sir," she said without really looking at him. With a firm jerk she felt the lace rip. "I can manage on my own."

The lace gave and she tumbled backward, finally free but off balance.

The tall stranger's arm went around her, breaking her fall before she hit the mud. "Careful now, miss," he said calmly as if her tumbling were an ordinary event in his day.

Rose straightened and pulled away. "I'm fine."

The stranger tipped his hat and grinned. "I can see that. My mistake to have even attempted aid."

As if by instinct, he offered his hand to assist her from the street to the walk, but Rose ignored it as she pulled her bag and hat close and rushed for the hotel entrance.

When she reached the huge double doors, she turned feeling obligated to thank him for his help.

Hard gray eyes stared at her a moment before he disappeared into the crowd. Winter eyes, as frosty as the day.

He'd been handsome in a cold kind of way and maybe a bit offended that she hadn't accepted his help or even thanked him. She was surprised to see such a gentleman in this wild, untamed town. In the menagerie of people, he didn't seem to fit in somehow. Too clean, too polished.

"May I take your bag?" The doorman reached for her luggage as he touched the brim of his hat.

Rose slipped her carpetbag to her other hand and frowned. "No, thank you, but I've a trunk you might pick up before the driver leaves."

The doorman nodded and waved his gloved hand toward

a younger man waiting in the corner. "Of course, miss. You'll be staying with us then?"

"I'm expected." Rose walked through the door he held open wide. "I'm with the Chamberlain wedding party."

The doorman raised an eyebrow. Rose wondered if he'd met the bride, Victoria Chamberlain, and pitied anyone arriving for her wedding. Tori, as Rose and her sister Emily called Victoria, was her own brand of complicated. She'd sent a telegram to Whispering Mountain twenty-four hours ago sounding near panic.

One week until the wedding and big problem. Come quickly. I may not live to wed.

Rose was the only one able, or maybe willing, among the McMurrays to answer the cry for help. She'd tried her best to talk everyone on the ranch into coming with her, but no one felt at twenty-five she needed a companion. Her father insisted she take extra cash. Her mother gave her advice and her best hat, and her uncle, the Texas Ranger, gave her a gun that fit nicely in a hidden pocket of her skirt. They all knew Tori and had decided years ago that Victoria's crying wolf was more a theme song to her life than any real alarm.

Rose started to question her judgment as she signed in at the desk while the doorman headed upstairs with her trunk. She couldn't help but wonder what Tori had gotten herself into now. At school, crisis followed her like an echo.

Though they'd been roommates in finishing school, she hadn't seen Victoria but once since graduation. Rose had been excited to bump into her in Austin at the Governor's Ball year before last. At twenty-three they might have been much changed from the girls of sixteen, but the friendship was still there. They'd chatted during the ball, loving the closeness between them that remained intact.

Rose remembered being surprised when few men asked Tori to dance. She'd even made her cousin Duncan dance with her friend, but neither looked like they enjoyed the one waltz.

It seemed Victoria Chamberlain, always a beauty, had become polished glass. Men admired her as though she were a painting and not a person. Her friend looked sad even while dressed in the newest fashions.

They parted that night, promising to write, and had every month since the ball, but Tori's letters grew formal, without the warmth Rose felt when they'd talked face-to-face. Something was wrong. Rose felt it in the letters. Tori was lonely, so lonely she may have rushed into first an engagement and now a marriage.

Rose had been shocked last month to get a wedding invitation. Tori claimed that since Rose was her closest friend, her husband-to-be, August Myers, had agreed to one bridesmaid and, of course, one wedding guest to attend with her. Tori went on to explain how they wanted to keep the wedding small.

So, here Rose was in the grandest hotel in Fort Worth a week before the wedding. Rose was a person of order. Emergencies bothered her. Worry seemed the constant side dish to her life, and with friends like Tori and cousins like Duncan McMurray, the servings were large.

The hotel clerk made Rose jump as he read her signature on the ledger and rushed around the desk. "You're Miss McMurray? The major told us to expect you early this morning. We have your rooms ready."

Exhaustion tightened her shoulders as she climbed the stairs. She hadn't slept on the train. If she calculated correctly, she'd been up twenty-seven hours. Maybe that would explain why she was so on edge. She was no longer a child; big cities and strangers shouldn't frighten her.

"Your suite of rooms is on the left, Miss McMurray, with a connecting door to Miss Chamberlain's suite off the sitting room." The clerk rushed ahead to unlock the door. "Miss Chamberlain's maid instructed me to tell you her mistress should be back by lunch. She's at fittings this morning, but the maid is pressing your bridesmaid's dress for your fitting this afternoon. She said she'd bring it up before Miss Chamberlain and her father, the major, get back." He leaned forward slightly as if whispering a secret. "All they've done since they arrived two days ago is shop."

Rose let out a long breath and felt the weight of the Colt in her pocket for the first time. It seemed Tori was in no immediate danger other than being gossiped about by the staff. If her father were with her, Tori couldn't be suffering any pain . . . other than being talked to death. The major's two favorite pastimes were spoiling his only child and rattling on about politics.

Rose almost laughed. She'd wasted hours trying to imagine what might be the problem that had prompted the telegram. Maybe it was nothing more than wedding jitters.

The clerk opened the door and waved her inside as if the small orderly rooms were a grand palace. "You see, you'll share a lovely sitting room facing our balcony. Your bedroom, a bathing chamber, and a maid's quarters are just beyond that door. The second-floor balconies on this side overlook the gardens and are considered our jewel among—"

"I'm sure I'll love them. Thank you." Rose smiled but closed the door giving him no more time to talk. All she wanted to do right now was wash up and sleep until lunch.

Tossing the hat on the arm of the nearest chair, she removed her traveling coat as she stepped into the bedroom. She pulled the Colt from the hidden pocket and deposited it on the dresser, then unfastened her heavy wool traveling skirt and let it fall. The world was getting far too civilized to worry about train robberies these days. The small gun in her purse should be enough; after all, it was 1876.

As she tugged the pins from her hair and let the midnight curls free, she caught her reflection in a ceiling-high mirror.

The long leather-covered legs of a man resting on the bed behind her made her jump for the Colt.

"Before you get any more undressed, maybe I should say hello?" a deep voice said as the cowboy leaned forward until she could see his face. "I don't think cousins are supposed to see much more of each other."

For a second, Rose considered lifting the Colt and firing. She could claim she hadn't recognized him before she shot. But reason won. "What are you doing here, Duncan?"

"Watching you strip. Please, now you know I'm family, continue." He might be considered good-looking by most, but she'd always thought his grin a bit wicked. His curly brown hair never had any order and his blue eyes seemed to smile even when they were fighting.

"You need a haircut and a shave."

"You, on the other hand"—he winked—"look perfect, dear cousin Rose, as always."

"We're not kin, so drop the 'cousin' bit," she demanded. "I'm a McMurray because my mother married into the clan when I was five and you were found in an outlaw camp and brought home wild as a bear cub. We may be in the same family, but there is no way we are related." He'd pestered her since the day she first saw him, and two decades later she was still mad at him. His last attempt to marry her off had almost driven her to drink before the suitor Duncan sent finally gave up courting her and left.

Duncan shrugged as if he'd read her thoughts. "Don't blame me for Weathers; I thought he was a count."

She glared at him, then grinned. "I'm not sure he could count. But you, Duncan, didn't even check. You just sent him to meet me."

"I'm sorry," Duncan said with little remorse. "I'll do a better job next time."

"Forget it. I don't want a next time. Stop playing matchmaker."

He nodded, but she doubted he'd stop. All the McMurray men were stubborn. He might not have been born to the name, but he'd been absorbed into the family.

"I still wouldn't mind watching you undress." He changed the subject. "Come on, Rose, in twenty years I've never seen one of you girls without layers of clothes on. Hell, Martha, that old witch of a housekeeper, permanently dented my head once for even trying to look in on you bathing."

She fought down a smile, remembering how Duncan

used to fight baths when he was little. He'd slip from his clothes when his adopted mother tried to bathe him and run around sometimes for hours before one of the McMurrays caught him and dropped him in a tub. "I'm afraid I can't say the same about you. I can smell the trail dust from here."

He leaned back on the bed and crossed his boots as if he wasn't listening. "How about we both compromise and take off all our clothes. Then I'm willing to call it even."

"Get your boots off my clean bed, Duck." She used the name they'd called him as a boy just to irritate him. No one but his mother had been permitted to call him that since he was ten and had been told by Rose that it wasn't a proper name for a boy. "What are you doing in Fort Worth or, more accurately, in my bedroom?" She knew asking how he got in would be a waste of time. She'd learned a long time ago that if a squirrel could slip inside a place, so could Duncan McMurray.

"I'm waiting for you. I heard you were heading to Cowtown. Emily wrote and told me how you got pushed into coming to this wedding and how everyone back home begged off on tagging along. I was in Dallas delivering two outlaw brothers to the sheriff when I got a telegram from your dad telling me to check on you. So I rode most the night to get here. Just because no one wants to be around Victoria doesn't mean they're not worried about you. That crazy friend of yours is her own kind of strange."

She walked to the edge of the bed. "You're checking up on me before I even have time to get into trouble."

He met her eyes and as always Rose guessed that he knew of the fears she tried so hard to hide. He might have been a pest, but she remembered once when they were in the second grade, she'd refused to go into the crowded schoolhouse for a program. When she'd claimed she was sick, Duncan had sat in the wagon with her. He hadn't said a word. He'd just kept her company. They'd wrapped up in a quilt until everyone came back.

Rose didn't argue with him now. He was probably right about Tori. The whole family met Victoria Chamberlain one summer when she visited the ranch while Rose and Emily were in their second year of finishing school. Down to the dog, they all hated Victoria. She was spoiled, whiny, and demanding. She wanted her breakfast specially made twenty minutes after she awoke. She never picked up anything or offered to help. At fifteen, she thought she was a queen, but when Victoria told Duncan to wipe the sweat off his horse because she didn't want to look at it, Duncan swore he'd never speak to her again.

"I don't need any help." Rose sat down on the other side of the bed and tugged off her boots. "I'm sure Tori was just overreacting when she sent the telegram begging me to come early. But if you really want to help, you could always go to the wedding with me. She said I could have a guest."

"No way, Rose, and don't bother trying to talk me into it." He pulled off his boots. "I may be tired, but I'll be dead before I ever agree to be in the same room with that woman. That time you made me dance with her, I politely bowed and asked if I might have the honor again sometime. Hell, I was just being nice. She gave me her usual 'drop dead' look and said, 'Not in this lifetime,' like I'd asked for her hand."

Giggling, Rose whispered, "Don't tell me someone finally turned down the handsome Ranger McMurray. I thought you always got the girl. Some say you've broken the hearts of half the unmarried women in Austin."

He thought about it a moment and whispered back, "I haven't had time to break any hearts in Austin or anywhere else. As far as her turning me down, I might have been hurt if I'd cared one way or the other. I swear, I can't believe she found one man to marry, even a braggart like August Myers."

"What's wrong with him?" Rose leaned against the pillows.

"Nothing, according to Victoria's father. They're made from the same muddy cloth, if you ask me. Southerners who don't think the war is over and plan to bore everyone else alive in the South with their theories about how it will rise again any minute."

Rose closed her eyes, for once too tired to pester him. "Tell me about the outlaws you caught this time, Duncan."

He settled his shoulder against hers. "Jeb and Owen Tanner are half Comanche and half German, or so the story goes. Neither race will claim them. Some say they have no idea who their old man was, only that he tanned hides during the days of the buffalo hunts. Hauling them from Waco to Dallas was like trying to march rabid squirrels through quicksand."

"What did they do wrong?"

"Everything. Train robbing is their favorite target, but they'll do anything to get money. I swear I should have just shot them when I first saw them. They were arguing over a pair of boots they'd just pulled off a gunfighter before the doc had time to pronounce him dead. I would have probably never caught them if they hadn't been busy trying to kill each other and all their gang were making bets on which one would survive."

Duncan kept talking, reliving every dumb thing the Tanner brothers had said. Finally, he swore and added, "I was with a band of rangers who almost caught the gang once. We lost two good men and the Tanners lost a brother in the fight. Soon after that the gang started pulling jobs that took some brains to plan. The two left alive are too dumb to stop a drunk duck, much less a train, so they're getting advice from somewhere." Duncan absently played with one curl of her hair. "I asked Jeb if he could read and he answered, 'What for?'"

Just before Rose dozed off, she heard him say that he knew a driver who'd take her anywhere she needed to go while she was in Fort Worth. He promised to check on her every time he got the chance.

"Promise me," Duncan said as he bumped her shoulder lightly. "Promise me you won't leave the hotel without the driver. I don't trust any of the hack drivers in this town. The guy I picked has never let a ranger down. He'll watch over you."

"I promise," she said as she relaxed into sleep.

CHAPTER 2

DUNCAN LISTENED AS ROSE'S BREATHING SLOWED. HE smiled. She might be all grown up, but she hadn't changed. She could fall asleep in the middle of a sentence. They used to laugh that it was a waste of time to read her a bedtime story; she was gone by the title page.

He laid his big hand over her small one, remembering a time when they'd been the same size. They'd hated each other since the day they met at five years old, but whenever he was at Whispering Mountain he always knew where she was. She was bossy even then and declared him completely wild, but he kept up with her.

He'd told himself it was in self-defense so he wouldn't run into her too often, but in truth, he liked knowing where she was and what she was doing. Rose was as much a mystery to him as he was to her. They might not be blood kin, but they were bound together by something and most of the time he wasn't sure if it was love or hate. If he'd been more practical, or she'd had one ounce of recklessness in her blood, maybe, just maybe, they might have been a match, but at twenty-five they were both too set to change. He'd never settle down and she'd never take a risk. But that fact didn't keep him from caring.

With the mess going on in Dallas, Duncan knew he couldn't watch over her for a few days, but he'd made sure she'd have a driver who could protect her. If he told her what danger she was in, she'd worry herself sick. Two nights ago a woman walking only a few blocks away had been killed. He didn't mention it to Rose. He figured this little wedding drama was about the most she could handle and it would keep her busy until he got back. The Tanners would also be a threat until they were locked away for good.

As he was a Texas Ranger, it wasn't that unusual for an outlaw to promise to kill him, but Jeb and Owen Tanner had both whispered that they'd murder every McMurray in the state. Reason told Duncan that all his family was safe . . . all except Rose. She'd come alone to Fort Worth with the Tanners and their gang only thirty miles away.

He'd guard the two during their trial, and then once they were locked away for good, he'd ride back here. Who knows, he might even let Rose talk him into going to the wedding before he put her back on the train heading back to Whispering Mountain.

Duncan smiled and closed his eyes letting a calmness blanket his tired mind. A stillness always settled inside him when he knew she was all right. They might fight more than talk, but he'd do whatever he had to do to protect her.

From the day he'd seen Travis McMurray, the man who became his father, Duncan knew deep down that he was one of them. He didn't remember anything about his first family, the raid that must have killed his folks or being tied up in a camp as if he were no more than a dog or pig they planned to sell. He only remembered being cold and alone for what seemed like forever.

Then he'd stepped onto the McMurray ranch and known he was home.

As he fell asleep, he remembered the report he'd seen about the man Rose's friend would marry in one week. If the documents were true, Rose might need one of the pistols she carried. The husband-to-be wasn't an outlaw the rangers needed to worry about, but Duncan wouldn't be surprised if every time he grew he didn't leave a snakeskin behind. Proper, spoiled Princess Victoria might never see his true colors, but Rose would. She'd always been good at sizing up people.

He rolled to his side and kissed her hand lightly. The family all thought she hated leaving the ranch because she had no sense of direction, but Duncan knew it was more than that. He'd ridden all night just to let her know that he was near, even if she'd never admit she was afraid. Rose was a mouse in a state packed with lions.

Now that he knew she was safe, he'd go do his duty and then get back as fast as he could. As much as she hated the thought, she might need him, if for nothing else but to take out the trash that was about to marry her friend.

He rolled from the bed and moved silently across the room. Her carpetbag sat open on the table. Without a sound, he tugged the letter from his vest pocket and smiled. It was addressed to him, but with all his bravery he couldn't force himself to open it. He slid it into the secret fold in the lining of the bag. If he ever mustered up the courage to see what the state registrar's office discovered about his family, he'd want Rose with him for the news so he might as well leave the letter with her.

As he slipped from the room, he thought about why he'd want her to know if the state records showed his real name and age. Maybe because she'd been his best friend when he was growing up or maybe because he knew it wouldn't matter to her what kind of people he'd come from, he'd always be her family.

Aggravating or not.

CHAPTER 3

Friday
Second Avenue

ABE HENDERSON STEPPED OUT IN THE ALLEY AND looked over his shoulder at the back of the Grand. Only ten feet separated him from the fancy hotel, but there might as well be a hundred miles in between. Second Avenue had been the first main road, but when the traffic moved one block over, Second slowed to a small-town feel of merchants and shopkeepers. The stockyards were nearby along with old homes, businesses, and boardinghouses, but all the hotels and gaming houses sprung up on Main Street, where the road was wide and traffic flowed in a steady stream from dawn till dusk.

Abe Henderson liked the slower pace of Second. No hurry, no panic. Nothing ever changed.

He always opened his mercantile early on Fridays, and he watched for Killian O'Toole to show up on the bench outside his store. He and Killian had been friends most of their lives and he knew if the Irishman was in town, he'd be stopping by. They'd both been shy boys in school who traded books, and they'd both joined the Confederacy in 1863 when they turned seventeen so they wouldn't miss the war.

Abe came back wounded before the year was out. Killian had met up with his older brother at Vicksburg and stayed to the end, then walked home alone and half-starved but without a wound. Folks talked, saying they'd heard tell of Killian and his brother, Shawn, facing a huge battle a few months after they got together. The Rebs were outnumbered when the O'Toole boys manned a cannon. Folks said Shawn held the line for two hours before he fell, his face so bloody not even his family could have claimed the body. The gossips said that Killian ran when commanded to take his place and spent the rest of the war driving a hospital wagon without a weapon at his side.

No one had proof. The story of O'Toole was just hearsay, but behind his back, some of the veterans called Killian O'Toole a coward. Others said he was simply mad, driven there by a war he was too young to understand. Folks claimed after twelve years he still talked to his brother as if Shawn O'Toole walked by his side, and Abe Henderson knew enough not to argue.

Abe didn't care about gossip. Killian O'Toole was his friend and that was all that mattered. The war had been over for a long time and neither of them ever mentioned it. Both were terribly scarred, Abe with a limp and Killian with rumors that never ended.

When Abe saw him sit down on the bench outside his store, he poured two cups of coffee and moved slowly to the door. At five past seven they'd see few people on the street. They could talk. If one of Abe's regulars did come in, he could get what he needed and leave the money on the counter. For both men, this hour once a week was all they had in the way of true companionship.

"Morning." Abe smiled at the long-legged man in black. "I swear you look more like an undertaker than a circuit judge."

"Jobs are about the same," Killian answered, without

meeting Abe's gaze. "I'm guessing I put about as many men in the ground as most of them do. Difference is, no one yells at an undertaker for just doing his job."

"Plus, don't forget you get to go down to Austin once in a while," Abe said, remembering how his friend always seemed happier and maybe a little more at peace when he took a few days off and made the trip. Maybe in getting away from his home and people who knew him, he somehow slipped away from his memories.

"I may not be going as much from now on. Things seem to have changed."

The shop owner knew his friend was still hung over from the night before. Killian, if nothing else, was predictable. He worked hard all week riding from town to town, sometimes holding court all day, then sleeping in the saddle so he could make the next town by morning. Every Thursday or Friday night he'd circle through Fort Worth and collect his mail. Then he'd rent a room in a good hotel, take a bath, have a shave, and stay drunk for two days before heading out again.

"How's Shawn?" Abe decided to change the subject. A ghost was all the family either of them had, so they always made polite conversation about him.

"He's fine. Says I'm getting too old to live on the road." Killian downed a swallow of hot coffee. "Thinks I should settle down and get married to some fat woman who'll keep me warm at night."

Both men laughed. They'd had the discussion before about marriage and decided no woman would want either one of them.

Killian lit a thin cigar and took a deep draw before adding, "This morning, I bumped into a pretty woman having trouble getting out of a carriage. Little bit of a thing with midnight hair and fiery eyes. I offered help, but she wouldn't take it. Looked at me like I was a devil for even talking to her."

"Were you sober?"

"More or less. I had to come in early this week. A newspaperman I got drunk with a few times when I was in Austin is getting married and I've agreed to be the best man. When I got the telegram asking me if I'd stand up with him, I was surprised he even remembered my name. All I can figure out is I must be the only person he knew in Fort Worth."

He didn't say more, but his frown left Abe wondering just how much of a friend the guy could be. Killian looked more like he planned to be a pallbearer than a best man.

Killian shrugged. "I got to wondering if I haven't reached the age where I frighten women and children. Every time I do meet a woman she tells me I'd make a good friend. Maybe I'm getting too old to even make attempts at being social. Remember Old Mr. Daily who lived at the edge of town? He scared a year's worth of growth out of me more than once."

Abe nodded. "He chased us out of his pumpkin patch with a shotgun. I thought that was a little much."

Killian nodded. "I used to think he was older than dirt. Last week, on the road, I got to thinking that he couldn't have been more than thirty-five or forty when we were kids. Hell, I'll be his age before I turn around."

"Maybe you should buy a place and start planting pumpkins?" Abe fought not to smile.

The judge just swore and smoked. "You and my brother are ganging up on me. He keeps telling me to forget about women all together. He thinks I should hang a shingle up here and go to work behind a desk." Killian laughed. "The last time he picked me up in the gutter, Shawn told me he felt like knocking some sense into me. Before I passed out, I thought of daring him to, but hell, I'd probably be beaten up by a ghost with my luck."

In the quiet dawn both men watched the schoolteacher walk across the street. She minded her steps, avoiding mud until she reached the steps of the little schoolhouse. She moved like a willow, Abe thought, and never offered a smile to anyone but her students.

"How old is she?" Killian asked as if just making conversation.

"I don't know. She looked almost too young to be a teacher when she came here eight years ago, but they said she'd already taught at a school up north for a year. I'm guessing now she's twenty-seven or -eight."

"Well on the way to being an old maid," Killian said. "She ever had any suitors come calling?"

Abe shrugged. "I've never noticed any man dropping by. She walks past my place heading back to the boarding-house every evening. I've never seen anyone with her."

"Kind of a shame. She's not exactly pretty, but she's not homely either."

"She's far too thin for you." Abe lowered his voice.

"I know. Plus she's the proper type. Probably wouldn't let my brother hang around. Some women start acting funny when I tell them he died a dozen years ago. They seem to be of the opinion that he shouldn't still be waiting around before passing on to the hereafter. I've told him a hundred times that he should go, but he says he's got to stay around and keep me company."

Abe continued to watch the schoolhouse door even though the teacher had disappeared. "If you ever do find one who doesn't mind Shawn, marry her no matter how thick or thin she is. She'd be one in a million, I'd guess." He almost added that he'd do exactly that if he ever found a woman who didn't mind his limp.

They were both silent as they watched the teacher open the windows. The winter day promised to be warm and Abe guessed she wanted to air the place out.

"She's more your type, Abe." Killian held the cup almost to his mouth when he spoke.

"Not likely, but I will say she's a worker." Abe shook his head. "It's a week before school starts back and she's already getting everything ready. For what they pay her she should only work a few hours a day, but she's in that room from dawn to dusk."

Killian tossed his cigar in the mud. "You ever talk to her?"

Abe shook his head. "Only when she orders supplies.

You'd think in the eight years I've been watching her go back and forth to work I would have thought of something to say besides 'How many do you want, Miss Norman' or 'I'll have it in a week.' "

Killian refilled his half-empty cup of coffee with whiskey from a flask. "Maybe you should grab her and kiss her. If she likes you, she'll kiss you back. If she doesn't, she'll slap you. Either way, you'll know how she feels."

"Where'd you get that advice?"

Killian winked. "Shawn told me. I haven't had a chance to test it. Most of the women I meet are defendants."

Abe ordered in a low voice, "Tell your dead brother to stay out of my love life."

"You don't have a love life," Killian corrected.

"Neither do you, and bathing only when you hit town isn't a good plan if you ever want one."

Both men laughed, something either rarely did. They talked on about the weather and work, but both knew the importance of this hour they spent had little to do with what they said. It was the one time they both could almost believe their world was normal and they were just like everyone else.

CHAPTER 4

Main Street

Rose SHIFTED AND TRIED TO PULL UP NONEXISTENT covers. Slowly she awoke as she became aware she wasn't in her room in the new wing of the ranch headquarters.

She realized immediately that Duncan had disappeared—as usual. Part of her wondered if he'd come to pester her or help. With him, she was never sure. He might be a lawyer, but he still loved riding with the Texas Rangers. Though tall and broad in the shoulders, he sometimes seemed more boy than man. Most of the time she felt a hundred years older than Duncan. They were playing a game they'd played since meeting. Because he was wild and did whatever he pleased, she had to be the sensible one who kept everything in order, everything grounded. He had all the adventures and she listened to his tales.

Rose stood and shook the dust from her skirt before putting it back on. There was something improper about two adults taking a nap together, but it didn't seem to bother either one of them. From the time they were small, she and

Duncan had taken naps together under the big trees behind the house. As they'd grown older they'd sometimes met in the same spot, both with a book to read. Often they didn't even talk; they just didn't seem to want to be alone.

As she began unpacking, a knock startled her. It couldn't be past midmorning, far too early for Victoria to be back from her fitting. If Duncan came back, he probably wouldn't bother to knock.

Rose opened the door to the maid Tori had employed since they were in school. Betty Ann was ten years older than Rose and Victoria, but she followed around after Victoria, picking up like a mother hen, and never saw her job as one of guidance to the young girls. If Tori wanted to jump off a bridge, Betty Ann's responsibility was simply to make sure she was dressed properly.

"Hello, Betty Ann." Rose stepped back so the maid could enter. "Good to see you again."

"Morning, Miss McMurray. I brought your dress for the wedding."

Rose grinned. That was about as friendly as Betty Ann had ever been and Rose learned a long time ago that she'd only fluster the maid if she tried to engage her in any conversation.

Betty Ann carried a bright yellow dress, with white roses of lace curled along the sleeves. Without a word, she crossed the sitting room and laid the gown on the bed. "I was told to bring this over as soon as I knew you were here."

Rose stared. She guessed Betty Ann thought her overwhelmed by the bridesmaid dress, and she was, though not by its beauty but by the message it delivered.

Betty Ann marched to the door. "I got things to do. If you need anything else, you might want to hire your own maid. I ain't hired to pick up after no one but Miss Chamberlain." She looked pointedly at Rose's open trunk. "You'll be needing someone to help you once the wedding party starts. The major doesn't let his daughter show up less than perfect and I don't think he'll be too happy with you all wrinkled. He told Miss Victoria that he plans to dine in style every night until the wedding."

"I understand." When Tori and Rose had shared a room in school, Betty Ann would pick up Victoria's dresses even if she had to step on Rose's to get to them.

Rose stepped closer to the yellow dress, fighting to slow her breathing. Her friend was in trouble. Deep trouble. Though she had no idea what was going on in Tori's life, she knew one fact: Victoria Chamberlain did not want to get married.

As young girls going to their first parties and dances, they laughed and swore against two things. Rose promised she'd never wear yellow, not even to her own funeral, and admitted she hated roses. Any kind of roses from fresh real ones delivered with notes that read, *A rose for my Rose*, to paper ones in cards or even lace curled to look like the flower. Tori had said she'd never wear purple or shoes taller than one inch. She loved being petite and said purple was a color sensible women wore when they weren't brave enough to wear red.

"Does Miss Chamberlain know of this dress?" Rose asked the maid.

"Of course, miss, she picked it out yesterday. Her father wanted another one with less lace, but she insisted." Betty Ann made a face. "He gives in to her more than he should. I imagine that will stop after the wedding."

Rose ran her hand over the yards of yellow material, barely listening to the maid. Tori hadn't confided in Betty Ann and so Rose would say nothing.

The maid didn't seem to notice her silence. "It will still be a few hours before Miss Chamberlain gets back. The groom was expected yesterday, but he didn't show up. He's an important newspaperman and probably has more important things to attend to than holding the bride's hand." The maid huffed. "I'm guessing that's your job now, Miss Mc-Murray."

"Fine," Rose answered. "I've a bit of shopping to do before the fitting. Let the bride and groom have some time alone." She opened the door, leaving Betty Ann no choice but to exit. "And I think you're right—I do need a maid."

Betty Ann walked out mumbling to herself. "If they spend time alone waiting for you, it'll probably be the first time they've spent without the major around. If I didn't know better, I'd swear them two were getting married and Miss Victoria is just decoration for the cake. The way she's been buying clothes you'd think she was stocking up for years and not just leaving for Galveston after the wedding."

Rose didn't ask questions. She had a feeling if Betty Ann thought she wanted any information about August Myers or the major, the maid would take great pleasure in hiding it.

As Rose hurried down the stairs, she planned. Whatever the trouble, it wasn't something she could discuss with anyone. She needed to know the good guys from the bad ones as fast as possible, and for that she'd need an expert. Too bad Duncan hadn't stayed around to help, but she'd manage. For once her fear had to take the backseat to helping a friend, and she needed to know what was going on as soon as possible.

At the desk, she asked the chatty clerk, "I understand Ranger McMurray hired a coach for me if I needed to move about town. Has anyone reported in?"

"Yes, miss, about a half hour ago. He said he'd be waiting whenever you needed him at the north door." The clerk pointed down a long hallway toward a back door, then hesitated and added, "The man the ranger sent, miss, he's not an easy man to look at, but he's honest. We use him mostly for hauling because our guests have trouble looking—"

"I'm not interested." She found people who judged others by looks far more difficult to face than any scar or deformity she'd ever seen.

"Yes, miss." The clerk's eyes met hers and she knew his opinion of her had just risen. "If you need anything, Miss McMurray, just ask for me, Hanson Rogers."

She nodded. "I will. Thank you, Mr. Rogers."

A few minutes later she stepped out of the north door and onto the side street where one worn buggy waited. Fort Worth had been a sleepy little town with its share of saloons and troublemakers, but with the railroad coming and cattle drives passing through, it had grown not only larger but rougher. The town fathers didn't try to clean up the bars and gambling houses but simply restricted the worst of it to one area everyone called Hell's Half Acre.

That was exactly where Rose knew she'd find the help she'd need.

The driver was tall, three, maybe four, inches over six feet. With his wide shoulders and thick legs, he seemed powerful more than overweight. He didn't offer to help her up when Rose approached the old wagon with benches tied into the bed. Duncan was wise to pick nothing fancy, nothing that would draw attention.

Rose walked to the front of the wagon and swung up easily on the bench beside the driver.

He turned his face away as he mumbled, "Where to, Miss McMurray?"

"Before we start out, turn around." At least he knew her name, but she'd look at him directly before she decided to go anywhere with him no matter what Duncan thought of the man.

He swiveled slowly as if bracing himself for her reaction.

Rose stared straight into his eyes, barely making note of the scars crossing his face like a crowded road map. "I understand you are a man to be trusted."

A bit of the anger left his eyes. "I am."

"Good. I need more than a driver. I don't know what I'm stepping into here, maybe nothing, but if there is trouble, I need to have someone I can depend on."

He studied her for a minute and she expected him to ask details, but all he finally said was, "Wherever we go, I'll not come out without you. I'll see you safe back to this door, miss. You have my word." He lifted a corner of his mouth in almost a smile. "Duncan McMurray is one of the few men I call friend and you matter to him. That's all I need to know."

"Fair enough. I'll expect you at this door when I need you."

He smiled. "I sleep in my wagon anyway. Might as well do it here. They call me Stitch, miss. That's the only name I got."

"Were you in the war, Stitch?" If he was, the surgeons had done a poor job. She couldn't help but notice that his hands revealed the same white scars that crossed his face. It was hard to guess his age, but by the lack of lines around his smoky blue-gray eyes she thought him under forty.

"I fought for a short time with Terry's Rangers. When I was hurt, I would have died if I hadn't been taken prisoner. A Yankee doctor fixed me up, sewing up holes so I wouldn't bleed all over everything. When I got where I could walk, they gave me a choice. Stay in prison, or sign up for the frontier. I served the rest of the war out on the fort line. Out there it didn't matter if you were Reb or Yank. You were fighting to keep settlers alive."

Stitch thought for a minute, then added with unexpected forthrightness, "I got a start on these scars from my father. He used to like to cut things when he was drunk. I was the oldest and the one he always came after."

"That's unforgivable." Anger caught in her throat as she forced the words out.

"That's what I told him when I killed him just after I turned nine."

"Self-defense," Rose whispered simply.

"I thought so too, even if he was snoring at the time." Stitch took a breath as if knowing he'd have to finish his story before she'd stop asking questions. "My ma had a baby on the breast at the time and didn't want to have to go to town and explain, so she just buried him. I don't remember any of the neighbors even asking how he died. Don't reckon they cared."

Rose fought down a gasp. She'd just hired a killer. A

killer who'd defended himself at nine. She didn't know whether to be worried or proud of him for being honest. "Do you know where the red-light district is?"

He barked a laugh. "Everyone in Fort Worth knows that, miss."

She was glad he didn't add something about such a place not being for the likes of her. With an overprotective father, three uncles—all bossy—and an older sister who thought she was a second mother, Rose did not need advice from strangers.

"I wish to go to a dress shop on the north end near that district. I don't have a street or number, but my uncle told me it was called Hallie's Dresses and it faced the river."

The big man set the team in motion. "Only one street it could be, I'm thinking. This time of the morning the roads in that part of town will be empty so we should be able to move fast."

Rose gripped the side of the seat. Stitch was a good driver and he didn't waste time. As the streets passed she had the feeling she was going down a well. Everything dulled and seemed covered in grime. Once, when Stitch stopped to drag a drunk out of the road, she tried to see anything bright, but the world seemed to be cloudy everywhere.

Finally the bars and saloons faded and small houses, two and three stories high, crowded by the river. The buggy stopped at a door even before Rose noticed the small sign at the corner of the house. HALLIE'S PLACE. DRESS OR UNDRESS.

"I don't think this is a dress shop," Stitch mumbled as he stepped down and lifted his hands to her.

She let him swing her from the buggy as she asked, "But it has to be?"

"No, miss, I think Hallie lets men dress her however they like . . . or undress her." He looked away obviously embarrassed at having been so bold.

"Really?"

He didn't face her. "There are probably stranger things

going on down here, but I ain't talking about them so don't ask."

He'd just supplied her with the oddest thing she'd ever heard. "Will you stay close?"

"I will." He straightened as she pounded on the door.

After several tries a chubby auburn-haired woman, maybe five or six years older than Rose, answered the door. She had sleepy eyes and very little clothes around her rather rounded body. Rose guessed the next customer must be one coming to dress her. When she saw Rose, she pulled a see-through robe around her and just stared as if it were far too early to be bothered.

"Are you Hallie Smith?"

The full-busted woman shrugged. "That's a name I've used."

"Ranger Travis McMurray is my uncle and he told me if I needed help of a certain nature you might be able to do me a service. He said he hadn't seen you in years, but he thought you owned a dress shop in Fort Worth." Rose knew she was rambling, but Hallie Smith looked like she might slam the door at any moment.

"That ranger saved my life once when I was more girl than woman. If you're his kin, the least I can do is listen to what you want. Come on in." When Rose passed, Hallie held the door. "This one with you?"

"Yes." Rose grinned. Stitch was taller than the door frame.

Hallie looked him up and down boldly and he returned the favor. Each seemed shocked by the other.

As they moved down the hallway to a tiny sitting room, Rose heard Hallie whisper to Stitch that she didn't give samples and he answered that he wasn't asking for any.

Hallie offered her a seat and didn't seem surprised when Stitch remained framed in the doorway. "Would you like some tea?" Hallie's tone seemed rusty, as if she knew the proper words but hadn't used them in a long time.

"Thank you. That would be nice," Rose answered. In truth, she needed a few minutes to wrap her mind around the idea that this dressmaker her uncle sent her to was something quite different from what she'd originally thought. He'd simply said, "If you need help with clothes or sewing, or even a good pickpocket, you might try Hallie Smith. When I knew her, she was a woman of many talents." He couldn't have known what she was doing, Rose felt sure of it.

While Hallie was gone, Rose surveyed the room, deciding Stitch must be wrong about the woman. There was a sewing machine in the corner and stacks of material next to it on the floor. A huge button jar sat beside her chair, and a worn sewing kit rested on the table. Maybe the sign, DRESSED AND UNDRESSED, meant she made clothes for both day and nightwear.

Glancing at Stitch, she noticed he was staring straight ahead as if afraid of what he might see if he let his gaze wander.

Hallie returned with a tray. She'd slipped on a proper robe and combed back her wild hair. She totally ignored Stitch as she poured tea. When she passed Rose her cup, she began, "I was still in my teens when your uncle caught me picking pockets. Turns out I'd lifted money from the outlaw gang Travis McMurray had come to round up. They were considering cutting off one of my hands when he stopped them."

She took a sip of her tea and added, "I haven't seen him for years, but I wrote him once telling him I had a dress shop in Fort Worth. Wanted him to know I was doing fine. Of late, I've found other work on the side."

Rose felt her cheeks warm. "Do you still pick pockets or, um, do anything else illegal?" It was a horrible thing to ask, but she had to know.

"No. I pick pockets now and then just to entertain customers. I still do some sewing but not for ladies like you." She seemed to be fighting to hold on to her pride. When she looked up, she met Rose's gaze. "You got kind eyes like your uncle. He always looked at folks straight on. Treated me just like I was a lady the last time he arrested me."

Rose smiled at her as Hallie offered her a biscuit from a tin. "Thank you," Rose said. "I'm here to offer you a job, but I have to know that we'll have no trouble with the law."

Hallie set her cup down, suddenly very interested. "I'm not a prostitute. I have a small group of men who come here a few times a month just to watch me dress and undress. It's easier than being a scrubwoman, and with a criminal record, I've not much chance at getting a job as a lady's maid. In exchange for the viewing, they give me gifts and help me sometimes with the rent. They're mostly gentlemen who only want to watch. If they did want more, they know to go down the street."

"I understand," Rose lied. She had no idea why a man would pay money to watch someone take off their clothes, and from what she knew of wives, very few were willing to undress in front of their husbands. Maybe that was why they came to Hallie, to see how it worked. "I must ask that nothing said here goes beyond this room."

"I'm all for that, with the bargain including not saying anything about me to your uncle. I kind of like the idea of him thinking of me as just a dressmaker."

"Fair enough." Rose liked this strange woman. "I'll hire you to act as my lady's maid while I'm in Fort Worth. I'm to be in a wedding in a week and will need to attend several events before the wedding itself." She didn't miss Hallie's interest. "I've need of your pickpocketing skills in an investigation I'm doing. You'll be paid double wages."

She had Hallie's full attention so she continued, "I believe my friend, who is to marry in six days, is in some kind of trouble. As my maid you'll be able to move unnoticed around the hotel. Whatever you palm, we'll return quickly so you'll be in little danger of being caught. If I find proof that her fiancé is not what he claims to be, I'll do whatever is necessary to stop the wedding."

"Give me an hour and I'll be ready." Hallie obviously wasn't a woman who dallied on discussions.

"But we haven't settled on a price?"

"It doesn't matter. I'm sure you'll be fair. I can't imagine a McMurray being otherwise. I've got a dress that will work perfect. I've only put it on and taken it off a few times, so it's almost new. I'll play the part of your maid better than a real one ever could."

Rose thought of asking why she'd jumped so quickly into something that might prove dangerous but then saw it in Hallie's eyes. Rose had just offered her the first ray of sunshine in her colorless life.

Standing, Rose thanked her for the tea and promised to send Stitch back in an hour.

Hallie surveyed the huge doorstop blocking her parlor door. "You sure I'll be safe with him?"

He raised his head. "I was wondering the same thing about you, ma'am."

Hallie laughed, but Rose just watched Stitch. Something in the way he stood told her that, though Hallie might have been teasing, he wasn't.

Rose returned to the hotel to find a note Tori had slid under her door saying she knew Rose needed to rest after the train ride and she would see her tomorrow if time allowed. Rose didn't know whether to be angry or relieved.

CHAPTER 5

Second Avenue

ABE HENDERSON FOLDED THE COLORFUL INDIAN blankets along the north wall for the fourth time since he opened the mercantile that morning. School would be starting back soon; the holidays would be officially over and his place could get back to normal.

Lightning flashed across his front windows. Every mother in town had been shopping today despite the weather and every kid had tracked mud across his floor. They'd bothered, fingered, and messed up all areas.

As he worked, he thought of the crazy advice that Killian's ghost brother had given him. Maybe he should make a New Year's resolution to just grab the first available single girl and kiss her. At least he'd have something to remember about this year besides just its passing.

"One more hour." He nodded toward Henry at the counter. His one employee was already antsy wanting to get home to his ever-growing family. "If this rain keeps up, we might think about closing early. No one would come in anyway."

"I don't mind staying and helping you clean up," Henry offered.

Abe shook his head. He'd be up till midnight getting the place back in order, but unlike Henry, he had nowhere to go. A bowl of soup and three-day-old bread was all that waited for him upstairs. *And the nightmares*, he added to himself.

He'd been seventeen when a Yankee bullet exploded into his leg a dozen years ago. If his mother hadn't gotten to him in time, he would have died in the hell they'd called a hospital prison. She'd argued with half the Union army officers that her dying son needed to go home. Abe wasn't sure if they gave in because he looked so bad or they couldn't stand against one southern widow about to lose her only child, but she brought him home more dead than alive. Then, more on a mission than out of love, he thought, she nursed him back as she ran the store all by herself.

He'd recovered, a skeleton of the boy who'd left to fight a war he thought would bring him glory. The town claimed he was a hero, but Abe Henderson felt more like a coward. He seldom left his family store since his return. Here, behind the stacks and counters, he could pretend he was whole. Here he could move so that the limp wasn't so noticeable. Here he could pretend he was normal.

His mother had lost her husband the same year he'd been wounded, and he'd wondered a thousand times whether she would have come after him if she could have found anyone else to help out in the store. *Love* wasn't a word he'd ever heard her use.

Abe sometimes reminded himself he was barely out of his twenties, but inside he felt old. Too old for dances or courting or even church suppers. He'd never attended a party or even walked down the street to a saloon for a drink. This was his prison. The store was his world.

He'd done well, enlarging his store in both directions when other businesses closed, but he'd only increased the prison. He planned to use the abandoned bakery next door, his newest acquisition, to enlarge his hardware space. He'd keep the door between his place and the new space so men could go in and look at tools while the women shopped. The men could smoke, maybe even pass around a bottle on cold days. It made sense that if both the man and wife came in, the shopping would increase.

So far the plan was only in his head, but once winter settled into spring there would be enough men looking for work that he could enlarge quickly.

"Here come the Donnely dozen," Henry announced as a batch of children hit the door. "The old man probably made them work all day in the rain before letting them come do their shopping."

Mrs. Donnely, as wide as the door, wiggled her way in. "Mr. Henderson!" she yelled. "Every other kid needs new shoes, and the boys get two pair of trousers, one new shirt, and three pairs of socks. The girls have their lists. I didn't have time to shop for Christmas this year so I gave them all promises." She pointed at one boy a few inches taller than her but still short of being a man. "Only my oldest needs a new coat. Any one will do as long as it's warm. I know it's a lot to buy, but I won't have folks thinking the Donnelys don't have enough to outfit them all. What we can't find in an hour, we'll do without until we slaughter another hog."

Abe almost swore as the arguments started. Old man Donnely, who obviously stayed home, thought shoes should last two years and there were always younger kids to pass them down to. The offspring might not argue with their father, but they thought nothing of yelling at their siblings.

Mrs. Donnely sat down on the stool by the boxes of shoes, slapping away children who were not eligible for a new pair. "All you get black lace-ups except for my Carol Ann. She's thirteen and almost marrying age so she can pick out a girl's shoe."

Three girls giggled behind him and Abe looked at them trying to figure out which was the oldest. None showed any sign of developing into "marrying age."

"You interested?" Mrs. Donnely smiled an almost toothless grin.

"No," Abe answered. "I don't plan to ever marry."

Momma Donnely looked disappointed as Abe tried to help a few of her brood while others pulled pairs off the shelf and began trying on whatever they could reach.

He heard Henry threaten a few by the counter. The youngest girl, about three or four, Abe guessed, was sitting among the bolts of material. Her crying blended in with the chaos, and he didn't miss the fact that every few minutes she blew her nose on the end of one of the bolts of material. He planned to roll off a half yard and send it home with Mrs. Donnely.

Forty-five minutes later the place was a total mess, the counter was head high with the Donnelys' annual clothing purchase and Abe was seriously considering drinking the vanilla even if it was only twelve percent alcohol.

The front door chimed. *Let it be Marshal Courtright coming to arrest all the candy thieves,* Abe thought. He should have weighed the lot when they came in and again as they left. He had no doubt at least five pounds of chocolate had been consumed.

No sheriff, though. The one person he prayed wouldn't come in until the mail run tomorrow morning stood just inside the door looking as if she'd just stepped into an ant bed.

"Evening, Miss Norman." One of the Donnely boys pulled off his hat and stepped out of the schoolteacher's way.

Abe watched as she moved in her proper little march toward him. He noticed the noise in the place dropped. Wild children paused in mid-rampage. For them, this one lady had more power over their world than anyone alive.

She smiled at each but didn't say a word until she stood a foot in front of him.

"Have the last of my supplies arrived, Mr. Henderson?" If she weren't a woman, he swore she'd be a general. She seemed to be willing her things to appear by the commanding tone of her voice.

In the eight years he'd known the schoolmarm, she'd never been anything but formal, even cold, to him. Never a hair out of place or a smudge on her clothes. Pretty washed down to plain, he'd always thought. Hair too tightly knotted. Not a touch of makeup. Clothes in only browns and dull blues. Women respected her and men never gave her a second look, except him maybe, when he thought she wouldn't notice.

Only today, for some insane reason, Abe found himself mesmerized by her mouth. The woman frightened him almost speechless, but he liked the way her mouth moved, when she wasn't pressing her lips together in impatience.

"Well, Mr. Henderson?"

"No," he managed.

She pointed a finger at the storage room behind his long counter. "I saw a wagonload of boxes being delivered earlier."

He forced himself to think, but exhaustion weighed against him. "I haven't had time to check the shipment, but I'm sure your things are not among the boxes." Staples came by train and were delivered by one of the men who worked at the depot. Her supplies were ordered by mail.

She looked disappointed and he saw a hint of doubt in her eyes. The proper Miss Norman didn't believe him. In some ways, he knew all about her, from what she ate to the tiny bottle of perfume she bought herself for Christmas each year, yet she didn't even know him well enough to believe him.

Lightning flashed again and the Donnely children woke up from their moment of silence. Henry and Abe had their hands full counting and boxing up as Mrs. Donnely screamed at them to finish or they'd be left behind.

When Abe had a second to look up, the schoolteacher had vanished. He'd probably think of what he wished he'd said to her tonight as he fought sleep. Now and then he'd concentrate on her face and will himself not to dream of the war. She might be about his age, but she wasn't the kind of woman who would ever look at a man like him. No woman wanted to step out with a man who relied on a crutch when he walked beyond the walls of his store.

Ten minutes later, he locked the door behind the Donnelys and turned to Henry. "Go on home and have your supper. It's late." Abe pulled the shades down and turned off the lights as he heard Henry running out the back door.

Moving through the empty store, Abe knew just where to put his hand on a counter or shelf or pole so that his weak leg never had to take the weight when he walked. Outside he might be crippled, but in here he almost appeared to be walking.

Smiling, he remembered how his mother taught him the trick when the store was small. He'd never been sure if she wanted him to be independent or just needed him to move faster. After she died and he expanded the store, he made sure he could move about so there was little chance of falling.

As he turned out the last lamp, a sound came from the back behind the counter. His first horrible thought was that Mrs. Donnely had accidentally left one of her crew behind. Or had someone slipped in and hidden until he was alone, waiting to rob him? During the early years when Fort Worth was wild after the war, he'd been robbed twice. Both times he'd handed over the money. No danger, no amount of money, would be worth picking up a gun again. One robber had said he was sorry and left, but the second robbery had been committed by two men. They'd taken the money, beat him in the head with the side of a gun until he passed out, and then ran, leaving Abe bleeding badly.

The sheriff had mentioned the robbers were probably the Tanner brothers, the same men who had been caught for robbing trains of late. The paper said that though they could be tied to more than a dozen robberies, they had no money on them when apprehended. One report described them as ragged when they were hauled to jail by a Texas Ranger. The two brothers were either very poor robbers or terrible money managers.

After the second attack, Abe swore if he ever got robbed again, he'd at least fight.

Now, in the shadows of his store, he picked up an ax he

kept leaning against the opening to the storage room and moved slowly toward the noise.

One hand braced the doorframe and the other held the ax high as he stepped into the back of his store. In the shadows between boxes he saw someone lifting a weapon.

Abe shifted his weight as the figure moved toward him. Just before he swung, the shadowy weapon lowered to the top of a box as if to pry it open and a frustrated huff whispered in the air. The big arms he'd seen became puffed sleeves and the tall form appeared shorter when he recognized the outline of a hat.

"Miss Norman?" Abe lowered the ax, not believing what he saw.

She turned toward him, a crowbar in her hand. "I'm only trying to help find my supplies."

"No one is allowed back here." He took the bar from her hand as if disarming her.

"The supplies have to be here. I can't start school without them." Her angry voice echoed his. "If you don't have time, I'll look myself."

"No one is allowed back here." He repeated the words slowly, anger building. He'd almost hurt her, maybe even killed her, and all because she was somewhere she didn't belong.

He moved closer, stumbling slightly when he dragged his weak leg. With his movement in the cramped space, he inadvertently shoved her against the boxes stacked higher than her shoulder. The sudden contact stilled them both.

For a moment, neither moved.

"You're not supposed to be here." The nearness of her washed over him. He hadn't been so close to a woman in years. To his shock, she seemed shorter, softer, and so much more vulnerable than he'd ever thought of her as being.

"I'm just looking . . ."

He could feel her stiffening against him as if preparing for battle. Her slight movements made him aware that she was a woman fully developed.

"What are you going to do, Mr. Henderson? Arrest me?" Her voice shook a little as he felt her words close to his throat. "I think I have a right to look for my things."

If she planned to argue, Abe knew he didn't have a chance. He wouldn't get in a word much less make a point. Before he could think, he leaned into her and pressed his mouth over hers. For a heartbeat, he thought she'd jerk away and slap him, but she remained perfectly still. He could feel her drawing in quick breaths as the awkward kiss continued.

He put his hands on either side of her, pinning her against a box as he moved his mouth an inch away from hers. "I think, Miss Norman, that I'm going to kiss you again."

She opened her mouth to protest and he silenced any argument. Her mouth tasted like heaven. He could feel her full bottom lip tremble. All she'd had to do was turn her head, but she remained frozen as if what he was doing was so out of the realm of possibilities, she had no defense.

He took his time kissing her the second try, remembering how a woman felt from a time when he'd been far more boy than man and kissed a few girls behind barn dances.

When she struggled against him, he broke the kiss. "Not a word. This is not open for discussion," he whispered against her cheek, "or I kiss you again." He couldn't stand the thought of her sharp words after the wonder of kissing her.

Abe stilled and watched her slowly straighten away from him. "Don't come back in the storage room again unless you want this to continue between us." Bracing himself for a slap, he didn't move.

He saw her nod slightly as he made room for her to pass. Her body brushed his as she moved away, and he felt the longing of her leaving as if in the few minutes they'd shared she'd become a part of him.

She lifted her chin and stared at him as lightning flashed from the high windows. He'd expected to see fear or hate. He guessed she'd threaten to have him arrested. After all, one doesn't go around kissing proper young women, and a schoolteacher was one step down from being a nun. If it went to trial, his only defense would be that a ghost told him to do it.

But he saw no fear in her eyes, only anger, before she turned and stormed out of his store.

Abe followed, moving easily between the displays in the darkness. He stood at the open door she'd left, wondering how he could ever face her again. She'd been a teacher for years across the street from his place and they'd never said a word that wasn't necessary. Nothing beyond "good morning." He'd had no right to kiss her, and to kiss her the way he had was probably unforgivable. If he had any sense, he'd apologize tomorrow. But how could he apologize for doing the one thing that had made him feel alive since the war?

He didn't sleep at all, thinking about what a fool he'd made of himself. When the mail came the next morning, he counted out her order and asked Henry to deliver it, even though the store was as busy as it had been the day before. "Tell her I'll put up the blackboard tomorrow." Sunday, he reasoned, the only day she never came to the school. The only day he could work without someone watching him.

Henry raised an eyebrow, but as always he didn't question the boss. Abe had given him a chance when no one else offered him a job.

Abe watched him go, wishing he could pick up the box and hurry across the street. If he could have, he might have talked to her again. He might have asked her to step out one evening. He might have had a chance with such a woman if he tried.

At noon, as Abe always did, he closed the store for lunch. Henry went home and Abe ate his meal alone in a little room in the back his mother had always called his study, as if they had a real home and were wealthy enough to have a real study. She had started the practice of closing the noon hour because he needed to rest his leg, and over the years it had become a habit. Everyone in town knew the store hours and respected them.

As he walked toward the back, Abe thought of trying to catch a nap in the old leather chair beside his collection of books he kept in "his study." Henry would wake him with a tap on the back door if he did happen to fall asleep.

He moved past a desk in the hallway, which served as his office, so he could watch for customers while doing his accounts. In the daylight, the windows high along the back wall offered plenty of light. As he slid his hand from the desk to a railing, Abe caught a glimpse of Miss Norman standing beside the stairs.

She wasn't looking at him. She stood still as stone, holding her hands in front of her so tightly together he could see them turning white. As always, she stood as proper and perfect as a model in a window of a ladies' store.

"Drop your hands to your sides," he said in little more than a whisper. He hated to think that she was hurting her fingers in her effort to remain still.

She lowered them and looked up at him, her gaze a mixture of fear and longing.

He didn't know how to make small talk. He didn't even know how to be kind. But she already knew that and it wasn't the reason she was standing before him now.

Leaning his hip against the desk so that they were close to the same height, Abe lifted his hand to her cheek. "Remember, not a word, Miss Norman." He wasn't sure he could stand chatter. "Do you understand? You're not here to talk."

He could feel her shaking, but she nodded as he slipped his fingers behind her neck and pulled her to him. Her body was stiff, almost fighting him as he lowered his mouth to hers. The need to touch her again had been building in him like a fire all morning.

She'd come back to him. That one fact made him feel half-drunk. She'd returned for another kiss, but she wasn't going to make it easy. Maybe, if it were possible, she knew even less about this than he did. They weren't courting or flirting. Neither knew how.

Circling her waist, he pulled until her breasts flattened

against his chest. Her arms remained at her sides, but he could feel her with each breath. When she tried to put an inch between their bodies, he tugged her back against him without breaking the kiss. "No," he whispered against her mouth. "I want you close against me."

He let the feel of her rock through his entire body.

The second time, she remained close even when he lessened his hold. He smiled, lightening the kiss to barely a brush of his lips against hers. "That's the way, Miss Norman. Now I can feel the way you react." His words brushed her cheek. "I can feel you."

With slow caressing strokes, his fingers crossed her face, tilting her chin slightly. His thumb brushed her bottom lip, pulling it open so that he could feel the moisture just inside. "You want this between us?" He had to be sure.

She nodded again. Her eyes were closed, but her short breaths and trembling body told him she was terrified of the unknown. Yet all she had to do was pull away. He might be touching her, but he wasn't holding her. "Move against me then," he whispered near her ear. When he stroked her back, she followed orders.

"Don't move away until we've finished. I'm not going to hurt you, Miss Norman, I only want you near." He parted her lips once more with the touch of his thumb, lowered the kiss over her full mouth.

She let out a little sound and he deepened the kiss giving her no time to protest his boldness. His arm tightened around her, keeping her so close that her every movement, no matter how slight, imprinted on him.

For a few minutes he kissed her hard, demanding, taking what he'd been afraid to even want for as long as he'd known her, and then he slowly relaxed his hold and the kiss turned soft. He expected her to pull away, but she remained where he'd put her, pressed solidly against his chest.

As he kissed her, he removed her hat and plowed his hand into her beautiful hair. Curls tumbled to her shoulders as pins tinged against the wooden floor around them. He lowered to her throat needing to taste her skin and she let out a sigh. He was drowning in pleasure. Not even his wildest dreams had been as wonderful. Miss Norman was in his arms and he had no idea why, nor any intention of stepping away.

When she finally gulped for air, he turned her around and crossed his arms just below her breasts as he pulled her back against him. This time she didn't protest, didn't pull away even one inch, but remained close. She seemed so soft and comfortable in his arms. He felt as if he were molding her to him, forever matching her form to his.

In the silence of the dusty room, she slowly relaxed against him, as lost in her thoughts as he was in his. The feel of another so close was too foreign to either of them to allow muscles to relax, but still he held her, letting his mouth drift along the smooth, soft line of flesh just below her ear. Then he twisted his fingers into her hair, tugging gently when he wanted her to offer her throat for another kiss. She responded to his request silently, but now and then he'd hear a soft sigh and he'd tighten his grip around her middle, letting her know he was still holding her, still hungry for her. The weight of her breasts resting atop his arm drove him slowly mad.

He'd asked her if she wanted this and she'd nodded, but he wasn't sure she had any more idea what *this* was between them than he did. He tugged an inch of lace away from her high collar and kissed new flesh, then whispered against her ear, "I swear I'll never hurt you. I just need to hold you awhile. When the tower clock chimes the hour, I'll let you go. Is that satisfactory, Miss Norman?"

He felt her draw a long breath. "Yes," she whispered. "I think it most satisfactory."

He hugged her as the hour passed, sometimes kissing her, sometimes whispering in her ear, and sometimes simply holding her. He'd just moved her arms so that they rested on his shoulders when the clock chimed.

"When you come back, wear your hair down." He twisted her slightly in his grip until he could kiss her one more time.

"You can redo it in the room just beyond that door." He pointed to his study. "I have to go reopen. Wait until you hear people in the store before you slip out the dressing room door. As you leave my study, turn out the light. There's a crack between the ceiling and the wall of supplies. From the store I'll see the light go out and know you're gone. From that moment on, know that I'll be missing you and wanting you like this.

"If you want to wait in there next time, I'll know you've come back when I see the light." He moved his hands down her sides as he let her go. "I'll be waiting."

She didn't look back as she disappeared into his study. He wondered what she'd think of the small area, the corner reading area with a comfortable old chair, the small stove he kept burning on cold days for tea and to warm his leg that always ached worse in winter. An old bench held a dusty washbasin and empty towel rack, and back in the corner, hidden away, was the cot he'd used during the healing year when he couldn't climb the stairs to the living space above.

On the other side of his study door were two dressing areas with only curtains separating them from the far entrance to the main floor. He kept all the ladies' things in that corner so they could shop and try on with privacy.

He guessed that was how she'd managed to slip into the storage room both times. He walked to the front door and unlocked it, knowing there would be no nap or lunch. Though he watched as he worked, he didn't see her leave the store, but by dark his body ached for her again.

After Henry went home for the night, Abe checked the storage room, knowing she wouldn't be there. He put the finest brush and comb set he sold in the little extra room along with hairpins, a new washbasin, and clean towels. When she returned, if she returned, he'd have everything ready for her. He didn't want his Miss Norman leaving looking like she'd been kissed.

His Miss Norman? He laughed at himself. She'd never

be his even if, for a few minutes when he held her tight, he wished she were.

When he hung a mirror on the back of the door, he looked at himself. All he saw was a fool.

A fool already dying of hunger for another kiss.

CHAPTER 6

Saturday
Main Street

ROSE WAS AMAZED HOW QUICKLY HALLIE FELL INTO the role of maid. She'd arrived dressed exactly like the finest lady's maid would dress, right down to her practical, polished shoes. Once they were in the sitting room, Rose ordered tea and the two women talked about every detail of Rose's plan to learn about her friend's groom.

A man might have thought Rose was overreacting to the yellow dress and lace roses, but Hallie agreed it had to be an important cry for help. The telegraph was examined, another clue.

Hallie also mentioned two facts that Rose hadn't considered. One, Victoria must have known the man for only a very short time or she would have mentioned him in her earlier letters, and two, why have the wedding in Fort Worth when they both lived in Austin? In fact, Major Chamberlain was a very successful businessman in the capital; wouldn't he have wanted a huge wedding for his only daughter?

"Something's not right," Hallie said as she finished off another sandwich. "As soon as the man arrives, I'll go through his things. I learned a long time ago that most folks carry a tale. Some small thing that tells them who they really are. A wedding ring. A picture. A coin. A bullet they thought meant for them. Find the tell and we find a clue to the secrets he carries."

"Makes sense," Rose agreed. "Like maybe a badge or a piece of a uniform they once wore."

"Right. We find whatever it is and then we go to work."

Rose decided she liked this woman. "If Tori won't or can't tell me what is wrong, we'll have to investigate. I know she wants me here."

Hallie smiled. "You can count on me."

As the hours passed, Rose began to do what she did best. She organized. "If you'll stay here, I'll go to the telegraph office and see what anyone may have noticed two days ago when Victoria sent me the message. Was she alone? Was she nervous? Frightened?"

"While you're gone I'll go next door and introduce myself to the maid. Maybe I can learn something. You'd be surprised what women in the same trade tell each other."

Rose laughed. "Good luck. I've never been able to get more than a few words out of the woman."

As she stood, Rose noticed Hallie wrapped the remaining sandwiches in a napkin. "If you don't mind taking Stitch these extras. I'd hate to see them go to waste."

Pulling on her coat, Rose took the napkin. She'd just learned something new about Hallie Smith. No matter what else the woman was, she was kind.

One step out the door, Rose collided with a tall figure blocking her path. He stumbled backward, surprised by her attack, and she lost her footing trying to slow. They both seemed to be dancing an odd scarecrow kind of movement a moment before both tumbled to within inches of the wide stairway.

She yelped in fear as the stranger stood, pulling her up

with him. The napkin of sandwiches went flying across the steps.

"Pardon me," she said as she looked up into cold gray eyes. "I wasn't watching where . . ." She recognized the man.

"You again," he said without loosening his grip. "Are you aware, miss, that you might be a danger both to yourself and others?"

"You don't look too damaged." Rose resented the fact that this stranger, who'd helped her yesterday when she'd arrived, might think she was normally clumsy. Though what he thought was of little matter to her, she reminded herself. "What are you doing here? Are you following me?"

"I might ask you the same question. Though it's obvious you're stealing food."

He picked up one of the little snacks and, to her shock, ate it. "Not bad, but if you can afford a suite, surely you can pay for your food."

"I did pay for it and stop eating my tea sandwiches. What are you doing hanging around outside my door? I should call the management."

"Not a bad idea, miss. Maybe one of us should switch rooms." He held up his key and pointed to the door next to hers. "Since I was the one attacked, I'll ask to be reassigned."

"Good."

She made it three steps before someone below shouted, "Rose!"

A vision in furs and silk rushed up the stairs. "Oh, Rose, I'm so glad you're here. I just couldn't wait any longer to see you even though my future husband seems to have a hundred things for me to do before the wedding."

Rose heard something in her friend's voice that didn't ring true. A note of panic or fear, or maybe just pre-wedding nerves.

With sudden emotion, Victoria whispered, "I don't know what I would have done if you'd been unable to come."

Rose hugged Victoria Chamberlain. She tried to smile, but the feeling that something was off center was still there. Tori's smile was too bright, her hug too tight. As always she was dressed to perfection, but for a woman declaring her joy over her dearest friend's appearance, she didn't even meet Rose's gaze.

The possibility that she was the only one who didn't know that she was in a play haunted Rose. Something was wrong with Victoria.

Rose almost laughed. According to her family, something was always wrong with Victoria. But there were shadows beneath Tori's pale blue eyes and she clung too tightly to Rose's arm.

She reminded Rose of a woman near panic.

Victoria continued her act. "I see you've met Killian O'Toole, our honorable circuit judge for this district. August's friend couldn't make it back from Washington in time for the wedding and he talked Killian into standing up with him as best man. Isn't that grand?"

Rose looked at the tall man dressed in black. Somehow she wasn't surprised to find him mixed up in this mess. The gray-eyed man bothered her. He seemed almost stoop-shouldered from the bundle of secrets he carried. Killian O'Toole appeared to be as tall as her driver Stitch, but his frame was far slimmer. She doubted Killian could protect himself much less anyone else.

When she noticed his confusion, she couldn't help but wonder if he wasn't another bit player cast in this production. The poor man must have hit his head in the fall because he just stared at Victoria as if all the rest of the world had faded to black. "I agreed to stand with August Myers before I knew who he planned to marry. I had no idea it was you, Miss Chamberlain."

His confession was whispered. Victoria didn't seem to hear it, but Rose had. She couldn't read the man, but she suspected that if he'd known who the bride was he might not have been a part of the wedding party.

Victoria grabbed his arm and pressed against him. "I

wanted to surprise you." She laughed as she moved him along like some giant puppet. "Killian, you must join us for lunch. You're going to love my very dearest friend, Rose McMurray."

Rose stared straight at the silent man, but her words were for Victoria. "He's already eaten."

"Nonsense, he has to join us. My father is getting us a table and August promised to stop by if he can. He's covering a very important trial so he won't be able to stay long before his train leaves for Dallas. He says the news doesn't stop for weddings, so he must work."

Without another word they moved down the stairs and into the dining room. Rose knew it wouldn't be worth arguing over. Victoria always got her way. Even if the thin man had wanted to run, he wouldn't have had a chance with Tori clinging to his arm in what looked like a death grip, and Rose felt just as trapped.

As they walked to the table, Rose heard Tori whisper to Killian, "Give my father time. He never likes anyone at first, but I know eventually he'll warm up to you."

Then, as if tossing out an old toy, Tori shoved Killian toward Rose and ran to hug her father.

Killian stood staring at Victoria. It was Rose's turn to help him along. She locked arms with him and tugged him forward. "She's beautiful, isn't she?"

Killian didn't take his eyes off Victoria. "Yes, she is. Even more beautiful than I remember." He finally seemed to notice Rose and added, "You both are. She told me about you writing her from your ranch. I think you mean a great deal to her."

Rose couldn't lie. "In truth, I doubt I'm her best friend. We've only seen each other once since our school days."

He turned his attention to her. "I think, Miss McMurray, that you are her only friend. I've never heard her mention another."

"You know her well?"

"I met her a few years ago when I was called to Austin. I found her crying on a hidden bench in the back of an old cemetery. I thought she was beautiful then, but here, now, is something different. It's like she's an ivory angel and not real flesh and blood."

"I know what you mean. I've seen her like this once before. Most women shine when they've been polished, but Tori—she sparkles. It's like she's playing the role of queen and we're all peasants."

There it was again, Rose thought, a feeling that all was not as it seemed. Part of her wanted to yell for everyone to stop pretending they were living some kind of adventure. Rose didn't like adventure. She liked order.

"You know her fiancé?"

"I've meet him a few times when I visited Austin. Apparently I'm the only person he knows in this area who's willing to fill in for the best man. I was shocked when he asked me. He said all of his friends couldn't spare the time off and his bride had insisted the wedding be in Fort Worth."

"Why?"

Killian shrugged. "I have no idea. In fact I didn't even know she was the bride August wrote about. I think it was pure luck that a big trial is going on in Dallas—otherwise he would have had to travel from Austin."

Rose glanced out the floor-to-ceiling windows along one wall of the dining room. A mixture of rain and snow was splattering against the glass. "Probably she wanted it here because of the weather."

He looked from the windows to her. "Why didn't I think of that?"

As she and Killian neared the table, he seemed to straighten back into the cold, polite stranger she'd met before.

While Victoria listened to her father, Killian O'Toole leaned down close to Rose's ear. "Tell me, Miss McMurray, does the major bite? I swear every time he looks in my direction I hear him growl."

She fought down a giggle. "Yes, I think he does." Deciding she might like this best man, she added, "Can we start over? I'm Rose, and don't count on me to know much about anyone here."

He took her hand. "I'm Killian, and if possible, I know even less about what's going on." He lifted his wine. "I think I'll give up trying to figure out anything and just drink."

Rose wished she'd had time to ask more, but suddenly Major Chamberlain drew all her attention. His time in the military must have taught him to bully and bluff his way through life as though everyone were under his command. Rose had never been sure she even liked the man. Talking to him had always seemed more like being interrogated than conversation. He professed his beliefs as if he had his name on a book in the Bible.

"How is your family, Rose?" He snapped the question to her.

"Fine." She didn't want to say more, but he pushed.

"Your father? He still running that huge ranch?"

"Yes."

"I hear about your uncle now and then. The famous Texas Ranger who went into law. Very unusual for a half-breed."

Rose wasn't sure that was a question so she said nothing, but a smile tickled at the corner of her lip. If the McMurrays heard the major call Travis a half-breed, they'd probably take turns beating him to death. The three brothers considered themselves double blessed by being both Irish and Apache.

The major continued, "Times are good finally. The McMurrays must be making the money. Of course, with all the kids running around, it probably costs a fortune just to outfit the clan, or should I say *tribe*."

He waited, as if expecting her to give him an accounting. In truth, he barely knew her family. Her papa met him once when he'd picked up Emily and her from school at the same time the major collected his daughter. Teagan McMurray had said very little to him. Papa Teagan seldom talked to people he liked and was usually silent to those he didn't.

Killian lifted his glass, drawing the major's attention. "I've heard of your family, miss. A fine family of heroes and statesmen."

The major frowned, but Rose smiled at the thin man. He'd willingly saved her by drawing fire.

Victoria quickly pulled her father back her direction and rattled all the way through lunch, first with plans of the wedding and then all about how dear Rose was to her.

Rose tried to smile. She even felt a little guilty about thinking so rarely of a woman who apparently claimed she loved her like a sister. She thought of all the crises she and Emily had helped Victoria through, but she couldn't think of one time Tori had saved her, or even tried to cheer her up. Yet she couldn't deny Tori had a kind of magic surrounding her. She lived life in her own kind of world and looked at things differently than anyone Rose had ever known.

Halfway through dinner, the major was called away on business, leaving Rose alone with Killian and Tori. Before Rose could think of anything to say, Victoria touched her arm. "I know you have a fitting so I'll meet you upstairs in a few minutes."

She stood like a queen and walked out of the dining room behind her father.

Killian had stood when Victoria rose, but she hadn't even looked his direction. Rose watched as he almost ran toward the garden door, straight out into the rain.

Left sitting alone at the table filled with half-eaten lunch plates and half-empty wineglasses, Rose decided it was going to be a long week until the wedding.

CHAPTER 7

Sunday
Second Avenue

ABE NOTICED KILLIAN SITTING OUT FRONT OF HIS MER-
cantile as he restocked his shelves on the only day the store
was closed. Killian never came for a visit in the afternoon.
The weather had turned colder, but Abe doubted either of
them would mind as long as they had a cup of coffee in their
hands. So he poured two mugs, put on his coat, and stepped
outside.

"Afternoon, O'Toole." Abe handed his friend a cup of
coffee, then nodded toward the empty space next to him on
the bench. "Afternoon, Shawn. Nice day for a visit."

Killian growled. "Don't talk to either of us. One of us is
an idiot and the other is dumb enough to hang around and
be his brother."

Abe knew better than to laugh. "Long morning, I'm
guessing. You start drinking early for some reason?"
Killian liked to drink; it seemed his balm for all the loneli-
ness in his life, but he usually didn't start until dark. "You
want to talk about it?"

"No. Just knowing I'm a fool is fact enough." He laced his coffee with whiskey and offered Abe the bottle. "And I didn't start early. I started last night and haven't quit."

Abe shook his head as he fought down a smile. "Good. Since you don't want to discuss whatever's got your goat, how about we talk about me? I took your brother's advice."

"What advice?" Killian straightened slightly out of his self-pity.

"I did just like he said. I grabbed a woman and kissed her."

"What'd she do?"

"She kissed me back."

Killian sobered a bit and stared at Abe. "The school-teacher really did that?"

"I didn't say it was the schoolteacher."

"You didn't have to." Killian shook his head. "I've watched you moon over her for years. You really got the nerve to kiss her? You really did it? How? When?"

"Yesterday and I told her not to come back in the storage room unless she wanted more." Abe grinned. "She came back."

They leaned back and drank their coffee, both amazed at the possibility of what might happen next. Finally, Abe broke the silence. "You think I should ask her to marry me? Or maybe I should be asking your dead brother since he steered me right the last time."

"No," Killian said after a long pause in thought. "You'll frighten her. If she lived through the shock of you grabbing her and kissing her—twice—there's no telling how much more her heart can take."

"So you think I should go slow?"

"Hell, no. Abe, if you go any slower, you'll probably be using the same flowers for your wedding and your funeral."

Abe frowned. "Then what do I do?"

"Shawn says you should kiss her every time she comes back, only be more demanding every time. Show her who's boss."

"I don't think so. First, I already know who's boss—she

is. We only kiss when she comes back. I don't have any say over when. And second, I think your brother may be a little out of his depth. How many women did he know before the war?"

"None that he ever mentioned, but remember he was right about grabbing her and just kissing her."

Abe still didn't look convinced. "Well, ask him how long I should wait to ask her to marry me."

Killian was silent for a while, then answered, "Before any kid who'd call you Pa comes along." He leaned his head back bumping it hard on the window frame behind the bench. "But you got to give me some time before you ask her. I don't think I could take being best man twice in one year. This first one may kill me."

"What first one?" Abe frowned. "And what makes you think I was going to ask you to stand up with me?"

Killian rubbed his head. Finally, he answered, "You'd ask me because I'm your only friend."

Abe agreed, never one to argue the obvious.

"As for being best man, I said I'd help out a guy from Austin I barely know. He's a half-crazy newspaperman who's always shouting wild ideas about relocating the South down in South America and how the Confederacy may rise again any day. After a few drinks I only listened to every tenth word or so. To tell the truth, I didn't think he'd even remembered my name until he asked me a week ago to stand up with him. This morning I found out that he's marrying a woman whose hand I was once brave enough to ask for. And, before you ask, I was stone cold sober at the time."

"She turned you down?"

"No, her father did." He swore. "Apparently they both said yes to this nut with a pen in his hand. We were all supposed to meet here in Fort Worth yesterday, but the guy took a turn at Dallas so he could cover some big trial going on. So I'm stuck in that Grand Hotel across the alley with the bridesmaid and the bride. To top it all off, Shawn hasn't shown up for hours. He thinks I should try talking to the bride, maybe make one last plea for my case. Or maybe I should run. Her father didn't even meet me, but he sent a man to threaten me if I ever tried to see her again. I'm too much a coward to do either. If I talk to her, she'll just tell me why this newspaperman is a better choice than me, and if I run I won't ever see her again. I'm in hell."

Abe shook his head. "You're right, Killian. You are a fool and you shouldn't talk about your problems. We should have stayed on mine. To tell the truth, I don't blame your dead brother for not speaking to you. I swear, Killian, your problem makes my brain hurt."

Abe decided not to bother the ghost with any questions either. Who knows, he might be as drunk as his brother.

There seemed no solution to O'Toole's mess, and all Abe wanted to do was kiss the teacher again.

Smiling to himself, Abe let his thoughts wander down that road. He'd liked the way she'd felt against him. He wouldn't mind doing that again as long as she was willing.

"Well?" Killian broke into Abe's daydreams. "Any advice for me other than stay drunk until the wedding is over?"

Abe gave it a shot. "Yeah. Grab her and kiss her. What have you got to lose?"

Both men laughed, knowing that the world was no longer ruled with logic.

They finished off the coffee and talked about how cold it was getting. Abe never asked details about the bride-to-be and Killian never offered any. The shopkeeper might have his nightmares to live with, but he had a feeling Killian had his own share of demons to fight.

A little before twilight they watched the schoolteacher walk down the street on her way home from church. She didn't so much as glance in their direction. Not once.

"You sure you kissed her, Abe?"

Abe didn't bother to answer. He could almost taste her. The need to hold her again ached all the way through his body. She'd come to him twice, and he guessed she'd come again but not tonight.

Killian emptied his flask and wandered off, saying

something about going back to his hotel to sleep. The judge was still a long way from being drunk, but Abe had a feeling he'd get there by midnight.

Abe went inside and collected his tools and the extra key he kept to the schoolhouse.

Slowly, he made his way across the street to put up the blackboard. This would be the only way he'd feel near her tonight.

As he worked, the setting sun weakened, and finally he stopped to light the lamp. He found a tin of matches high on a shelf behind the teacher's desk. He smiled. *Smart,* he thought. *Out of reach of any children.*

As he pulled the tin down, a polished wooden carton about the size of a cigar box tumbled with the matches to the floor. He picked them both up and lit the lamp, then looked inside the box to see what might be so dangerous that she kept it tucked away on the top shelf. He found a few pages of inexpensive stationery and several cards postmarked from Maryland, along with a thin little notebook.

Abe knew he shouldn't, but he turned the first page and scanned down a list of things she planned for the year. *Work harder with Tim on his penmanship. Try to get school board to allot more money for supplies. Save money for a visit home by next summer.*

Then there was her "never" list for the year. *Never sleep before the grading is done. Never eat the boardinghouse fish. Never lose my temper at Mr. Henderson.*

Abe smiled and read on, but he wasn't mentioned again.

When he turned the page, he saw the "dream" list for the New Year: *Be more open to tasting life. Have an adventure. Allow someone else to make decisions now and then. Don't always have to be in control.*

He stared at the page for a while, knowing that she couldn't have written them long ago. Maybe only a day or two before he'd kissed her.

He flipped through the stationery to where she'd written the beginning of a letter to her mother.

Dear Mom, she'd started. *I promise I'll try to make it*

home this year. I miss you terribly. I got your last letter, and you're right—I fear I will never marry, but the way I see it there are worse things. I see many women unhappy, old before their time with work and too many mouths to feed. I have a mission here and do good work with the children. That is enough.

I do wonder what it would be like to be cherished. To be held. To be treated as though I were not plain and ordinary.

Now don't worry, I haven't gone mad. Like I promised, I still keep to myself and never speak to a man unless absolutely necessary.

She stopped there, as if distracted, and never returned to the letter. Maybe she wrote her Christmas note in the boardinghouse or maybe she just had no more to write.

Abe moved his fingers over the writing. How could she think she was plain? He now knew why she'd let him kiss her. Why she'd come back to the storage room again. It hadn't been about him at all. She'd only wanted a taste of life, nothing more.

As he closed the box and placed it back on the shelf, he made himself a promise. If she returned to him, he'd do all he could to make her feel cherished, if only for a blink in her controlled life. If there was never to be a "them," he'd make their time together about her. If there would never be a future together, at least they'd have a memory to share.

CHAPTER 8

Main Street

THE EVENING AIR DRIFTED OVER ROSE LIKE A THIN blanket of damp cotton as she opened the door to the long balcony that ran in a wide U-shape along all the second-floor rooms. The day had been endless and frustrating because she never found one moment to be alone with Victoria. The bride seemed far more worried that her new wardrobe wasn't altered than that the bridegroom hadn't bothered to show up. In fact, Tori and her father rarely mentioned him. August seemed just a detail of the wedding, no more important than the cake knife or the altar flowers.

Rose leaned against the doorframe and stared out into the shadows. She could hear Hallie snoring away in the maid's quarters just beyond her bedroom. The undercover maid had spent the evening with Betty Ann helping with the alterations, but for all her effort she learned only one fact. Victoria had cried herself to sleep every night since she agreed to marry August Meyers.

The thought occurred to Rose that maybe August was blackmailing her or somehow forcing her into the marriage, but that made no sense. The major was a powerful man. August, on a newspaperman's salary, couldn't even keep Victoria in shoes. Also, even if August were a bully, he wasn't here now to force Victoria to do anything. He'd apparently jumped trains and headed to Dallas to cover some big trial. A man in love wouldn't be thinking about work a few days before his wedding.

Rose thought of the line of men who'd tried to court her over the years. Some were just looking for a wife, any wife. A few were far more interested in a slice of her family ranch than in her, and three swore they'd fallen hopelessly in love with her. Two of those she'd made the mistake of accepting an engagement ring from, hoping that she'd either grow to feel the same way or that they'd lose interest. In the end, she'd broken both engagements long before the date was set. She didn't know why, but they just weren't right.

The curtain moved as Duncan walked in from the balcony. "About time you opened the door. I thought I might freeze solid out there." He was dressed in a suit tonight and what looked like a new gray Stetson. Clean-shaven and washed he made a handsome ranger.

But Rose frowned at her cousin. "Too bad I didn't know you were there. I would have gone to bed early and forgotten about needing fresh air. Besides, you don't feel the cold like most folks do. Ever occur to you that one of your parents might have been cold-blooded? Maybe a lizard or a frog." She brushed the frost from his windblown hair.

"Or alligator." He grinned, shaking his head enough for bits of cold rain to sprinkle her face. "Any chance you'll order room service? I didn't want to come through the front door. Right now I'd just as soon make sure no one knows where I am."

Rose didn't ask why. In truth, from the time he was five no one usually knew where he was. "I told them an hour ago to deliver a late snack for two."

He raised an eyebrow. "You couldn't have known I was coming."

"I didn't. It's for my maid and me. The major insisted we all go to dinner tonight. My dress was laced so tightly I couldn't eat more than two bites. Hallie said that was the style and promised we'd eat later. Only she dozed off on me before the food arrived."

"Since when did you ever have a maid, Rose?" He looked her over from nose to toes. "There's nothing wrong with your body like it is. Why would you want to lace up any part of it?"

She opened her mouth to answer, but a tap on the door forced him back out on the balcony while the tray was delivered. Then he joined her and began eating both plates of food. Rose drank her hot chocolate and watched.

"Want to tell me why you're here? And don't bother saying it's to watch over me. You've got Stitch and probably half the hotel staff doing that."

"I came over to tell you that the trial will drag on through Monday at least. I figured it would only take a day or two to find the Tanner brothers guilty, but the press is going crazy, so the lawyers are talking every murder and robbery out detail by horrible detail so the reporters can get it all. Everyone knows the Tanners are guilty, but the longer it lasts, the more papers sell."

"So? Why are you here, Duncan? It's a long ride from here to Dallas and back. If you're working a twelve-hour shift guarding, you're losing almost half the downtime traveling."

He set his fork aside and seemed to be picking his words carefully. "Rose, the longer this thing goes on, the greater the chance is that one guard will look away at the wrong time or take a bribe, and two of the worst outlaws I've ever come across will break free. A few of us believe the Tanners are working for someone. If they are, he might find a way to break them free."

"You don't think they'd come here?" She grinned. "As far as I know they're not on the guest list for the wedding."

He didn't laugh. "I don't think they'd come here, but I'd feel better if you were back at Whispering Mountain."

"Why?" She leaned closer. "The truth, Duncan. Don't you dare lie to me."

"All right. If they got free, and that's a big if, they might have it in their heads to kill me or any McMurray they could find. I'm top on their list to murder right now and you're second."

"I'm not surprised you are." She shook her head. "But me? You think they might want to kill me? That's ridiculous. I don't even know the men and don't plan to."

Duncan wanted to take back his words, but it was too late. He'd come to check on her, not frighten poor timid Rose half to death. But he could never lie to her, never fool her. She was smart and what he was telling her didn't make sense.

He stood, pacing the little room. "Just be careful. That's all I'm asking." Dropping into the nearest chair, he added as if to himself, "Not that you would ever be anything but careful, Rose. In a family of wild reckless people, you're the only one who always prepares, always takes precautions. You're the only McMurray no one ever has to worry about, so heaven knows why I'm worried about you now."

Rose straightened her dressing gown, playing with the material as if she could brush her misgivings away. "It's not like I didn't already have enough to worry about with Tori and her August. I haven't told you that I have my suspicions that they don't love each other. Forget that now. Now I have to worry about outlaws murdering me."

She looked up, hoping he'd reassure her.

Duncan didn't seem to be listening. He stared out the balcony window at two figures moving in the shadows.

For a second, Rose felt her heart stop beating, then she realized Duncan wasn't reaching for his gun. If danger lay just beyond the glass, he would have the Colt ready to fire.

"I don't think you have to worry about your friend being in love," he said, his words so low they barely reached her. "Not from the way someone is kissing what looks to me like Miss Victoria Chamberlain right now."

"Really?" Rose rushed to the window. A couple stood in

the far corner of the long balcony, locked in one another's arms. Branches from the trees and vines that surrounded the garden crossed over them as if protecting them inside their own world. His black hat blocked both their faces, but she had little doubt what they were doing. There was no mistaking Victoria's long midnight cape that she'd worn to dinner.

Rose leaned against Duncan's chair, knowing she shouldn't spy but unable to look away from the beauty of two lovers holding one another. Both bodies seemed like porcelain figures swaying to music she couldn't quite hear.

"Isn't it beautiful?"

"I wouldn't know," Duncan answered honestly. "Every woman I love turns me down or joins the nunnery."

"I wouldn't know either. I probably never will. I'm beginning to believe there is no man for me born in this lifetime." She frowned at Duncan. "It could happen."

Duncan tugged her to the arm of his chair, the couple outside holding no interest to him. "Well, it's not from my lack of trying. I've sent you half the eligible men in the state and you bounce them all back. I swear, Rose, couldn't you pick one so my dad and uncles will stop asking me if I know anyone right for sweet, dear little Rose?" He played with her braid as he'd done for as long as she remembered.

"I don't bounce them back. They just all leave. Besides, I don't want you picking a husband for me." She patted his arm as if he were a spoiled child. "You can't even pick your clothes, Duncan. Look at you. No one in the state would guess you're a lawyer. I'd be willing to bet none of your clothes have ever seen a pressing and your boots are two winters muddy. Most of the time you look like you've been trailing cattle for a hundred miles. Don't you think the rangers should have a dress code?"

"We do. We have to wear them."

"Seriously, you could use a few more . . ."

"Forget my clothes, Rose. I'm talking about you." He put his arm around her to steady her on the chair arm. "You make the men I send leave, Rose. You know what they all

say. They say you're too perfect. Couldn't you burn a few
meals or get a little dirt on the hem of your skirt or cuss
now and then? Men don't know how to handle perfect
women. They can't measure up."

He was on a roll and she knew there would be no stopping him. One of their favorite pastimes seemed to be re-
making each other and it was his turn.

"Maybe you could take up smoking—men hate women
who smoke cigars—or drinking, only it would have to
be hard liquor." He brushed her hair braid with his hand.
"Cut your hair lopsided, or maybe some makeup could ugly
you up a little. Start thinking only about yourself, maybe
even talk in the third person like you're the queen of something."

"Stop it." She shoved him and would have fallen off the
chair arm if he hadn't held her safe. "You're making me
sound like Victoria."

"You're nothing like her. She's like a glass statue. I
swear I could feel a norther coming in when I danced with
her that once. You're flesh and blood. You're a good woman,
Rose. So good you make a man see his own imperfections."

"She's not much of a statue tonight," Rose said as she
looked back to the window. "She looked very warm-
blooded in the arms of that man in the shadows. I guess we
can stop worrying about her fiancé making it to the wedding on time if he made it in to kiss her tonight."

The couple had vanished. Probably disappearing into
one of the rooms or down the wrought-iron stairs to the
garden. The memory of them seemed to linger in the shadows of branches brushing the railing.

Duncan stood and tugged her to the opening. "I like the
silence of this place. We're in the middle of town, but here,
walled in by the hotel, the garden seems magical."

"I know what you mean." She'd felt it too. "I see why
people stay here. In this place it's easy to believe the world
is beautiful and you can be or do anything you want to."

"You can, Rose. Just stop being afraid to try. Take a

chance. Go wild." He smiled. "Who knows—for you that would probably be eating dessert first."

"I couldn't . . ."

"You could."

When he winked, Rose pushed him out the open door afraid of what he might suggest next.

Duncan stumbled acting as if she'd hit him a blow and not a tap. Before he could recover, he collided with a tall thin man passing along the balcony walkway.

Rose squealed with laughter when she recognized Killian O'Toole.

"Attacking another unsuspecting stranger?" Killian said calmly as if just stating a fact.

Rose fought down a giggle. "No, Judge O'Toole, this time I was attacking my cousin and I promise you he deserved it. Please step out of the night and meet him."

Duncan stepped back inside, straightened, and offered his hand to the man. "We've never met, Judge, but I've heard of you. My father says the West could use more men as dedicated as you."

"Ranger Duncan McMurray." Killian accepted his hand and set his black hat on the back of the nearest chair. "You're a legend and I'm told you brought the Tanner boys in. Fascinating. I'll bet the trial is interesting."

As the two men talked of the trial going on in Dallas, Rose felt invisible. Out of habit, she began to tidy the sitting room. When she opened the door to the hallway to set the tray out, Major Chamberlain stood with his hand up preparing to knock.

"Major, I'm afraid you have the wrong room. Victoria is next door."

"She's not in her room," he huffed like the big bad wolf. "I was told she was seen on the balcony with a man."

Rose started to agree but hesitated. The major seemed far too upset to be simply checking on his daughter.

The father of the bride looked past Rose to the two men standing by the balcony windows. "Did either of you see my daughter?" He moved into the room waving Rose aside as if she were no more than a doorman.

Both men stepped out onto the balcony as though they planned to help the major in his quest.

"I was told she was seen out here with a man." The major stormed back and forth as if in front of his men. "When I ran into the garden, I saw a couple embracing, but they seem to have vanished."

Rose joined them. Even in the shadows she didn't miss the look that passed between Duncan and Killian O'Toole.

The major seemed to be building steam. "She'd better not be . . ."

"Wait a minute, sir, did the couple look something like this?" Duncan grabbed the black hat from the back of the chair and tugged Rose a few feet into the night.

Before she could react, he lifted the hat to cover their faces, tugged her against him, and lowered his mouth to hers for a light kiss.

The major swore. "They looked exactly like that, Ranger McMurray. You have my apology for interrupting you. Your cousin, Rose, is obviously not held to the same standards as my daughter."

Rose didn't know which one of the men to fire at first. Duncan had no right to kiss her on the lips. A kiss on the cheek or forehead would have been proper but not a real kiss. And . . . the major had just insulted her.

Duncan, the idiot, just smiled at her and said, "It was just a friendly kiss. Though we both took the name McMurray, we're not related by blood. I guess you might say we're just kissing cousins."

If Killian O'Toole hadn't decided to come alive and step between them, she might have killed Duncan.

"Well, ladies and gentlemen, I think it best if I call it a night." Killian yawned. "I just stepped out for a smoke. Maybe the garden downstairs would be quieter."

As Killian passed Duncan, he took his hat and disappeared into the night. The major couldn't have noticed for he stormed across the sitting room and began pounding on the far door leading to Victoria's bedroom.

After three knocks, a robed Victoria appeared looking as if she'd just awakened. "Father," she mumbled, "is something wrong?"

The major cooled. "No, dear. Sorry to have woke you. Go back to bed."

Victoria followed orders, as she'd done all her life. She turned around, walked into her room, and closed the door.

The major left the way he'd come without saying a word.

Rose turned on Duncan, but he was already backing away.

"I think I'll join Judge O'Toole for a smoke. Good night, Rose."

To have her say, she would have had to yell, and Rose told herself a lady never yells. So, as calmly as she could, she said good night and closed the balcony door.

Once alone she blew out the lamp in the sitting room and went to her bedroom. As she got ready for bed she wondered if the judge had seen the couple kissing in the corner of the balcony. Probably not, she decided, or he would have mentioned it. He seemed a cold, hard man who might have interrupted the loving couple and threatened to charge them with public displays of affection, if there were such a crime.

Then Rose remembered the hat Duncan had used to re-create the couple's scene. Killian's black hat.

Could it be possible that the judge and the ice princess had been the two lovers on the balcony?

Logic told her no, but in an odd way the possibility of their pairing was the first thing that had made sense in days.

CHAPTER 9

After a few drinks with the judge, Duncan decided to spend the night in Fort Worth. The rain had stopped, but the water on the roads was already freezing. The trail to Dallas would be much easier to follow in daylight and he didn't have to be on guard until noon.

He rented a room across the street from Rose's hotel. It was a noisy place with rooms above a saloon, but he felt more at home here than at the fancy hotel. The memory of the sweet kiss he'd given Rose lingered in his thoughts. He had a feeling when she thought about what he'd done there would be hell to pay, but in truth, he really didn't care. Kissing her had been in the back of his mind for years.

She wasn't right for him. He doubted any woman ever would be, but every time she sent a man packing Duncan saw a sadness in her eyes. She was a woman who should be kissed, but he knew none of the men who courted her would ever measure up to her standards . . . to what she deserved. And neither would he. Even the black suit he'd borrowed hadn't impressed her. She wanted polished oak, and he was in the rough, with the bark still on.

Even with the whiskey floating in his brain, he couldn't get the taste of her out of his mind. Maybe it was the rainy night or the couple kissing in the shadows, but he'd felt a need to hold her tonight. She'd always seemed comfortable when they took naps together on the long porch at the ranch or under the trees in Austin on hot afternoons, but he figured she'd draw the line at sleeping next to him tonight. He'd probably broken one of her thousand unwritten rules.

He knew he'd never be the man for her, but every time they were together he found himself hating the thought that one day she might find a man who would be right. A man who'd make love to her like he never would.

She wasn't the type of woman he needed either, all soft and sweet, and he'd never make her happy roaming around the state. He didn't remember his real parents, but they must have had Gypsy blood in them. If they'd come to Texas so early, they probably loved adventure. He liked the made-up image he had of them and wasn't sure he wanted to know what was in the letter tucked safely away in Rose's traveling bag. He thought of them as like him, wild and free, hating the idea of settling down.

Frustrated, Duncan went back downstairs to the saloon. Maybe all he needed was a woman, any woman. He'd never been a man who frequented the services of soiled doves, but tonight he might make an exception.

The saloon was almost empty. A few drunks sleeping on the tabletops and two groups of gamblers settled in to play the night away. Several pretty girls sat at a table near the back. Their dresses were low cut in front and short enough to show off their legs.

He walked up, tipped his hat to the group, and held his hand out to the nearest black-haired beauty. She had on too much makeup and her eyes weren't brown, but in the dark she'd do.

She gave him a tired smile and took his hand. Without a word, they walked back to his room. Just inside the door, he removed his hat and gun belt while she stood silently watching. Then, with one hand, he pushed her against the wall and kissed her hard as he tugged the straps off her shoulders.

Her dress slipped even lower as she leaned her head back giving a view of what promised to be large and lovely breasts. He leaned his body into hers and she made a practiced sound of pleasure.

Duncan hesitated an inch away from kissing her again. She waited, in no hurry, for time was money in her line of work.

She had a pretty face and a soft body that fit nicely against his, but he smelled the hint of cigar smoke in her hair and knew he wasn't the first to dance with her tonight.

After one more kiss, he pulled away. She'd done nothing wrong. She'd done nothing right. He handed her a few bills and opened the door for her.

"That's all you wanted, cowboy?"

"That's all," he answered.

She wasn't in the habit of questioning customers. With a shrug, she stuffed the money down her dress and left.

Duncan dropped on the bed and stared at the ceiling. He had enough real problems to worry about. One more day of trial to deal with and he still hadn't gotten around to telling Rose about Victoria's groom.

Yesterday, after the trial had ended for the night, August Myers had walked over to the nearest saloon, spent ten minutes writing notes and the rest of the night drinking. He didn't act like a man who had a bride waiting thirty miles away. Duncan had taken his turn guarding the Tanner brothers, but one of the rangers later reported that the newspaperman spent the evening drinking with three of the saloon girls. He left at closing time, pulling the drunkest one along behind him toward the alley. When the bartender tried to stop him, Myers said he'd pay for her services but that he didn't want her in his bed. He claimed the alley would do fine.

August Myers didn't sound like the kind of man who'd marry Victoria Chamberlain. Though he had enough money to drink and his clothes were expensive, he didn't seem to fit with Victoria. She'd listened to her windbag of a father for twenty-five years, and it looked like she'd be spending the next fifty doing the same thing with a husband. Both were radicals and she'd always just be an audience for their rants.

Today Duncan had left right after his guard duty, hoping to reach Fort Worth before dark. For August to make it in time to be kissing Victoria on the balcony, he would have had to ride faster than Duncan. Impossible. Not with the kind of horses rented at the livery.

Which left one possibility: The man kissing Victoria wasn't August. Judge O'Toole's black hat was all the proof he'd needed. When they'd shared a drink, neither mentioned the couple in the shadows, but for a man who'd just kissed a woman the judge didn't look very happy. When he said good night, he looked like a man walking back to an empty room, not a man who had an unlocked balcony door waiting for him.

Duncan closed his eyes knowing he'd be back in the saddle heading toward Dallas before dawn. He'd worry about Killian O'Toole and August Myers after the outlaws were sentenced and handed over to the federal marshals. With luck tomorrow would be the last day of the trial. If the Tanners planned to make a break, they'd make it before dark.

CHAPTER 10

Monday
Second Avenue

ABE WATCHED MISS SARA NORMAN AS SHE RANG THE school bell and welcomed her students back from their holiday break. If she'd glanced up, she would have seen him standing in the doorway. He told himself he'd wave when she noticed him. Then maybe she'd nod slightly or even wave back if he were lucky.

But she never looked his way.

All day he found himself stealing looks out the window toward the school, wishing, hoping to see her returning them. But it never happened. The weather was too cold for the children to go outside. He'd seen them eating their lunches at their desks and then marching around the room on parade like a small band, laughing and clapping.

When he saw her like that, a teacher—a good teacher—he couldn't think of her as an almost lover. It wouldn't be right. She was smart and caring and too good for a crippled-up man who rarely left his store.

That evening, he watched her light burning late in the

little schoolroom. He knew she was working, but that didn't stop him from wanting her. Seeing her all alone at the desk made him think of the lists she made for herself and the letter she'd started to her mother. He thought of her as lonely, maybe as lonely as he was, and he wanted to hold her.

When she finished, she blew out the lamp, locked the door, and walked home to her boardinghouse without looking his direction. He'd feared she wasn't coming back to him. Maybe he'd been too bold. Maybe he'd been too mean, too demanding. He made up a hundred *ifs*. If he'd moved slower, maybe asked to hold her hand. If he'd just talked to her and not told her he was going to kiss her. He couldn't remember saying one nice thing to her. He'd only demanded she remain silent while he kissed her like he was sure no gentleman ever kissed a lady.

Maybe she wanted to forget the whole thing. What had meant so much to him might be nothing more to her than a memory she'd like to forget.

He went about his job, waiting on late customers just getting off work and stopping by to pick up things before heading home. A few of the girls from the saloon on Main Street came in. They probably hadn't felt comfortable in the fancy stores a block over, but this time of night no one would notice them buying a few necessities. They giggled and talked among themselves. When they finally made their selections, they walked shyly to the counter.

Abe always treated them like fine ladies and they always thanked him as properly as if they lived in one of the big houses and not in the back of a saloon.

Nights were the worst for him. Abe wished he could have at least walked Sara home. In his mind he would try talking to her, though even there he struggled with words. *You're every thought I have*, seemed a little much, and *How are you?* didn't seem nearly enough. So he'd remained in his prison with his nightmares of the war and his days filled with thinking of things he wished he'd said. Before holding her in his arms, he felt like he'd been asleep through his days. With one kiss, she'd awakened him and he learned how lonely his life was.

The air had turned icy when he finally locked up. He wanted to stand at the corner of his porch and look down the road where he could see the windows of her boarding-house, but Abe forced his mind on other matters. He'd decided not to remodel the bakery next door. Sara often used the space for her own supplies because the little school-house lacked room, and he liked the thought of her visiting the storage area from time to time to retrieve desks and chairs and whatever else she needed. He'd even had Henry take her a key to the old bakery door just in case she ever needed to pick up something when he wasn't around. As if that would ever happen; he was always at the store.

As far as he knew she'd only been over to the storage space a few times with a couple of the older boys to help carry desks. He'd checked and she'd always made sure to lock the door before leaving.

He turned the sign and pulled down the shade on the door. She would be eating supper at the boardinghouse about now. He had no idea which room was hers and saw no way to find out, but he liked to think that she could see his lights above the store from her window.

When he moved through the empty store, he was glad she'd gone home before the rain had turned to ice. In her way, she worked as hard as he did, and he admired that about her. If he were honest, he admired everything about her and he hated the way he'd been hard and cold to her. The one lady who mattered to him and he hadn't treated her like a lady. Maybe she'd come back that second time think-ing that he'd be kind.

He turned off all the lights except the one over his desk and almost stumbled as he noticed the dim glow from the study lamp just behind the store's wall of shelves. His first thought was that he'd left it on, but he never left it on by accident.

He slowly moved into the storeroom and opened his

study door. The possibility that she might be there frightened him almost as much as the fear that she might not.

Sara Norman stood still and silent as if waiting for a train. Her long cape, a hunter's green, covered her completely. She'd lit the lamp but not the stove. The room was more in shadow than light, making it seem even colder.

With no greeting, he moved to the stove and lit the fire inside. He thought of telling her he'd kept everything ready, but he wasn't sure he wanted her to know how dearly he'd hoped that she would come again.

When he faced her, she'd lowered her head so that most of her face was hidden by her hood. The rain glittering off her shoulders told him she'd just arrived. She must have gone home, maybe eaten dinner, then slipped back into the night and walked the shadowed walkways to him.

Moving around his study chair, he gripped the leather arm for support. When she didn't look up, he lowered her hood, hungry for the sight of her.

Her hair hung long and rich over her shoulders as she looked down at her hands. She was a woman fully grown, but her shyness made her seem younger. Moving his hand over her dark hair in a slight caress, he waited for her to look up.

She'd come back to him. The joy of it made his heart pound so loudly he was surprised she couldn't hear it.

When she didn't look up, he knew what he had to do. He had to tell her he was sorry. He had to be kind, when all he'd ever considered himself was simply fair and honest. "I'm sorry," he whispered as he lowered his hand to his side. "You're a lady. I shouldn't have . . . We shouldn't have . . ."

Raising her gaze, she stared at him, her eyes wide with surprise.

He fought to find more words about how he felt while she studied him as if looking for something that was no longer there.

"I shouldn't have . . ." he began again. The way he'd touched her had been far too bold.

One tear bubbled and moved slowly down her cheek. She began to shake her head and back away. When her hip bumped the washstand, she looked at the door behind him as if waiting for a chance to run.

He saw all he needed to see. His words made her frown. They were turning her away. An apology hadn't been what she'd wanted.

She pulled her hood up as she tried to inch around him without touching him, as if she'd returned and found nothing of interest.

With a sudden stab to his heart, Abe knew he hadn't given her what she'd come to him for. He'd thought of a hundred reasons why she'd let him behave as he had toward her, but never once had it occurred to him that this was simply what she wanted. Someone else to take charge. Someone who told her what he wanted and acted without discussion or debate.

She'd set the rules. She made the choice to come here, and apparently she wanted him to do the rest.

He caught her wrist just before she was out of his reach. "Where do you think you're going, Sara?" He used her first name to remind her she wasn't just anyone to him, she was special. "We've only just begun."

Tugging her toward him, he ignored her protest as he lowered into the chair and pulled her atop him. When she was on his lap, he moved his hand along her arm and over her shoulder until he reached her throat and closed his fingers gently around her cool skin. "Close your eyes and open your mouth. I plan to kiss you long and completely before you go." His voice came hard and demanding as he drew her to him.

Before she could say anything, his mouth covered hers. She pushed at his chest, but his arms held her. When she tried to turn her head, he grabbed her jaw and held her steady. "Don't move, Sara. Don't try to pull away from me. I know you didn't cross the night to run away from me now." He could feel her tears falling, but he didn't let go of her. If she didn't want his apology, he'd try this. Either way, he might lose her forever.

After a hard kiss against her closed mouth, his fingers dug into her hair and tugged, pulling her an inch away. "Kiss me back," he ordered. "Kiss me back."

He could feel her heart pounding wildly against his as he loosened his grip on her hair to a caress.

She timidly moved her lips to his. For a few heartbeats she barely brushed his mouth with hers. He didn't move. He wanted her to come to him willingly, and slowly she did. She was fighting her own shyness, her own hesitation, her own fears, not him.

When she finished another kiss and leaned a few inches away, he said simply, "That's the way to do it, my love. Now again." His fingers caressed her face. "Kiss me, Sara."

He thought he saw a smile a moment before her mouth touched his. With a laugh, he drew her near and deepened the kiss she'd offered.

As the room grew warm, she melted against him without protest. He pulled off her cape, letting it fall on the floor. Underneath she wore only a blouse and skirt, not her normal suit. He set her a few inches away. Her eyes were bright as she watched him, gulping for air as she waited to see what would come next.

"Be very still," he said, his hand moving along her jaw.

She nodded slightly.

He tugged at the scarf she'd knotted almost like a tie around her throat. As it gave and drifted to the floor he felt as though he were opening a wonderful gift. He'd watched her for years, even spent time trying to think of how to talk to her about something other than school supplies. Only tonight, here she was, sitting on his good leg, letting him touch her. His fingertips brushed over her face, needing to know every line, every curve, and loving the feel of her warm skin.

She remained still even when he kissed her lightly.

His hands settled around her waist, liking the feel of her

without a jacket or coat. "Unbutton the top button of your blouse."

When she didn't move, he whispered his request again. "I've a need to taste your throat," he added. "Such a beautiful throat. Unbutton the top for me."

With trembling hands she loosened the first button.

He kissed her quickly, then pushed her back in place against the arm of his chair. "And now the next button."

She leaned back, closing her eyes as he continued to move his hands over her. "You're a woman who needs to be touched, Sara." His fingers moved into her hair, pulling slightly as his free hand spread out over her blouse just below her breasts.

She held his gaze as she worked the next button free. When she'd finished, he whispered, "Well done. Open your mouth, dear, so I can kiss you again." His fingers brushed beneath her breasts and he caught her cry of surprise in a kiss.

As she grew comfortable with his long kisses, he pulled away watching the blush in her cheeks and the slight smile on her slightly swollen lips.

He moved close so that his words brushed her cheek. "I plan to kiss you tonight until I've had my fill of this soft beautiful mouth. I don't know the words to say or what a woman needs to hear. You matter to me. Even if you never come back to this room, you matter to me. Do you understand, Miss Norman?"

Smiling slightly, she nodded and whispered, "I understand," and was rewarded with a kiss that moved slowly down her throat and back up to her mouth.

He left her breathless before he whispered, "Now work the next button free. It's time for our adventure to begin."

When her hands hesitated at her collar, he moved his fingers over hers and gripped the cotton a moment before he tugged hard, breaking buttons down half her blouse.

As she cried out in surprise, he cradled her close, this time molding her body against his while she calmed.

"Hush, Sara. It's all right. I've got you." He moved his hand over her back in a gentle caress, knowing this was as new to her as it was to him.

When she finally stilled, he said simply, "I couldn't wait any longer." He brushed his fingers down her slim neck. "Do you have any objections?"

She leaned back against the arm of the chair, closed her eyes, and she answered, "No, Abraham."

"Then stay with me awhile. I've waited years to touch you, to feel you in my arms, and I plan to take my time."

He thought he caught another smile touching her lips as his hand moved slowly down the V of her blouse. Her hips shifted atop him.

Laughing, he patted her hip gently then allowed his hand to remain there. "Be still while I look at you. I know you've a grand mind, but it's the beauty of you I want to see tonight."

He felt her tremble as his hand moved down the trail of broken buttons. He stopped there for a moment, then brushed his fingers down the middle where they almost met. Her breasts were bigger than he'd thought and softer than anything he'd ever touched. They might be bound tightly with lace, but pure creamy skin pushed up.

As she lay back against the arm of the chair he watched her breathe. Gently, he moved his hand over her hip. "You make me feel like the luckiest man alive, just to be allowed to look at you like this, Sara." He patted her hip. "The wonder of you, the feel of you, makes me forget to breathe."

He watched her cheeks warm with a blush and he couldn't resist kissing her tenderly. When he finally straightened, she smiled with lips wet and swollen from his kiss.

The tips of his fingers brushed over the swell of her breasts. If one more button had fallen, her breasts might have been exposed. He pushed the blouse back so that he could see the cotton lace of her camisole ride the rise and fall of her breasts.

"You're perfection, miss, pure and simple," he said,

amazed at how her skin warmed and reddened to his slight caress. "When you return to me, I want your blouse open exactly this far. We'll begin where we leave off tonight."

She didn't open her eyes as he moved his fingers along her jaw and over her cheeks. Lifting her hair up and over the arm of the chair, he watched it tumble to the floor. He studied her as she seemed to sleep in his arms. His hand returned again and again to the rise of her breasts above the lace. Then, his kisses turned loving, saying what he couldn't say with words.

When she moved, he molded his hands over her body to settle her back where he wanted her. Her damp clothes did little to hide her curves. From time to time he grew bold, barely letting her get over the shock of one touch before another took her breath away. Each time he'd kiss her tenderly and rock her in his arms until she calmed, and then he'd take her to another high.

He moved his mouth to her throat, knowing their time was growing short. "It's almost time for you to go."

She nodded and straightened.

She didn't look at him as she stood and pulled the blouse together. He knew without asking that this was far more than she'd ever shown a man.

He stood behind her. "I know it's late, but lower your hands. I can't end this yet."

Slowly she moved her hands to her sides and he reached around her and opened the blouse once more. "Now lean your head back against my shoulder for just a moment more."

He circled his arm and turned her toward him as she closed her eyes. Just as her left breast brushed against his chest and began to swell with her intake of air, he placed a kiss above the lace, then moved to her mouth and kissed her, learning how she liked to be kissed by the movements she made and the little sounds of pleasure.

Finally, she cuddled against his heart and he held her tightly, lost in the wonder of her so near. When she finally turned back to the bench, he lightly brushed his fingers down her throat to where the cotton of her undergarments blocked his path.

She didn't move.

Fighting to keep his hands from shaking, he slowly moved over the material and cupped her breasts in his hands.

He waited for her to react, but she remained so still he wasn't sure she was even breathing.

His fingers tightened over the cotton covering her and he lowered his head to kiss her cheek.

When he stepped back, she lifted the brush he'd left for her and began to straighten her hair. He didn't miss the way her hand shook.

"Our time tonight is over," he said as he forced his voice back to the cold, impersonal tone he always used. "I'll leave you to dress and tie up your hair. You'll find what you need on the washstand. From now on leave your cape on the peg by the door."

She nodded as he stepped away. She seemed suddenly shy, turning her back to him.

He watched her at the washbasin. Her movements were slow as if she didn't want the time to end. He came and stood behind her one last time.

"Turn around," he said sharply, his hands already resting lightly on her waist.

When she did, he pulled her against him. For a few minutes, he just held her, growing used to her with every sense. When the clock tower chimed ten times, he let her slip from his arms.

He left the study and crossed to the button display. Returning, he shoved a few cards of his best buttons in her pocket, then stepped into the blackness beneath the stairs.

Closing his eyes, he listened to the door open and heard her footsteps leave. For a long while he remained in the darkness. If he'd gone any closer, he would have held her again. If he hadn't let her go now, Abe wasn't sure he'd ever be able to let her go.

How could such a woman need anything so personal from him?

He'd given the orders. He'd demanded she kiss him and let him touch her, but Abe was under no illusion he held the power. For the hour they'd been together he'd been in charge, but now all he could do was wait and hope she'd return.

When he crossed to the study, he noticed she hadn't taken the brush and comb or even the hairpins. Walking closer he found the cards of buttons beside the brush. She hadn't wanted his gifts.

For a moment he was angry, but then he realized something.

All she'd wanted tonight was him.

CHAPTER 11

Monday
Main Street

Rose awoke before sunrise, guessing that she would spend another day alone at the hotel. Victoria always seemed in a hurry or had her father by her side. She talked of dresses and wedding plans but never about why she'd asked Rose to come in early.

Hallie was making more headway with Betty Ann. Through Victoria's maid they were able to keep up with when the Chamberlains were in the hotel. Not that it mattered. Hallie had gone through everything in both of the major's rooms and found nothing of interest except that the major seemed to be leaving the country after the wedding. Also, Victoria's trousseau was packed in new luggage and each bag was locked. According to the maid, Victoria wasn't even allowed to look at anything until her wedding day.

Rose's new maid also broke into the room that was supposed to be the bridegroom's and nothing of his was even there. He was four days away from his own wedding and he didn't seem in any hurry to show up.

Everything seemed in order, except for the yellow dress hanging in Rose's closet and the telegram Tori had sent. The couple on the balcony was still a mystery, as was the reason Tori cried every night.

Rose sensed that her friend was in some kind of trouble, but Victoria stood a canyon away, unable or unwilling to cross and tell Rose the truth. The only strategy seemed to be for Rose to wait, ready to stand as a friend when needed.

Monday came wrapped in fog. Victoria had promised to get up at least in time to dress and have brunch with Rose, not in the huge restaurant downstairs or even the coffee shop that served simple meals but in the sitting room between their bedrooms.

Finally, they'd have their time alone. Time for Rose to ask questions. Time for her to get some answers.

As Hallie put on the pot for their morning tea, a pounding on the door leading to Tori's rooms made them both jump. There was no need for Tori to announce her arrival into what was as much her sitting room as Rose's.

Hallie straightened her uniform and answered the knock with all the proper manner of a fine maid.

Betty Ann exploded into the room. With her nightgown and robe flying, she ran to Rose and dropped at her feet. "Help me, miss. You have to help me. The unthinkable has happened and I'm going to get blamed."

Rose knelt beside her. "What is it?" She could feel the maid shaking as she tried to lift Betty Ann to her feet.

"Miss Victoria is gone. I don't know when or how, but she didn't wake me this morning to help her dress, and when I checked on her, the bed hadn't been slept in."

Betty Ann began to cry. "She's been kidnapped. That has to be it. In ten years she's never gone anywhere without me dressing her first. I had my curse last night. She made me warm tea with a bit of whiskey and told me to rest." The maid sobbed, mumbling something about how much money the major had and how they'd all feared a kidnapping.

Rose looked up at Hallie. "Get the major and any security the hotel has."

Hallie nodded and disappeared. Within minutes Rose's sitting room was packed with men asking questions that no one knew the answers to. For the first time, the major couldn't think of anything to say, he just paced the little room like a caged lion.

Rose stood back near the balcony doors and tried to piece together the facts. The couple on the balcony kept flashing across her mind, but she didn't say a word. If Victoria ran away with her August Myers a few days before the wedding, Rose owed her loyalty to her friend, not to the father who'd pushed her all her life. Over the past few days he'd said a dozen times that this marriage will take place as if there were some invisible army just beyond the doors waiting to invade and ruin his plans. The woman on the balcony didn't look to be held against her will, so the couple couldn't have been part of a kidnapping.

Within minutes the staff from last night were all ordered in and interrogated. Most must have slept somewhere in the hotel and looked like they'd been awakened into a nightmare. The hotel security made the poor workers feel like they were hiding something, even though one by one they all told the same story. No one was allowed on the balcony but guests of the hotel. The garden gates were locked at dusk. Miss Chamberlain could not have possibly passed down the stairs and across the hotel lobby without staff seeing her.

After his second cup of coffee, the major started issuing death threats to each of the staff if he found they were lying. Between interviews he screamed at the sheriff.

The sheriff tried to stay calm, but the major's outbursts began to get on his nerves.

Everyone talked about how they understood he was a panicked father, but Rose didn't miss how they all walked a wide circle around him. Rose couldn't help but get the feeling the major was more upset that his plans had been changed than that his daughter was missing.

Rose, though still in her gown and robe, moved among the men doing what she always did—playing hostess and listening.

Betty Ann checked and reported nothing was missing except a pair of slippers. Apparently Victoria left without any clothing. Even the robe she'd had on the night before when her father woke her was folded across the bed. Rose found the fact that Victoria left behind her half dozen trunks of new clothes far more shocking than the kidnapping. She could almost imagine Tori being led away at gunpoint and demanding to have her luggage travel with her.

Rose ordered breakfast brought into her sitting room, which had somehow become headquarters for the investigation. Hallie went with Betty Ann to count everything, including socks to make sure nothing except one pair of slippers was missing.

The hotel detective questioned the poor maid so harshly that Betty Ann started crying and screaming she wasn't positive about any numbers on the undergarments. Miss Victoria might have bought more. She was always buying things. Or she might have tossed one away.

If Hallie hadn't taken her out for another count, the poor maid would probably have been arrested for being an idiot. As they left, Rose caught Hallie's glance and guessed her maid was looking for clues the detectives might have missed.

Once the room was reasonably quiet, Rose excused herself, went in the bedroom, and loaded her gun. Then, as calmly as if it were an ordinary day, she dressed and slipped the gun into the hidden pocket of her skirt, not because she thought she might need it, but simply because she believed in being prepared.

As she opened the wardrobe to put away the box of bullets, she looked inside, aware that something was missing but for a moment not being able to think of what it might be.

Rose stared as she let out a long breath and realized Tori hadn't left without taking anything but shoes. She'd left wearing the yellow dress. She'd left everything behind that she owned but had stolen Rose's terrible yellow dress.

If this were a kidnapping, it had to be up there as the dumbest one in Texas.

The lawmen were one room away. All she'd have to do was shout and they'd come running. But Rose simply closed the wardrobe door, realizing that her friend hadn't bought the dress for a bridesmaid after all.

Victoria Chamberlain bought it for her getaway, but from whom or to whom, Rose had no idea.

When she returned to the sitting room, the sheriff was telling Betty Ann that if Miss Victoria were lucky she'd be returned after the ransom was paid. He said there had been another woman murdered in the streets of Hell's Half Acre last night.

The news only made Betty Ann scream louder.

CHAPTER 12

"STITCH, YOU OUT HERE?" A WHISPER LOUD ENOUGH TO wake the drunks a half block away echoed off the buildings bordering the alley behind the Grand Hotel.

"I'm here, Miss Hallie," Stitch mumbled as he sat up from the bed of his wagon. He could hear the rustle of her starched apron even before he saw her. When she took form out of the fog, for a moment his memory saw her almost nude, like she'd been the morning they'd met. She might look all proper now in her maid's uniform, but Stitch remembered every curve.

"I'm sorry I'm so early bringing you some breakfast, but you wouldn't believe all the mess going on upstairs. I decided to come down here to the quiet of the alley."

"I overheard some of the staff talking. They found Miss Chamberlain yet?" He took the basket she carried with a nod of thanks.

"No. The poor girl's just plain disappeared. She didn't leave out the front door. No one saw her even come downstairs, and the desk clerk said he never left his post. There's a night guard near the back and he says no one can leave the closed-in garden at night. So all I can figure is she jumped over the wall and ran off wearing nothing but her slippers."

"I seen that ranger do it."

"Do which part?" Hallie wiggled her eyebrows. "The running, the jumping, or the wearing nothing?"

Stitch laughed. "I seen the ranger jump over the wall."

"What ranger?"

"The one who hired me to drive Miss Rose. He swings up in a tree and walks over the wall on a branch like it was nothing more than jumping a puddle. Miss Rose says he's her cousin. Told me yesterday when we were riding around that he used to hang from the rafters like some kind of wild animal when he was a kid."

Hallie giggled. "I must be going blind. Miss Rose is having a man visit and I didn't even notice. Men climbing eight-foot walls and brides disappearing—it's a strange place, I'll say that much."

"If Miss Chamberlain came out the north door, I would have noticed her. Not much gets past me out here."

"Eat your breakfast." Hallie tapped the basket. "I got you hot rolls with ham as fine as you've ever tasted stuffed in them."

"Bossy, aren't you," Stitch said as he sat down on the wagon gate.

She joined him. "I guess I am, but somebody needs to tell you a thing or two. Stitch, there's a whole world out there and you're hiding away in this back alley. Sure you got scars, but they ain't so bad folks wouldn't get used to them if you gave them a chance."

"You don't need to keep bringing me meals just so you can tell me how to live. I can manage on my own. The cook will even let me order from the back door after the restaurant closes."

Hallie crossed her arms over her large breasts. "I know what you get when you do that . . . the leftovers. The bottom of the bowl or the scrapings off someone's plate."

"It's not bad eatings."

She frowned at him. "Miss Rose wouldn't think it's

good enough for you. She says you're an honorable man, and honorable men don't eat the leavings off plates."

"I don't mind. I'm not much more than a 'bottom of the bowl' kind of person, a man who's been cut up so badly he looks like he's made of scraps."

"Why do you say that?"

"I don't know. Maybe I've been hearing it all my life. I remember my pa telling me how worthless I was when I was little and couldn't do anything. He'd yell at me till he got so drunk he'd get crazy, and then he'd start cutting on me. He didn't want to kill me, just cut deep enough to make me cry. When I did, he'd start laughing, saying I was nothing more than a baby.

"After he died I helped my ma out until I got old enough to work cattle. I sent money home every month till the war came, and then I joined up."

"Did you see much fighting?"

Stitch shook his head. "Halfway through I got captured and was told I could spend the rest of the war in prison or wear blue and fight on the frontier. I picked soldiering at a frontier post, but the Yanks hated those of us who switched because we were Rebs, and when I came home the southerners hated me because I switched. I've seen the street and I think right here suits me fine."

Hallie hopped off the wagon gate. "Does this sad story come with hankies? You make me want to cry."

Stitch laughed. "You're not going to cut me any slack, are you, woman?"

"Nope. I decided a few years back I'd listened to enough sad stories to fill one lifetime and I didn't plan on taking the overflow into the hereafter. Way I see it, if you're still breathing, you're walking away from the table a winner."

"Did you grow up in a bed of rattlers? I was just talking to you, trying to be friendly."

She huffed. "Maybe I've had one too many men being friendly."

He had no reason to doubt her. "Fair enough. Thanks for

the breakfast. How about we just nod at each other when we pass and save arguing?"

"Sounds fair." She headed off toward the back door, then stopped halfway there. "Oh, I almost forgot, Miss Rose says she'll be needing you in an hour. She plans to go over to the sheriff's office and get everyone organized. Whoever kidnapped Miss Chamberlain is going to be real sorry when Rose gets through with them."

"What makes you think she was kidnapped? She might have just run off. If she waited until real late at night, the drunks in this town probably wouldn't notice a naked lady rushing by in her slippers."

Hallie shook her head. "I don't blame her. That's what I would have done with a father like the major, but the missus doesn't have any backbone."

CHAPTER 13

Tuesday morning
Dallas

DUNCAN MCMURRAY STOOD WITH HIS BACK TO THE
courtroom wall and watched the Tanner brothers' lawyer
shouting and pounding as if he thought the two worthless
outlaws were innocent. The first lawyer brought up the fact
that the brothers had both been in the war and fought for
the South.

No one in the room seemed impressed. Most of the men
present over thirty had done the same thing. A dozen years
ago they'd come home broken and penniless, but they
hadn't turned to a life of crime.

The other lawyer shouted that the men could not be con-
victed because not one dollar of the stolen money had been
found. The jury had listened to a dozen witnesses swear
that the Tanners had robbed trains they were traveling on.
One was a U.S. marshal and another two were respected
doctors.

Duncan stretched his long frame, wishing the trial was

over. He wanted to be back in Fort Worth . . . back with Rose.

When she'd first tried to convince him that something was wrong about the Chamberlain wedding, he'd thought she was overreacting. Who could possibly care about a yellow dress? Only after the major stormed into the sitting room last night did Duncan decide that maybe more was going on than he'd thought. Maybe no great mystery, but the beautiful Victoria did seem to be testing out at least one other man before she settled down with the groom.

Duncan allowed his gaze to locate August Myers in the fourth row with the rest of the reporters. For a man determined to report the news, he didn't look all that interested in the trial. Every few minutes he glanced back at a man standing near the door as if he were a second grader waiting for the bell. Duncan wished he'd told Rose more about the man. Maybe she would have tried to talk some sense into Victoria. Myers was tall and had been well built at one time, but his late nights and heavy drinking were taking a toll.

He couldn't blame Victoria for hoping for someone else.

Grinning, he thought of the couple on the balcony last night and hoped Judge O'Toole had been the lover trying to change her course. The young judge was a good man who kept mostly to himself. He hadn't seemed the type who would maintain a friendship with a man like Myers, but maybe he did so because of Victoria.

Duncan forced his mind back to the trial. It couldn't last much longer. The Tanners' lawyers had to run out of steam at some point. They reminded Duncan of trains huffing and puffing as they stormed from one side of the room to the other. Occasionally, the judge pounded with his gavel to hurry along one of the lawyers so he could find the brothers guilty and order the hanging, but words, like smoke and ashes, kept flying.

The Tanner brothers had given up even pretending to listen. Jeb was looking out the window the judge had ordered open because of the smell of too many unwashed bodies crowded in the room. Owen had fallen asleep a half hour ago for his usual morning nap. Even from across the room Duncan swore he could still smell the pair. The Tanner gang must have no sense of smell, he decided. He'd heard rumors about half the gang being in Dallas, hanging around the back streets. They'd have to be dumber than cow chips if they followed these two outlaws. The idea that someone else might be in charge of the gang tickled at the corners of Duncan's mind, but not one person had shown up to even visit with the Tanners.

One more day of guard duty, Duncan thought, *and I can take a few days off.* He was daydreaming about catching the train home with Rose and spending a week sleeping when a shot rang out across the courtroom.

People darted in every direction as they took cover.

Duncan headed straight for the Tanner brothers, pushing people out of the way. He'd return fire if he got the chance, but first he planned to make sure the criminals didn't try to leave the courtroom.

Owen was no trouble to find. He sat under the table, screaming between hiccups of swear words. He cradled his arms as he rocked back and forth. The second he saw Duncan heading toward him, Owen began to yell, "How'd you let someone shoot me? You're supposed to be here to protect me. I think I'm dying."

"Shut up," Duncan said as he knelt to look at the wound. "I'm here to protect the innocent, not the guilty." Pulling off his bandanna, Duncan wrapped the arm wound. "The bullet only grazed you. Have any idea where the shot came from?"

"How should I know?" Owen yelled. "I was asleep."

Duncan thought of asking again, but he could think of at least a dozen victims of robberies in the courtroom who wanted the brothers dead. Any one of them could have fired off a shot and disappeared in the chaos.

"You got to get me to the doc, Ranger!" Owen screamed. "I could die of poison blood."

"Oh, you will die, Owen, but not from a flesh wound on your arm. I'm surprised the bullet made it through the armor of dirt you've got protecting you." Suddenly Duncan looked up. "Where's your brother?"

Owen's face was blank. Duncan pulled his gun and pointed it at him. "Stay under that table or I'll shoot you myself. Understand?"

Owen managed a nod. He might be one bad outlaw, but he'd never been brave. He looked like he fully believed the ranger would shoot him if he moved and he was right.

Duncan turned his full attention to finding the other Tanner. By now people had either crawled into hiding places or run. Two other rangers were covering the door, so Jeb Tanner couldn't have gotten out.

The rangers, Slim Bates, and a new guy who called himself Waco Jones, began to move in, checking under every table and chair.

When they reached the middle of the room, Slim looked at Duncan and shook his head. Jeb Tanner had disappeared.

Duncan scanned the walls, but there was no corner deep enough to hold an outlaw. On his second scan, he saw the window Jeb had been staring at. A window from which someone could take a direct line of fire at Owen Tanner and an opening big enough for a six-foot man to jump through. Only Jeb would have had to do so a second after the shot blasted in while everyone was ducking for cover.

Two facts exploded through Duncan's mind. One, Jeb had escaped in the confusion, and two, his brother had been used as a distraction.

Waco moved closer and pulled Owen out from under the table. "I'll take care of this one," he said. "You two find Jeb."

Duncan ran for the window while Slim bolted for the door. The drop to the ground below was more than six feet but nothing Duncan hadn't done a hundred times, and, he figured, it probably wouldn't have been a challenge for an outlaw like Jeb either.

An overturned box rested against the brick, a convenient

prop for the shooter. The window opened onto a side street, but the shooter would have had to be fast to climb on the box, fire, and disappear before someone passing by saw him.

Fast and accurate didn't fit any of the Tanner gang.

Slim rode around from the front of the courthouse, leading Duncan's horse. "They wouldn't have come that way," he yelled, and pointed back with his head. "Street is too busy. Someone would spot Jeb."

Duncan climbed on his horse and both men rode farther into the alley. If Jeb was on foot, they'd catch him.

An hour later they'd lost any hint of a trail. The shooter must have disappeared down one of the alleyways and tracking on busy, muddy roads was impossible.

Slim swore. "I can't believe it. After watching him like a hawk he seems to have just jumped out the window and flown away."

"Jeb's not smart enough to have planned this on his own. He had help. Between the brothers, they don't have enough brains to fill one skull."

"But who? While they were in jail not a single person visited them except a few reporters wanting a quote. Even their lawyers wouldn't talk to the pair, and neither of the Tanners can read, so it wouldn't do any good for someone to slip them a note."

They turned back toward the sheriff's office as Slim added, "Let's go back and see if we can beat something out of Owen."

"He doesn't know anything." Duncan would bet on it. "Whoever did this just needed one Tanner, but why?"

Slim shrugged, then suggested, "It would only take one to lead him to the money. I heard they got a hundred thousand in gold at the last robbery, but we've been through every place they've held up this past year and haven't found a halfpenny, much less gold."

"The gang's probably already split that up." Duncan had shot two of them the night he captured the brothers. The others seemed to have vanished into the cracks like roaches.

"Nope," Slim said. "Way I heard it, the gang had to stay with them for a year to get a dime of the loot. The brothers were squirreling it away, wouldn't even use it for fresh horses."

Duncan had heard the same thing, but he had a hard time believing it. Easy money usually dribbled through robbers' hands like water.

Slim shook his head. "It don't make no sense. What would they be saving money like that for? But I'll tell you one thing, whoever planned this must have had Jeb on his side. Otherwise, why would he run toward the shooter and jump out the window?"

Duncan didn't have the answers. All he knew for sure was that he wouldn't be riding back to Fort Worth and Rose anytime soon. His plan to kiss her again just to see if she tasted as good as he remembered would have to wait.

When they made it back to the jail cell, Owen was hollering that he was going to die, and half the lawmen in the state were surrounding the building. The trial had gone from a daily article to front-page news.

Duncan stood in the back of the room, watching the outlaw being questioned. Owen spotted him as if he'd been waiting. "McMurray!" he yelled, ignoring the men asking for answers. "Jeb's going after you." He laughed. "You'll be one dead ranger come morning. He told me last night he didn't care so much about hanging, but he planned to take you into hell with us."

Duncan stepped out of the room. He'd heard it all before.

CHAPTER 14

Tuesday
Second Avenue

ABE HENDERSON FORCED THE COBWEBS FROM HIS brain and tried to focus on opening his store after a night of no sleep. Sara filled his mind to overflowing. The plain little schoolteacher had been beautiful last night, washing over him like a warm rain. The possibility of what might happen next between them blocked all other thoughts. He went through his usual routine with his mind still floating in the pleasure of last night. When he pulled up the shade over the door and turned the sign to OPEN, Abe wasn't surprised to see Killian O'Toole sitting out in front of his store.

After pouring two cups of coffee, he went to meet his friend, wondering if Killian would be able to tell how much his world had changed in the few days since they'd talked. Miss Norman had gone from being just a woman he watched to almost a lover . . . almost *his* lover.

"Morning, Killian," Abe said as he passed off one of the cups to the thin man in black. "You're early."

O'Toole didn't say a word. In fact he looked exhausted, as though he'd had even less sleep than Abe.

"What's wrong?" Abe lowered slowly to the bench.

Killian gripped his cup so tightly Abe wouldn't have been surprised to see the mug shatter in his hands. Abe knew without Killian saying a word that it was time to be a friend. A true friend.

He didn't hesitate. "Whatever you need, Killian, I'm here. Just name it and it's yours." He hadn't been friends with the man for this long to put limits on a favor.

Killian looked up with red-rimmed eyes. "Thanks," he said. "Is there still an apartment above that bakery you bought?" He pointed with his head to the next business down the walkway.

"There is. There has been since we were kids." An older couple from Chicago had lived there before the war. When the war broke out, they moved back up north, telling Abe they'd return when all the fighting was over. They never came back.

"Would you mind if I borrowed the space, Abe? I'd be happy to pay rent."

Abe frowned. "I don't mind. You can stay in the place as long as you need it. I'm guessing you know your way around in there—you played in that kitchen when your mother used to work at the bakery part-time."

Killian shook his head. "I'm not the one moving in. I just want to leave something there that is very dear to me. It's the only place that I think might be safe."

"Something?" Abe asked, thinking that he'd never seen Killian own anything besides a saddlebag in years.

"Someone," the judge corrected.

"I'll have Henry sweep it out as soon as he comes in."

"No. I'll do that. She'll be moving on as soon as it's safe for her to travel."

"She?" Abe had to ask.

"I can't say more." Killian looked exhausted. "If trouble comes, the less you know the better, but no matter what you hear, she'll be there of her own free will."

Abe smiled. "Then I'll ask no more. I'll get the key to the apartment and one to the back door of the bakery. Consider it yours for as long as she needs it. The only person who goes in there now and then is the schoolteacher. She stores extra desks in the front and she'd have no reason to climb the stairs."

Killian nodded and his long body seemed to relax a bit.

When Abe made it back with the keys, his friend gratefully took them. "You'll be needing supplies, bedding, food, a bucket of coal for the stove. Just leave a note and I'll deliver it to the bottom of the stairs."

Killian nodded as he stood. "Thanks."

"Don't mention it."

The judge put on his hat and held out his hand. "I'd appreciate it if you didn't mention this to anyone. It could be a matter of life or death."

Abe took his hand. "Done."

CHAPTER 15

Tuesday
Dallas

EVERY RANGER WITHIN FIFTY MILES STORMED INTO Dallas. Most of the older rangers had known the town before the war when the population had been under seven hundred. Now with the railroad bringing industry and commerce from every direction, a hundred rangers couldn't check every corner looking for Jeb Tanner.

Duncan McMurray knew he was just one of a few dozen men determined to find Jeb among the townspeople descended from artists and farmers. In Fort Worth they might have started by combing the saloons and gaming houses, but here Duncan wasn't sure where to begin. Jeb might have had friends willing to hide him for a price, or more likely, he could have broken into a place and made himself at home. They'd found one witness on the street next to the courthouse who said he saw a man fitting Jeb's description limping down the alley.

If that were true, Jeb must be hiding somewhere near the courthouse.

When Duncan left the sheriff's office, he had two missions. His first was to talk to August Myers to see if the man had anything to do with the escape, and the second was to begin searching from the window where Jeb had jumped and continue on to every building in the vicinity.

Talking to August Myers proved impossible. Apparently the reporter had run from the courtroom straight to the train station. The man in the ticket cage remembered August yelling for them to hurry because he had to be on the next train. For a man who claimed to be a war hero, he could sure run like a rabbit.

Duncan wasn't surprised to learn August had bought one ticket to Fort Worth. Either he was suddenly in a hurry to see his bride-to-be, or his mission in Dallas was finished. Logic told Duncan that August probably wasn't the brain behind the escape, but he might have been the messenger. Also, as a reporter, he traveled between the big towns and was probably more aware of the train schedules and maybe even shipments than most people.

Slim Bates went along with Duncan to search the alley. Other rangers were covering roads out of town and interviewing the hundred or so citizens who felt the need to come forward and report they'd seen what might have been the outlaw or heard strange noises that could have come from him.

"I'll take the left side," Slim said as they stepped away from the window, their eyes on the ground for any clue.

Duncan didn't have to tell the other ranger what to look for. He knew. A half hour later they'd found nothing. Most of the doors of the alley were securely locked, none had been broken into. The only clue they'd found were several drops of blood that probably belonged to a pack of meat being delivered and not Jeb Tanner.

When they stopped for a minute to plan, Slim rolled a cigarette and said, "We're in the old part of downtown now."

Duncan looked at the wood on the side of the building he was leaning against. "Looks pretty new to me."

"Oh, it is. The original buildings burned back in 1860. Some said the slaves, stirred up by the abolitionists, burned it down. The abolitionists were run out of town and the orders went out claiming every slave in the county had to be whipped."

"Folks did that?"

Slim shook his head. "I'm sure a few did, but I doubt many would."

Duncan frowned. He'd been too young to know of slavery before the war. The McMurrays had never had slaves. Any black man who came on the ranch worked for wages just like anyone else. After the war he'd seen freed slaves moving from town to town looking for work. He remembered helping his uncle plow up rows to plant extra food during the war and for a few years after, when it seemed most people didn't have enough to feed their own family much less the drifters.

"Did you ever own slaves, Slim?" Duncan asked just to give the older man a minute more to rest before they pushed on.

"No." Slim smiled. "I was too poor."

"But you fought for the South."

Slim shrugged. "I guess I thought since Texas joined the Union in '45, we had a right to leave in '60 if we wanted to."

"Still feel that way?"

Slim shook his head. "I gave up feeling years ago. Once in a while I see men still eaten up with the war and I don't want to be one of them. One night that reporter you talked to was mouthing off in the saloon that the Confederacy will never die like we are going to wake up one morning and everything will be back like it was years go."

"Would you like that, Slim?"

The older ranger shook his head. "You know what they say about the good old days, kid."

"What?"

"They weren't." He dropped his cigarette and crushed it out. "We'd better get moving."

Three doors later they found one unlocked, leading into

a small saddle shop. If Jeb made it to this door before they overtook him, he might have found his way out, or his way into hiding.

Slim pushed the door open slowly as Duncan stood ready. The back room was lit by one lamp over a worktable. The place was as silent as a tomb. One step inside the room and they saw a little man in a leather apron leaned over his work station. Blood spotted his white hair.

Slim moved closer and touched the old man's shoulder. "He's still alive."

Duncan fanned the shop making sure no one was hiding in the corners, then helped Slim place the old man on a cot near the back. The whole place smelled of leather and pipe smoke and blood.

While Slim ran for a doctor, Duncan knelt beside the injured man. "Can you talk?" he asked, hoping to keep him awake until Slim got back.

The man jerked, then settled when he saw the circle star on Duncan's chest. "Thank the Lord you're here. I've been attacked."

Duncan stood and collected towels from a washstand along with a glass of water. The man drank deeply.

It was clear to Duncan that a robber would have little to steal in such a place. When he knelt back beside the man, he asked, "You able to talk now, old fellow?"

"*Ja.*" The man's German accent lingered at the corner of his words. "A fella came blowing through the back door like all hell was after him. He grabbed my old flint lock and started hitting me again and again with the butt of the rifle." The old man let out a cry of pain as Duncan turned his head to see gashes cut to bone on the back of his head.

"Did he rob you?"

"Not that I know of. I passed out after several hits. I do remember hearing him complain about the gun not being loaded." The old man closed his eyes. "If it had been loaded, he would have shot me. I only keep it by the door to scare off kids thinking of starting a life of crime."

Duncan wrapped a strip of cloth around his head. "What do you remember about the man?"

The little saddle maker thought for a few minutes and finally said, "Thin. Dirty. When I was passing out, I remember him leaning over me. He smelled bad."

Duncan knew he'd found Jeb. "Did you see which way he went?"

"No." He patted Duncan's hand and closed his eyes. "I think I'll rest till the doc gets here."

Duncan went to the front door and waited. There was nothing more he could do for the old man and he couldn't leave until Slim returned. Jeb Tanner was out there somewhere on the streets, maybe wounded and armed with an unloaded rifle. Someone had helped him make his escape by shooting his brother. Why weren't they helping him now?

CHAPTER 16

Main Street

At dusk Stitch drove Miss Rose away from the sheriff's office and back to the hotel. He told himself he was keeping his word to Duncan by always staying beside her when she stepped out, but Stitch knew it was more than just a job. He liked the little lady. She'd stood up to the sheriff and fought to get all the help she could for her friend.

She seemed frustrated as they drove back to the Grand Hotel. "They have no plan," Rose complained. "A woman goes missing and all they said was that they saw no evidence of foul play so therefore she must have just walked away. The fact that we are three days away from her wedding seems to be as good a reason to run as any. One of the deputies felt the need to tell me he'd run out on his wedding years ago with the bride walking down the aisle. He bragged that it was the smartest thing he'd done in his life."

Stitch didn't say a word. He hadn't for the past half hour. He'd just gone with Miss Rose from one place to the other trying to find someone to investigate.

"To top it all off," she continued, "the major seems far more angry than worried. He keeps complaining that this latest spoiled tantrum of Victoria's would put him behind schedule. I get the feeling he's more upset about not having a wedding than he is about missing a daughter."

Stitch had to agree with her there. After making a huge scene at the hotel and demanding the hotel detective find her, Major Chamberlain walked out and hadn't been seen since. He said he had business that couldn't be delayed, which Rose found intolerable and said so.

The major's answer had surprised Rose. He'd told her that his only child was a coward who couldn't stand up to him. He'd said this wasn't the first time she'd run and hidden.

Rain was coming down so hard in the wind that it blew sideways. Miss Rose, to his surprise, didn't seem to notice. She was too busy talking her problems out.

"What am I supposed to do, Stitch? Apparently there isn't going to be a wedding. Do I follow the bride and vanish, or do I hang around with my flowers in hand and see if she comes back? I don't even have a dress to wear. Tori took my yellow gown when she ran . . . if she ran. It's starting to sound unlikely that she'd dress up for the abduction, and in my dress no less. And she didn't have to steal it—I would have given it to her gladly. Can you imagine asking me to wear a dress with roses on it?"

Stitch smiled. He hadn't been around women much in his life, but this one was precious. She rattled on like a broken music box, but there was no doubt her heart was in the right place. Miss Rose liked her world in order and a part of him wished he could break his rule of never getting involved and somehow help her out.

"I don't blame her for running. The major is a bully. I just wish she'd told me. I wish I knew where she was and if she's safe." She laughed suddenly. "I wish she'd taken me with her."

When they pulled up to the north door of the hotel, she turned to him and tugged on his sleeve. "Will you come up to my sitting room, Stitch? You could have lunch out of the

rain and I'd feel better having someone there on guard."
She hesitated as if molding a lie. "Hallie's been frightened
by all this. She's heard there have been women killed
lately."

"I'll take care of the horses and come up the back way.
They know me and always let me circle where most folks
aren't allowed to go." He grinned and followed her lie.
"You tell Hallie not to worry. I'll be there as quick as I
can."

He watched the little lady run through the rain to the
door. She had more grit than most men he knew. She'd
stood up to the sheriff and told him exactly what he needed
to do. When he'd ignored her, Stitch felt anger building in
him for the first time in a long while. She might not know
it, but she was brave and smart, even if she was afraid of
being alone.

Stitch decided to board his horses at the livery. He
wouldn't be needing them for the rest of the day and they
deserved a dry place to stay. When he made it up to Miss
Rose's sitting room, Hallie told him to leave his wet coat by
the fire and try not to get mud on anything. She didn't act
the least bit glad to see him or grateful he'd come to stand
guard.

Even though he growled at her, Stitch knew he didn't
frighten her at all. They might have agreed not to talk, but
that didn't mean she planned to stop feeding him. She
pulled a ladder-back chair by the fire and set a little table
beside him with a hot cup of coffee made strong. The great
luxury of having someone do for him made him smile even
if Hallie's tone was sharp.

"Thank you kindly," he said simply.

Hallie straightened suddenly as if his gratitude shocked
her. "You are welcome," she finally said in a softer tone
than she'd ever used when talking to him.

Rose came out of the other room. She'd changed into dry
clothes but was still storming about the lack of support
from law enforcement. She sat down at the little desk and

began to make a list of possible places where Victoria might hide.

After Hallie served them both a bowl of chili, she gathered her sewing and sat across from Stitch near the fireplace. Though she never looked up at him, he watched her. Her dress was all proper, but he couldn't help remembering how pretty her skin had been the other morning. The thin robe she'd answered the door in hadn't hidden her well-rounded breasts or the way her chubby body curved. Hallie's words might be hard, but her body appeared soft and touchable all over.

He laughed to himself. If he weren't careful, he'd be spending his hard-earned money just to watch her undress and dress. If fact, if she knew what he was thinking, she'd probably charge him for the daydream.

By midafternoon the storm still raged and Rose was busy writing letters. Stitch stepped out onto the balcony to smoke. The awning held back the rain but not the wind, and the sun seemed to have given up for the day. As always, Stitch moved into the shadows trying his best to make his big frame invisible. Over the years he knew most of the regulars who stayed at the hotel. Most he recognized by sight.

As he watched, a man stepped from the room next to Rose's and walked toward Stitch. It took him a minute to recognize Killian O'Toole with his hat low and his collar high. The woman curled beneath his arm was completely covered in a black coat with a lining of fur framing the hood. They looked like any couple rushing through the weather.

For a moment, Stitch started to step out blocking their path, but he hesitated. Stitch wasn't a man who spoke to many folks unless he had to. He pulled back against the wall, hoping they wouldn't see him.

As they passed, the wind caught the hem of the lady's coat and Stitch saw a flash of yellow before they began descending down the steps to the garden.

Without giving it any thought, Stitch followed the couple. Thanks to the rain, they wouldn't be able to see him even if they happened to look back, but he kept them in his sight. They crossed through the garden gate and rushed across the alley to the back of a business.

Stitch let them disappear inside, then waited a full minute before opening the unlocked door and following.

The storage room he moved into was dark and dusty. At one time it had been a huge kitchen behind a bakery. Stitch followed their wet footprints to a long hallway. At the base of the stairs were crates of supplies, and light shone down from above.

Stitch pressed against the wall when he heard someone running down the stairs. A moment later a man stepped from a doorway, leading to what looked like the mercantile.

"You all set, O'Toole?"

"All set. Thanks again, Abe. I think we may have just saved her life. If it hadn't been for the storm, I don't know how I would have ever smuggled her out of the hotel. Without you, I'm not sure where we would have gone. I heard her father has every road out of town watched and a woman like her doesn't check into a hotel without being noticed."

"Glad I could be of help."

When the store owner limped away, Stitch knew who he was. Abe Henderson. The man Killian sometimes talked too early in the morning. Stitch had seen them many times over the years as they drank coffee in front of the store a block away from the hotel. A few early mornings, when shadows were long, he'd moved to the edge of the alley and listened.

Without making a sound, Stitch now retraced his steps back into the kitchen and out the back door. He walked slowly through the rain trying to decide what to do. The woman in the yellow dress didn't look like she was being kidnapped. A judge wouldn't do that anyway. Killian would never break the law, not unless he had a real good reason.

Stitch figured he had two choices: Forget what he saw, or tell Miss Rose.

When he stepped back into the sitting room, Stitch almost yelped in surprise when he saw a man snoring on the settee. He was tall and well dressed, looking very much like a gentleman except for the ink stains on his hands.

"Hush now, Stitch, don't wake the man up." Hallie grumbled and frowned at the guest as if he were a possum who'd gotten in the house. "He came in here all a rage. I don't want him awake till my ears recover from the noise."

"Who is he?" Stitch whispered.

"The bridegroom. He finally made it here an hour ago and came in to find his bride is missing. Poor man almost exploded, and if he had, you-know-who would have had to clean up the mess. Me." She looked at Stitch's wet clothes. "You looked like you almost drowned having a smoke. Maybe you should give up the habit."

"She wasn't kidnapped. She went of her own free will," Stitch said before he thought. "And I already told you, woman, stay out of my life."

She didn't take offense at his order. "You're probably right about the kidnapping. If she knew this one was coming, she might have vanished. After listening to him for ten minutes I'd rather run away and live with the Apache than have to hear more of his high-and-mighty talk. He orders everyone around and was more upset that his room had been canceled than the fact that his bride was missing. Housekeeping promised to find him a place, but for right now we seem to be stuck with him. I swear Miss Rose's room is busier than a whorehouse on pay day."

Stitch noticed the bottle by the gentleman's head. "He been drinking?"

"Constantly. Told me to be sure and wake him as soon as the major got back from wherever he went. Like I was a clock and should just stand by chiming the hour."

Stitch laughed, glad she was picking on another male for a change and not him. "Where's Miss Rose?"

"She tried to talk to this one. The third time he interrupted her, she stood and walked like a lady out of the room and closed her door." Hallie giggled. "Only I swear I heard her let out a few not-so-ladylike words once she was out of his sight. Mr. Myers here might have heard them if he hadn't been busy ranting about how everything in this world is unfair. He was acting like God planned Miss Victoria's disappearance just to irritate him. I think maybe we should find whoever took her and demand he take the set of bride and groom. He needs to vanish as well."

"I could make that happen," Stitch said in a low voice. "I could lift him, couch and all, off the balcony. He's a good-sized man. Make quite a splat down in the garden."

Hallie smacked her lips. "Why, Stitch, when you say sweet things like that you warm my heart."

"Really?"

"No, not really. I don't have a heart." She took his hand and placed it between her breasts. "You want to try to feel it beating?"

Stitch froze, his big hand over her very proper uniform front. "I can't," he finally managed to say. "Mine is pounding too hard for me to feel anything." He met her eyes and wondered if she were flirting or teasing him. Women didn't usually come near him much less talk to him, and he had a strong feeling women never lifted a man's hand and put it on top of their breasts.

A movement came from the settee. "What do you two think you are doing?"

It took Stitch a moment to react, and when he did, it was in pure anger. "None of your business." He wasn't sure what to do with his hand, so he patted Hallie's breasts lightly and moved it away.

"I believe, as your better, anything done in my presence is my business. Who are you, sir, and what are you doing here?"

Before anyone could move, Rose stepped into the room. August Myers's voice rose as if an audience had just arrived. "On your behalf, miss, I'm calling the guards and having both these undesirables removed. A lady like yourself shouldn't even look at such a hideous man, and your maid is obviously nothing but a tramp for keeping company with this fellow who smells like he belongs more in a barn than a hotel."

Rose walked to the center of the room and looked first at Stitch, then at August Myers. "They have both been invited, Mr. Myers. You, on the other hand, have not. If the hotel doesn't have your room ready by now, I suggest you wait in the saloon across the street."

Myers turned his wrath toward her. "You're obviously not the lady Victoria thinks you are, Miss McMurray. When I find my bride, I'll inform her you simply will not do to stand beside us when we marry. No wonder her father never allowed her to visit you more than once. After meeting you and your staff"—he frowned pointedly at Hallie and Stitch—"I'm surprised the major even allowed her to write to you. I'm a man in deep sorrow over the disappearance of my intended and you are putting me out."

"Now might be a good time to toss the settee, Stitch." Hallie nudged him with her shoulder.

Myers stood and straightened his coat. "I'm not leaving until my room is ready. I've spent enough time of late among people far below my station. The two of you can leave and go about your duties, and I suggest, Miss Rose, you return to your room until you've decided to behave like a lady."

Rose walked calmly to the door and opened it. "Goodbye, Mr. Myers. I think you are right, I will not be attending your wedding and I strongly suspect neither will the bride. Now, do you walk out or would you like some help to leave?"

"Don't you dare threaten me!" Myers's tone turned deadly.

"I'm not. I'm simply asking a question."

Myers folded his arms. At over two hundred pounds, he looked like he was daring the little lady to make the first move.

"Good day, Mr. Myers," Rose said politely.

"If that freak of a man touches me, I'll have him arrested." August glared at Stitch.

Rose pulled the small handgun from her skirt pocket. "If he touches you, it will only be to carry out the body. As you pointed out, I'm only a silly woman with my shaking finger on the hair trigger of this gun. I suggest you leave as quickly as possible."

Myers opened his mouth to argue but reconsidered. He stomped out of the room and was on the first step of the long staircase when Hallie tossed his coat to him so hard he stumbled for several steps before gaining his balance.

Rose closed the door and they all broke into laughter as they took turns imitating the ever-changing expressions on Mr. Myers's face. Hallie stepped out to order tea and Rose sat by the fire with Stitch.

"What now, miss?" he asked after a comfortable silence.

"If I knew Tori was safe, I'd go back home. I don't think there will be a wedding, and even if there were, I wouldn't be invited. It bothers me why my friend would agree to marry such a man as August Myers in the first place. He isn't all that bad-looking and the major claims he's one of the best newspapermen in the country, but after only listening to him a few minutes I hate him."

Stitch leaned close to the fire letting his clothes dry as she continued. He figured women must need to talk out their thinking sometimes.

Rose stood and looked out the window. "How has Tori stood it the past two months? I have to find her and make sure she wasn't blackmailed or tricked into this marriage. That man seems capable of anything. Maybe he threatened to kill someone or maybe her father owes him a fortune. The major talks about how rich he is, but no one quite knows how he makes his money."

"You're just guessing at why she left." Stitch stopped her.

"I know, but until I find out the truth, I can't just abandon her. I have to know she's safe."

"What if I could tell you that she wasn't kidnapped or forced to disappear? What if you knew she left of her own free will?"

"I'd still need to find her and offer to help. If she did run away, the major won't be a forgiving father. He wants this marriage." Rose looked over at him. "Stitch, do you know something you haven't told me?"

"I think I do, but you'll have to trust me to make sure. It might have been another woman in a yellow dress and not your friend. Tonight I'll go find out. If it was Miss Chamberlain I saw, and she's safe, I'll take you there."

"And if she's somewhere that isn't safe?"

Stitch smiled. "Then I'll bring her back here to you."

"Fair enough."

CHAPTER 17

Second Avenue

ABE LOCKED THE FRONT DOOR AND MOVED THROUGH the shadowy aisles of his store. He'd been so busy he'd hardly had time to watch Miss Norman across the street. His friend Killian O'Toole had brought a woman to the small room above the bakery next door. She had to be in trouble, running from something, maybe even the law, but Abe knew Killian was doing what was right. He also knew that it wouldn't be safe for Sara to come to the store with others so close. Before, when they were alone in his study, there were always locked doors between them and the world, but there was no locked door between the apartment and his back room except the one at the top of the stairs. Killian and his lady could lock them out, but Abe couldn't lock them out of the back room.

He could think of only one thing to do. As he saw Sara close the schoolhouse door for the night, he pulled on his coat and stepped out on the porch.

When she walked by, he called, "Miss Norman, may I speak with you a moment?"

"Of course, Mr. Henderson," she answered just as formally.

She moved to the steps and waited. Close enough to be out of the mist now falling but not close enough for him to touch her.

"I . . ." Abe tried to remember what to say. "I'd like to offer you an umbrella."

"Thank you," she said and stepped closer.

He forced words out. "I would offer to walk you home, but, you see, I need a crutch when I'm not in the store and I couldn't manage it and the umbrella. So I'm afraid I'd be no use to you, but my umbrella will hold back the rain." He didn't want their short time to end. "I often watch from the corner of my store to make sure you get back to your place safely."

There, he'd told her why he couldn't walk her home and hopefully she'd understand that it was not because he didn't want to. He'd also told her he cared about her, though that should be obvious to her by now. "I have a friend staying with me for a few days. Judge O'Toole. You may know him. He'll be making use of the quarters above the bakery so if you need any stored things from there, don't be frightened if you hear noises above."

She nodded slightly at what he hadn't said. "I think I've seen him talking with you, Mr. Henderson. He's a tall man who always wears black."

Abe felt relieved. "Yes, we often have coffee early in the morning." No one was walking near, so he added, "I'll miss you while he's here."

She looked down at the umbrella in her hand. "Most of my walk home is covered boardwalk in front of the post office and the dress shops. I really don't need your umbrella."

He didn't want to take it back and people were walking too close for him to say what he wanted to say to her.

"When you walk outside the store, Mr. Henderson, do you need the crutch for support or balance?" she asked boldly in her teacher's voice.

Abe didn't want to talk about his leg. Now she'd see him as a cripple, not a lover. "Balance," he finally answered.

She raised her chin. "Then, if you'd like to walk me home, use my arm as your balance and I'll hold the umbrella. I'm not a small woman, Mr. Henderson, and my father used to look at my feet and say I had a great understanding." She laughed at her own twist of words. "I'll not topple over if you need balance."

She offered her arm and he laced his around hers until their hands touched. Anyone looking wouldn't have been able to tell if she held to him or he held to her. She lifted the umbrella and they began to walk.

They were almost to the boardinghouse when he broke the silence. "You're not to come to the study while O'Toole is staying with me. I'll not have your honor questioned."

She slowed, letting him take his time at a step.

He turned, his face level with hers before she stepped down. "But make no mistake, Miss Norman, I want you back and waiting for me as soon as possible after he's gone."

She lowered the umbrella, curtaining them away from the world as she leaned into him and brushed her cold mouth over his.

He fought to keep from touching her. Even with the night and the rain, this was far too public a place. "I'll be walking you home tomorrow night," he said, straightening away from her. "But there will be no more of that."

"Yes, dear," she whispered as if she'd had no say in the matter.

A few minutes later she handed him the umbrella and climbed the stairs to the boardinghouse. He walked across the street, guessing how long it would take her to get to her room, and then he turned and saw her light blink on. He now knew which room was hers and somehow after years of guessing that seemed a very private thing to know.

The walk home wasn't as frightening as he thought it might be. There were poles and railing along part of the boardwalk, and when he had nothing to hang on to, he used the umbrella as a cane.

When he got back to the store, Killian was waiting for him on the porch.

"I thought you never left this place," he said as Abe joined him on the bench.

"I decided to walk Miss Norman home."

"Who?"

Abe grinned. "The schoolteacher. I offered her my umbrella and she insisted on taking my arm."

Killian laughed. "Maybe you should offer her something bigger than an umbrella and she might take all of you."

"I'll consider it," Abe answered. "How is our guest upstairs?"

"I just left her. She was fighting back tears. We got everything moved in and cleaned, but I don't think it's what she's used to. She's pretty worried about being found. I have to leave her tonight and go back to my room at the hotel or they'll think that I had something to do with her disappearance. I hated leaving her alone."

"How much trouble is she in?"

"Nothing with the law, but she swears her father is making her marry a man she doesn't love or even like. He claims to know what's best for her, but she's no child."

"Do you know the groom-to-be?" Abe leaned closer so he could see Killian's face.

"Yeah, and I don't like him either. Right now I've got to go over and find the guy and probably drink half the night away, pretending I feel sorry for him. He doesn't love her. Hell, he doesn't even know her. The interest in marrying her is centered on her father's money."

Abe suddenly realized Killian was stone-cold sober. "Have you told her about your dead brother, Shawn?"

Killian laughed. "Of course, we've talked about him since the day we met in a cemetery. She asked me before I came downstairs if I'd have him watch over her tonight and I said sure."

Abe grinned. "You know you might have found that one in a million you've been looking for."

"Yeah, but I've got to stay alive long enough to make sure. I have a feeling if this gets out, both her fiancé and her father will take turns killing me. According to Victoria, both Myers and her father were great heroes in battle, and me, I seemed to be missing most of the time. My only battle plan was to try and be wherever bullets weren't flying. I never wanted to lead or follow anyone."

Abe didn't say a word. This was the first time Killian had ever talked about what he did in the war. He might not have been a great fighter, but he stayed and that was more than some did.

"Do you think you love her?" Abe asked.

"Sure. From the first moment I met her. Only problem is I doubt I'm what she needs in a man. She dreams of things and has ideas about life that have never crossed my mind." Killian frowned. "Do you ever get the feeling that women are born knowing stuff we'll never even know we don't know?"

Abe laughed. "O'Toole, you make more sense drunk than sober."

O'Toole stood and buttoned his coat. "I'm going to be drinking tea tonight. I figure I'll need all my brains to pull this kidnapping off and not get killed." He stepped away from the porch. "I'll see you in the morning."

"Good night, Killian," Abe said as he stood and went inside. When he passed the hallway leading to the bakery, he added, "Good night, Shawn." Just in case the ghost of Killian's brother was hanging around.

In the creaking windows and wind whispering through the shadows of the night, he almost swore he heard a ghost say, "Good night."

CHAPTER 18

Stitch moved through the clutter of the bakery toward the stairs. He'd seen Killian O'Toole and Abe Henderson talking on the porch and had no trouble slipping around back and sliding in the chute where coal had once been delivered for the ovens.

He'd grown up going to the school across the street years before the war and remembered the bakery well. His mother had worked there before she'd gotten pregnant with his little brother, and Stitch had the run of the place while his mother baked.

There were stairs along the far wall that had once been an outside entrance to the apartment before another store was built on sharing the wall, but originally a small winding staircase off the kitchen had been the inside way up to the apartment. Once the outside stairs were walled in, the other steps appeared to have been used for storage.

Stitch moved around the boxes and old pots to the top of the stairs. Through the cracks in a boarded-up door, he could see the little kitchen and the small area beyond. The only light offered to the living space was one from a streetlamp out front. The place didn't looked lived in and for a minute he decided he'd been wrong about where Killian had brought the woman, but then he noticed the bucket of coal by the little potbelly stove.

No one hauls up a bucket of coal to an empty apartment.

He waited maybe a half hour before Victoria Chamberlain walked into the kitchen. She still wore the yellow dress, but the midnight coat with the fur hood was missing. She was beautiful and so was the gown, Stitch would give her that. Not the kind of pretty he liked, but he could see why men might fight over her.

She sat staring out the window as she folded, then unfolded, what looked like a handkerchief. In the stillness he could hear her softly crying, not the heartbreak kind of crying but sad little sobs as if she'd suffered a loss and had to let the tears fall before her heart would heal.

For the first time in years Stitch wished he were another man and could go to her and comfort her. She might be a woman, but there was something childlike in the way she kept her weeping in, barely letting it out in tiny gulps. She was as beautiful as he was ugly, but he understood her kind of never-ending sorrow.

Stitch couldn't help but wonder at the wisdom of what Killian had done. Was he really helping the lady? Stitch couldn't see her marrying Myers, but putting her in this dark, tiny room seemed to be more torture than saving.

He almost jumped out of his skin when she whispered, "Are you there, Shawn? Please be there. I don't know if I can stand to be so alone." She cried into her hands as if fighting to keep a bit of control, then she said again in a voice so low he barely heard, "Please be there, ghost, or I fear I'll die a solitary death."

"I'm here," Stitch said without thought.

Even before the words were out he realized what he'd done. Holding his breath he looked through the darkness trying to figure out if he'd just scared the poor woman into the hereafter.

She leaned slowly back in the chair. "I knew you would be, Shawn. My Killian wouldn't lie to me."

Stitch thought about telling her that her Killian was an idiot for acting like his big brother's ghost was following him, but there seemed an overload of idiots around. Here he was standing in an abandoned bakery he'd broken into talking to a woman crazy enough to believe a ghost was watching over her.

Hell, he might as well go with it. He'd probably be shot for trespassing before dawn and then he could come back and really haunt the place.

"I was so afraid I'd be by myself tonight. In all my life I've never been alone. Even last night when I hid in Killian's room he was just beyond the door sleeping." She laughed softly. "I could hear him snoring."

Stitch frowned. Killian was not only an idiot, he was dumb as wet coal. What kind of man sleeps in another room when a lady comes to him for the night?

Stitch couldn't answer his own question. His experience with women was so limited he'd had no idea what Hallie wanted him to do earlier when she'd put his hand on her chest. What chance would he have with a woman who wanted a ghost for company?

His thoughts drifted back to Hallie. Did she want him to feel those large breasts of hers, or was she just making a point? Maybe he could ask her to do it again and see what she said.

The beautiful lady had been talking to Shawn the ghost while Stitch had been reasoning. He had no idea what the first of the sentence was, but the last thing he heard was, ". . . I've never been brave. Three days away from my wedding and I'm not sure I could have ended it if Killian hadn't come to me and asked me to think about what I want."

"Do you love him?" Stitch whispered, trying to figure out what she was talking about.

"Who?"

"Myers."

"No, but my father says I have a responsibility. He says Myers will be a very powerful man soon and he'll need a wife like me. The major said I'd do him proud if I married such a man." She let out a cry. "I don't think I've ever made him proud of me and it looks like I'm failing again. I'll bet he's furious at me about now, and when he's in a dark mood he can lecture me for days."

She was sobbing again. Stitch just listened.

"You know what the last thing the major said to my mother was?"

"No." Stitch was out of his realm again. Advice wasn't something he'd been too good at giving or taking.

"He said to her, 'Why couldn't you have given me a son?' And my mother's last words were, 'I'm sorry,' like I was the big mistake of their lives."

Stitch decided this woman's problems were way over his head. He knew nothing of dealing with fathers other than killing his while the old bastard was asleep. That didn't appear to be good advice to pass along to Miss Chamberlain, so he tried another angle. "Do you love O'Toole?"

She stopped crying. "I do. I think I've loved him since I met him, but he'd never kissed me or even touched me until last night. I thought he only wanted to be a friend."

Now they were in territory Stitch had had some recent experience with. "A friend is someone good to have. Some might disagree, but I think a woman can never have too many friends."

"Oh, but I didn't want him to be a friend. I wanted him to be more. He's the only man I've ever met who lets me be me. He makes me laugh."

Stitch was back to square one. Being a ghost adviser was hard work. No wonder the dead never bothered to do it. He thought he might as well toss in a question he needed answering. "So if a woman says she doesn't want to be friends, does that mean she wants more from a man or that she never wants to speak to him again?"

Victoria leaned her chin on her propped-up hand. "I don't know. I guess it depends on if she touches him or not."

"What kind of touch?" He had a feeling that putting a hand on a breast wouldn't be one of the multiple-choice answers.

"Any touch, I guess. I had no idea what Killian thought of me until last night when he leaned over and touched his lips to mine. It wasn't like any kiss I've had. I've had hello kisses and good-bye kisses on the cheek, but I'd never been kissed like that."

"Like what?"

He could hear the laughter in her voice. "Like he was making a promise there would be more. Like it was the first kiss of a million kisses."

Stitch leaned against the wall wondering what that kind of kiss would be like. Wondering if he'd ever find a woman who'd let him kiss her with a promise kiss. Probably not, he decided.

"Shawn? You still there?"

"I'm still here. I'll watch over you all night."

"Good. I think I can lie down now and sleep. Thanks for being here and for talking to me. You helped a great deal tonight. When I think about Killian's kiss, I'm not so afraid."

"I'm glad, honey. You go on to bed now. I'll be here if you need me. Nothing or no one will bother you tonight."

CHAPTER 19

Main Street

A BLOCK AWAY FROM THE BAKERY, KILLIAN SAT ACROSS from August Myers wishing he were drunk enough to act like he was listening without hearing a word. For some reason, the man thought they were alike. He claimed they'd hit it off during the saloon tour he'd taken Killian on in Austin the night they'd met a few years back.

In truth, Killian had just been happy not to drink alone that night and August Myers seemed to know everyone in town.

The newspaperman was good-looking enough to attract not-so-subtle stares from the ladies, and several men spoke of how brave he'd been in battle. Apparently, Myers had led charges at Vicksburg, Gettysburg, and Chattanooga and lived to tell about it. The brave captain's sharp pen constantly complained about Reconstruction and the carpetbaggers, drawing praise from some and frowns from others.

Killian hadn't cared about the gossip or politics of the capital that night, and he'd learned years ago that bravery is sometimes a hard thing to measure. All Killian wanted to know was simply what August Myers, the newspaperman, knew about the girl Killian had met at the cemetery that morning.

It had taken O'Toole an hour to get around to asking his new drinking buddy about Major Chamberlain and his daughter. He hadn't been surprised that Victoria was rich—everything about her spoke of money and breeding. Myers commented that she was cold, but the woman Killian had talked to had been warm and funny. They'd spent that day talking in the cemetery and walking among the headstones.

The night he'd met August Myers wasn't much different than tonight, Killian thought. Two years had passed and they were in Fort Worth and not Austin, but he was thinking about Victoria and Myers was still talking.

Killian fought down a laugh. He and Myers might have been raised in the same state but that was where the similarity ended. Only Myers didn't see it because he was too busy trying to tell Killian how to think. Why is it people who are terribly misinformed seem to believe the rest of the world wants to hear their opinion? It's kind of like people who are least open to listening are the ones most determined to talk.

A barmaid delivered another round of drinks and winked at Killian. She didn't mind serving him tea and charging him for whiskey.

Myers patted her on the bottom and asked if she was available later. The barmaid glared at him and informed him she was only there to serve drinks. Myers laughed as if he knew she were lying and just trying to up her price. The good looks and polish that had been there when Killian met Myers two years ago had faded . . . grayed into an alcohol wash.

Once the waitress was gone, Myers mumbled, "Ever since I got engaged, I have to have a different woman every night. Just the thought of settling down with Victoria makes me hungry for a warm-blooded woman."

"Why marry her?" Killian finally got his chance to ask.

Myers smiled as if he had a secret. "Between her father

and me, we hold all the marbles. In a few days, my friend, you're going to say, 'I knew August Myers before he became famous.'" The groom-to-be frowned. "All I have to do is find that stupid woman and marry her before she pulls another stunt. Fine time to play hard to get, but once I round her up, I'll ride her regular until she's pregnant. From that day on, I'll have the major and all his money in my pocket."

"Maybe she's not in too big a hurry to marry you?" Killian downed his tea and signaled for another round.

"She'll go along with what her father wants, she always has, plus I think the twit really likes me. She's usually speechless when we're together, and until today, she's done everything I've told her to do. The maid keeps me informed and she says Victoria has a room full of new clothes. Where we're going after the wedding there will be no shopping." Myers laughed. "Or, for that matter, anywhere to run."

"What if you don't find her?"

Myers puffed up a little as if proud of himself. "I've let it be known in circles the sheriff doesn't even know about that I'll pay well to have her back unharmed. A dozen men are out searching now and by tomorrow it may be a hundred. Her father swears she'll come back soon, crying and agreeing to his command."

"She always does?"

Myers grinned. "She always does. The major told me that when she was about five or six she'd break the rules now and then. He said he'd make her stand at attention, just like she was one of his troops, and lecture her until she passed out. He said she could never take much of his yelling, and before long she'd start saying she was sorry the moment he'd pull her into his study. He claimed he never laid a belt on her. Didn't have to. She gave in to every command."

When the next round of drinks came, Killian had no doubt Myers was now receiving the cheapest whiskey served. He was too drunk to tell the difference. As he talked on, Killian tried to think of where Myers planned to take Victoria. The man was a bone-and-blood southerner. He wouldn't leave the South.

An idea crept into Killian's thoughts. What if he moved south, far south? Killian had heard of a few men like the Knights of the Golden Circle. Men who couldn't let the southern way die, they claimed. A group like them had moved down to South America, along with their slaves and families, and started a colony. If the major had the money, he might have handpicked Myers to lead another settlement. But it made no sense—they'd have to have a fortune to make such a move, and no one in the South had money to invest.

Myers downed his drink and began to talk about Victoria. He went down the list of her attributes, all of which were physical, and complained that he hadn't seen as much of her as he should have been allowed to after the engagement ring was on her finger. He'd tried cornering her and getting a good feel a few times, but her father was always around or the maid was standing right beside them looking like she'd gladly bite any hand that roamed over the virgin bride.

"Do you love her, Myers?" Killian finally asked.

"Of course. I loved her the minute I set eyes on her. She's got a perfect body, small waist, nicely flared hips. It was all I could do to keep from shoving her down and climbing on, but I knew I had to wait. If she'd been anyone else's daughter, she'd already be feeling my bastard in her belly, but with her I get far more than a breeder."

Killian gripped the edge of the table to keep from hitting the man.

"I planned it out so carefully. I knew all about her father and his grand plan. I did my research. He's building an empire, and when I'm his son-in-law I'll be next in line for the crown."

"He thinks you're a great journalist," Killian added, wanting suddenly to talk of anything except Victoria.

"Of course he does. I'm spoon-feeding him his own

words. I learned a long time ago a reporter doesn't worry about telling the truth, just tell them what they want to hear and you look like a genius. I've even convinced him I'd be valuable to him as a newspaperman. My stories of where we'll be going will bring in recruits from all over the South."

Killian wondered how much of this August would remember in the morning. He was either too drunk to realize all he was giving away or he was smart enough to know that the game he'd played was over. Victoria was gone, and with her went some, if not most, of his value to the major.

The barmaid returned with double the drinks. "Last drinks are on the house," she said, smiling. "Drink up, boys."

Myers downed his first shot. "She wants me," he said, "and I might give in. After all, when we find my bride tomorrow I plan to stay at her side until we're legally linked." His words were so slurred Killian could barely understand him. "I'll have to settle down to one woman. The major said he'd shoot me if I wasn't faithful to his little girl." Myers made a face as if his whiskey, or his lie, tasted bad.

Killian raised his glass for one last toast. "To freedom," he said.

"To power." Myers downed his second drink.

His head hit the table at the same time his glass did.

Killian stood and collected his hat and coat, leaving Myers where he fell. As he walked out of the saloon the barmaid smiled at him.

"He's all yours," Killian whispered.

"Thanks. I'll have him tossed in a back room and we'll charge him for all the fun he thought he was going to have. He'll be too hung over in the morning to argue."

CHAPTER 20

Main Street

Rose woke Wednesday morning feeling like she'd been in Fort Worth a month rather than a mere five days. As she cuddled deeper into the covers for warmth, she realized something, or someone, lay beside her.

After the first bolt of fear, she turned slowly, ready to bolt.

She spotted the hat, then the leather coat atop the covers. Duncan.

He lay on his back, still wearing his coat, boots, and gun belt. He must have ridden through the storm late last night and collapsed next to her.

She didn't know whether to hit him until he woke or let him sleep. He looked exhausted, but in no way was it proper for a Texas Ranger, even one who was a cousin almost, to break into her room and sleep with her.

Slipping from the bed, Rose pulled on her robe, deciding to order breakfast for him before she started yelling at him.

She moved silently into the maid's little room. "Hallie?" she whispered. "Are you awake?"

Hallie, her hair tied up in rag knots, continued to snore.

"Hallie, I've got a sleeping Texas Ranger in my bed and I need you to slip down to the kitchen and order three breakfasts sent up and a pot of coffee. Hallie, can you hear me?"

The snoring stopped. "Sure. You're dreaming of having some man in your bed and all you can think about is we all should eat breakfast." Hallie rose slowly, rubbing her eyes. "I'm really not hungry this early. Why don't you go back to sleep?"

Rose laughed. "I'm not dreaming. There really is a ranger in my bed and the breakfasts are not for all of us. All three are for him. Once we wake him, he'll be as hungry as a hibernating bear."

Hallie walked to the connecting door to Rose's room and peered in to check for herself. She shrugged as if she'd seen stranger things and stepped into her slippers. "I'll be right back, miss. Don't poke the bear awake until I'm back. I can slip down the back stairs and come out in the kitchen."

Rose laughed. Hallie was probably right. The food should be on the way first. As Hallie slipped out her panel door that led to the back hallway, Rose added, "Ask if they can send up a bath in an hour."

Hallie mumbled something about not feeding wild animals.

Rose crossed back into her room. She took a moment to brush her hair and wash her face before she turned to Duncan. This was too much, she decided. What would people say if they knew he was in here? It was simply not something civilized people did. Not that Duncan would know anything about what normal people did. He was wild, always climbing in the rafters when he was five. By the time he was ten he'd vanish on Whispering Mountain land and not show up for a week. Her uncle and aunt, who'd adopted him, had to threaten to tie him to a desk the first week he went to school. If it hadn't been for Mrs. Dickerson's home-made candy he wouldn't have stayed even tied. He'd simply have gnawed through the ropes and been gone.

Now he was grown and educated to be a lawyer like his adopted father, but the wildness was still there. She crossed the room and touched his hair, another part of him that had never been tamed. "Duncan," she whispered. "Duncan." Her hand brushed his warm cheek.

He showed no sign of waking.

"Duncan," she said louder. "Get out of my bed. You can't just come in here and sleep with me."

He still didn't move.

She poked him on the shoulder. "Duncan McMurray, get . . ."

He rolled to his side with a low moan like an animal in pain.

As his jacket dropped open, Rose saw blood soaking his shirt. Bright red blood made his clothes cling to him like skin and the smell of blood and mud and sweat made her stomach turn over. She let out a small cry. "Duncan, oh, Duncan."

She tried to move him so she could find the wound, but he was too heavy. When she heard the click of Hallie's door, she yelled, "Hallie! Get Stitch fast."

In what seemed like seconds, Stitch was at her side. He didn't look like he'd slept all night. His clothes were more wrinkled than usual and dark circles shadowed his eyes. He took one look at Duncan and went to work without Rose having to say a word.

Rose ran around gathering towels and both basins for water. Then she put the small teapot, left in the sitting room, on the fireplace coals so water would heat as fast as possible.

Hallie rushed downstairs to send a runner for the nearest doctor and returned with more supplies.

Forcing herself to stand still and think, Rose watched Stitch carefully remove Duncan's coat. It looked even worse than she thought it might. She stepped closer to cut away his shirt and undershirt while Stitch pulled off his boots and gun belt.

When both stood back to look at the gaping hole high on Duncan's shoulder, Stitch whispered, "I can clean it, miss, if it's too much for you. He'll need a doctor to sew it up."

"No. I've helped my aunt doctor worse wounds. If you can keep hot water coming, I'll clean it." Then, in a whisper, she added, "It's bad, really bad, isn't it?"

Stitch stated the obvious. "The bullet's still in him. If a doctor doesn't get here fast, we'll have to pull it out. That could take a while and really do some damage. He's already lost a great deal of blood, miss."

"I know," Rose said as if she'd seen a wound like this before. "We'll clean all the blood off as best we can, then tie a bandage around him as tight as he can stand. Maybe that will slow the bleeding some."

An hour passed before a doctor finally showed up. He was so young Rose almost wouldn't let him near Duncan.

"Atamear," the young man said, "Dr. Atamear. I'm two years out of medical school so you need to step aside, miss, and let me do my work." He looked like he'd dealt with people not believing him before. "Now, with all your help, we'll do the best we can for this man." He smiled at Rose as he moved past her and began checking the wound. "We can talk about me being too young later. Right now, I've a life to save."

Stitch stood just behind her and whispered, "I'll stay close to him and make sure he does no more damage. You need to take a few minutes to wash up."

Rose looked down. Her arms and robe were covered in Duncan's blood.

The kid, who claimed he was a doctor, looked at them both. "I know what I'm doing, people. I've taken bullets out before."

"How many?" Stitch asked.

"A dozen," he answered without hesitation.

"How many of your patients lived?"

"All but one." The doctor opened his bag. "We've no time to waste. I'll need someone to hold this man down if he wakes and he'll need whiskey when I'm finished."

"He's not just 'this man.'" Rose straightened. "He's a ranger and his name is Duncan."

The doctor looked at her and added in a gentler voice, "Then we'll have to do our best for Ranger Duncan. Texas doesn't have enough rangers as it is. We don't need to lose one."

Rose reluctantly moved to the other room, thinking Duncan was so much more to her. Even though months often passed before she saw him, he was a part of her, a part of her life, a piece of her heart.

Hallie turned into a mother hen. She helped Rose bathe and dress. All the while the maid talked about wounds she'd seen over her life as if the subject might cheer Rose up, but all Rose's thoughts were on Duncan in the other room. Sometime in the night he'd been shot and he'd ridden to her before he collapsed. Something must have gone terribly wrong at the trial and he felt he had to make it back to her even before he took time to doctor a wound.

The world was spinning out of control. All her life she'd lived with order, everything in its time and place. She clocked her day in chores and routine. When trouble or crisis came, she always managed to keep everything running with her ability to concentrate on what needed to be done. Only this time it wasn't working.

First, Victoria had demanded she come early to a wedding, but she never explained why. And when she'd arrived as instructed, there was an absent groom, a father hurrying the wedding along, and a bride disconnected to her own life.

Then Duncan showed up, not to accompany her but to frighten her with stories of how bad the outlaws he caught were and how dangerous Fort Worth could be.

Before Rose could make sense of it all, Victoria vanished, and within hours her father rode off on some kind of business that seemed more important than finding his daughter.

Yesterday everyone had gone crazy looking for Victoria, and today Duncan showed up with a bullet lodged in his shoulder.

Rose tried to stay calm while the doctor worked, but she felt like she was in a whirlwind. In her mind, she tried to find a pattern in the trouble, but none formed. Reason told her somehow all that was happening had to be connected and if she could just find the thread that tied them all together she could stop it.

She decided the fewer people who knew Duncan was in her room the better, so she asked Hallie to step out and ask the doorman if the major had returned.

The maid came back ten minutes later and sat down next to the small desk in the sitting room.

Rose laid her pen down and waited for the report.

Hallie began with the facts. "The major checked out an hour ago but left two men on duty in the lobby in case his daughter returned. The doorman said he overheard the major tell the men waiting to make sure she was on the next train to Galveston when she came in."

"That's odd. Shouldn't he be working with the sheriff?"

"No," Hallie corrected. "The odd part hasn't been told yet."

Rose nodded for her to continue.

Hallie lowered her voice to a whisper as if trying to tell the story exactly as it had been told to her. "Apparently, the major has been led to believe that his daughter was not kidnapped but is simply playing games with her future husband. Last night, when he checked on her things looking for clues, all her trousseau was in her room. So the major told Myers he might as well start handling his wife. He left telling Myers to be sure to show up in Galveston within three days with his wife and her luggage in tow."

Rose figured Myers was probably the one who convinced the major all was well. The pompous man would never consider that Victoria might not want to marry him.

Hallie wasn't finished with her report. "One of the detectives told the doorman that the maid, who was fired, came down a few minutes ago saying that Miss Victoria's things had vanished. It had all been there when she went to bed, she said. Her best defense seemed to be that a ghost must have taken it because she locked all the doors. The hotel swore no one else would have a key to the rooms and no outsider would have ever been allowed up the stairs."

"So where is her luggage?"

Hallie shrugged. "I don't know, but the major and Mr. Myers are going to have a fit when they find out it's missing. Wherever it is, I'm guessing it found its way to Miss Victoria."

Rose smiled with the thought that Tori might be happy. She'd had a feeling from the first that there was a good chance Tori had chosen to vanish. Rose only wished her friend had trusted her enough to tell her.

"That's not all, Miss McMurray. The major made sure to tell the clerk that he would not be picking up the bill for you or Mr. O'Toole. Since there is no wedding, the two of you are on your own."

"I hadn't thought he would pay for me," Rose answered. "Have you any idea where Mr. O'Toole is this morning?" He seemed to be the forgotten one. Apparently, August Myers hadn't even thought to go into his best man's room to wait until a room was ready yesterday. If they had been friends, wouldn't Killian be with the grieving groom?

"The doorman said O'Toole is still staying here. Said he left the hotel early this morning." Hallie grinned, loving being the detective. "And August Myers hasn't checked out of his room either. So he must not be going with the major. But this is interesting: He didn't come in at all last night. Word is he's across the street, passed out drunk."

They drank the pot of coffee that had been sent up with breakfast. Hallie ate a few bites of the now-cold pancakes and said she wanted to talk to Betty Ann. Maybe the maid knew something to add to this mess of a wedding party.

Rose couldn't sit still. She walked back into her bedroom as the doc was finishing bandaging Duncan's shoulder and chest.

"How is he?" she whispered.

"If the fever don't get him, miss, he'll live, I'm thinking, at least till the next shootout. This is the famous Duncan

McMurray, isn't it? I was so consumed with what needed to be done I didn't put the name together with the legend."

Rose looked over to Stitch, wondering if it would be wise to tell the doctor.

Stitch nodded slightly.

"Yes," she said, "but we ask you to tell no one he's here. I'm not sure it would be prop—"

"Forget about proper." The doc laughed. "I won't tell anyone. I came in from Dallas last night on the train. Folks were talking about the shooting in the courtroom Monday. One guy claimed he'd heard that Jeb Tanner had his whole gang waiting for him as soon as he jumped from that courtroom and their single mission was to kill McMurray before they disappeared forever."

Stitch frowned. "Gangs like them don't disappear. They usually keep robbing until they get caught or killed."

The doc pulled the covers to Duncan's shoulders. "Keep him warm," he said as he gave Rose a small bottle of opium. "Give him this for the pain if you have to and take him home as soon as you can. The Tanners are coming for this ranger and I have a feeling every ranger in this state would have to block the door to stop them."

"Thank you, Dr. Atamear, for the care . . . and the warning."

The doc looked back at Duncan. "Have any idea how or when he was shot?"

Rose shook her head.

"I'll be back to check on him in a few hours. If the hotel staff asks, I'll tell them you're having female trouble." He grinned. "That usually stops all questions. Women don't like to think about it and men want to ignore it completely."

She kissed him on the cheek. "The McMurrays are in your debt, sir."

He suddenly looked very young again as he blushed and left the room.

CHAPTER 21

KILLIAN O'TOOLE DECIDED HE SHOULD GO BACK TO bed and start over. He'd planned on leaving the hotel early, collecting a couple of things for breakfast, and seeing Victoria before he had to begin playing his role of friend and groomsman to August Myers.

But before he had crossed the lobby, the major spotted him.

"Judge!" Victoria's father yelled. "Hold up."

Killian watched as Major Chamberlain ordered the bellman to load his luggage.

"I wanted to catch you and Myers before I leave. I absolutely have to be in Galveston as quickly as possible. I have full faith that August and the lawmen will find my daughter, but I wanted your assurance that you'll help in the search. As a judge, you must be able to put pressure to widen the search. The dumb girl can't walk a dog without getting lost. She couldn't be far."

"I'll do all I can," Killian promised, not admitting to the major that a circuit judge had no power. If he did, he wouldn't be spending the week riding from town to town.

"I know you will." Major Chamberlain patted Killian on

the shoulder. "I expect her to be in Galveston by the end of the week even if Myers has to tie her up and drag her across the state." The major smiled suddenly. "Any chance you could marry them? Judges do that, don't they?"

"We do." Killian felt sick at the idea. "I'll try to be of service to your daughter, sir."

"I'm depending on you." The major looked like he was waiting to be saluted. When it didn't happen, he stormed out of the lobby as if charging into battle.

Killian wasn't sure he'd said good-bye to him. The man's total lack of love for his child shocked him. Though Killian had no memory of his father since he'd died soon after his son's birth, he'd always thought that fathers were supposed to worry about their children.

An hour later, when Killian crossed through the wet grass and slipped out the back gate heading toward the mercantile, he still couldn't get the major's words out of his head. Victoria had no mother to raise her and no father who cared. He was glad he'd been brave enough to hold her and tell her he was on her side. He'd said simply, "If you don't want this marriage, walk away." She hadn't said a word, just kissed him and disappeared into the unlocked door of her friend's room. An hour later, she'd tapped on his door and said, 'I've walked away. Will you protect me?'

"With my life," he'd whispered, and meant it.

Now Killian couldn't wait to see her this morning. He wanted to hold her and let her know someone did care about her, but she seemed so fragile. Right now she needed a friend, not a lover. He knew Abe Henderson promised to leave the back door to his business unlocked in daylight so no one would suspect him entering the store, but they might think it strange that he had a key to an abandoned bakery.

"Morning." He waved to Abe standing at his tall desk halfway between the store and the storeroom.

"Morning." Abe grinned. "In a little while I'll close for lunch. I usually lock both doors and have a little nap. You make yourself at home if you need something from the store."

"Have you heard anything from above?" Killian pointed to where he'd left Victoria.

"Not a sound."

Killian headed down the hallway and took the stairs two at a time. At the top, he paused, unsure what to do. Finally, he tapped lightly.

She didn't answer.

Killian tapped again and said, "Victoria, it's me."

The door flew open and she was in his arms. Killian laughed. "I guess you're glad to see me."

She smiled. "Of course, but I'm starving. What took you so long? What's going on at the hotel? Is my father furious? Is poor Rose worried out of her mind?"

"Hold on." Killian pushed her gently into the apartment kitchen. "One question at a time. Why are you hungry? I brought up three boxes of supplies last night."

Victoria didn't meet his gaze. "I can't cook."

"Not even scrambled eggs?"

"Nothing. I can order meals in five languages, but I've never made anything to eat besides sandwiches out of cold meat and bread."

Killian found it hard to believe that an adult couldn't at least cook for herself, but Victoria was unique, unlike any-one he'd ever known. "I'm not much of a cook either, but I could make you eggs and toast." He held up the bag he'd carried over from the hotel. "While you wait, I have hot rolls and apples."

"Great." She took the bag and began rummaging. "Can you answer questions as you work? These aren't going to last long."

"Of course. I'm surprised you didn't go nuts up here without anyone to talk to." He tugged off his coat and hung it on a peg, then tied an apron around his waist. He smiled, thinking how good it felt to have someone need him.

Just as he cracked an egg against the skillet, she an-swered, "I would have been lonely, but Shawn kept me company. We talked for a while and he promised to watch over me until dawn."

Killian froze. A few times when he'd been drunk he'd thought he had seen or heard the ghost, but Killian had never known anyone else who did. "You saw Shawn?" he asked, forcing himself to move slowly while preparing for the next shock.

"No. Of course I didn't see him. But he talked to me. Told me he'd stay near."

Killian frowned. Shawn was his private ghost. He wasn't sure he believed in him except when he'd had way too much to drink. If he even hinted that Victoria might be crazy, he'd be condemning himself as well. "Did he make you feel better?"

"Yes. He made me feel not so alone. He called me 'honey' just like my grandfather used to do when I was little."

Killian smiled. If Victoria wanted to play like she'd talked to Shawn, what did it matter if it gave her comfort? He'd done the same thing since he'd left his brother's body on the battlefield. If he kept talking to Shawn, somehow he wasn't quite so alone in the world and Shawn didn't seem so dead.

When he'd met Victoria that day in the cemetery, he'd sensed her need to talk to someone, for she too felt alone. Their shared longing had pulled her to him even more than her beauty. Like him, she'd turned to books sometimes and between them they'd decided they'd read almost every book in the library.

As he cooked their meal, he told her all about what he'd seen and heard from the hotel. She didn't seem the least bit worried about her father or Myers. The only one she seemed concerned about was Rose.

"She deserves a better friend than me," Victoria finally said. "I asked her to come because I knew she'd be on my side. She was always like that in school. No matter what a fool I made of myself, she never laughed or turned away. I played on her kindness, I'm afraid."

"She's got a good heart." Killian put the food on one

plate. "Want to share my food?" he asked as he took the other chair at the tiny table by the window.

"I thought it was my food," she answered.

He set the huge plate of eggs between them. "All right, I'll share this time, but next time you have to help with the cooking if you want to eat." When she frowned, he added, "Or you could always do the dishes."

She took a bite. "I don't know how."

"Eat up, little princess." He grinned. "I'll teach you after we're finished."

They talked and planned as they ate the simple food. Neither of them was sure of what to do. Right now she was safe and not under her father's thumb. That seemed enough. Something inside told Killian that these few days might be all he had with her. The chances of them getting out of the city without getting caught weren't good, and if Killian went missing too, it wouldn't take a brain to figure out that they were together. So he'd play his role as August's friend for a little longer. Maybe in a few days the newspaperman would leave as Chamberlain had.

Wiping a touch of jelly off her cheek, he said, "I won't leave you alone, Victoria. I promise."

"I know. Since the day we met I've always felt I had a friend. Somehow, in the back of my mind, I knew if I could get to Fort Worth, you'd help me figure a way out of this mess."

"We will, together." He stood.

She laughed suddenly. "We also have Shawn to help. You're a good friend, but he may be the perfect one. He watches over me and doesn't eat half my food."

"I have to get back," he said as he pulled on his coat. "I have to play the part back at the hotel, but I promise, when I return I'll bring more food. Do you always eat so much?"

"Only when I'm happy."

"You're happy now?" To him, it seemed she was in the biggest mess of her life. He wasn't sure she meant her words or was simply acting the part she thought she was expected to play. He saw a kaleidoscope of feelings dancing in her eyes. The woman was fascinating, but the person below, deep inside, was the one he longed to know. The woman beneath seemed painted over by a hundred layers of polish.

"I have the promise of being free and that is more than I've had in years. I know it's only a flicker of hope, but it's more than I ever let myself believe in. I feel excited just thinking about controlling my own life and not having everything I do or say evaluated and reviewed."

She looked up at him with tear-filled eyes. "I should tell you that my father plans to leave the country in a few days. He thought the wedding would cover up some of his activity. That's why he allowed the wedding to be in Fort Worth. He's not so well known here. He's been moving money and supplies for weeks. When he relocates, he wants me with him, willing or not."

"I figured it was something like that."

"I'm only a small part of his plan. If he can't find me, he won't delay. He'll go on without me as soon as he gets the rest of his men and all the money he's been hiding away for years."

"What about August Myers?"

"I don't know. Without me on his arm I don't think he'll be too important to my father. The major thinks this marriage will give him grandsons . . . almost as good to him as sons. He's building an empire in South America. It's been his dream since the war. He thinks he can go back to living like he did years ago in Georgia."

"How long have you known about this?"

A tear drifted down her cheek. "I've heard plotting since he came back from the war, but I saw no part of it as involving me. I thought it was just a dream he had. Something he liked to talk about with his old friends. Only a few months ago when he brought August Myers home, I knew that I too was supposed to play a part. I'd met August a few times. My father asked me what I thought of him and I said that I thought he was good-looking. That seemed to be enough."

She moved closer to Killian. "Until you came to me on the balcony, I didn't think I had a choice."

He held her gently. "What made you change your mind?"

"You kissed me, Killian, and I knew I could never marry August. When August kisses me, I feel nothing but cold, as if I'm touching my lips to a windowpane just before it freezes over." She smiled as though she were telling a secret. "When you kissed me, I felt a warmth all the way to my toes."

He held her against his heart, trying to understand how such a woman would turn to him. How could he ever explain to her that he wasn't saving her, she was saving him?

Finally, he whispered in her ear that she didn't have to go back, but he wasn't sure she believed him.

When he pulled away, he asked, "What can I bring you? What do you need?"

She smiled up at him. "Besides you?"

"Besides me." He kissed her on the nose.

"A nightgown. A book to read. Shawn to watch over me."

"Fair enough. I'll be back as soon as I can slip away."

"And," she added, "if you get the chance, tell Rose I'm all right."

"I'll do that."

Killian almost ran from the little rooms above the bakery. If he'd stayed a moment longer he would have told her all that was in his heart. He probably would have sworn he loved her and wanted to bed her. He would have frightened her to death.

She'd asked for his help and that was all he'd offer until he knew she was safe. Only then would he tell her just how much she could mean to him.

A few minutes later when he passed Rose McMurray's room, he tapped on her door unsure how or what he'd tell her.

The maid answered the door, looking like she was bothered by the knock.

"May I speak to Miss Rose?"

The maid frowned. "She's indisposed at the moment. Perhaps you should try again later."

"Fine," Killian managed, and moved away with the strong feeling that the maid had just lied to him.

CHAPTER 22

Second Avenue

ABE SPENT A QUIET AFTERNOON WORKING ON THE books. Though the rain had stopped, the sky was still cloudy. Everyone on the avenue seemed to be moving in slow motion. Miss Norman even let the children out a little early.

About once an hour Abe would walk to the front of the store and look out to see Miss Norman working alone at her desk. Part of him wanted to stand at the door of his place and stare until she looked up and saw him, but he knew he couldn't. Someone would notice.

It crossed his mind that she'd simply come to him to have her "taste of life and adventure." He could be that if it was all she wanted. He'd make her blush. He'd make the decisions. Her taste of life might be a lark for her, but to him it would be his one favorite memory until the day he died.

He knew he'd never tell her so. Emotions and feelings weren't allowed when he was growing up, and when he lay almost dying after the battle, they seemed only a weakness he couldn't allow himself.

When the evening finally came, he let Henry go home and locked up early. He'd thought he would walk the schoolteacher to her door again tonight; but when he looked at the window she always sat by, the schoolhouse was empty and dark. He'd missed her passing the store. He'd missed his one chance to see her. To speak to her.

As he blew out the lights, he thought of walking over to the boardinghouse and asking to talk to her. But with the mud, he wasn't sure he could make it without falling. If he did make it to her door, she might not be allowed guests even in the parlor.

He could almost hear his mother's words snapping in his mind. *You don't need her, Abe, you don't need anyone.*

Abe moved to the back, an ache for her deep inside him. He'd thought walking her home had been the beginning of something, but he must have been wrong.

He was almost to the back counter when he looked up and saw the light on in his study. A thin beam of light shone high behind the wall of shelves. She'd returned. It didn't matter why. He'd be her taste of life if that was all she wanted and he'd count himself lucky.

When he opened the door, she was standing next to the mirror combing out her hair for him. She'd hung her coat on the door as he'd told her and she was using the brush he'd left her. For a while he just watched her, thinking of how lovely she looked. People build expensive buildings to house art, but nothing he'd ever seen could compare to Miss Norman combing her hair in the little room at the back of his store.

"I told you not to come," he said simply as he moved up behind her while he studied her face in the mirror. For a moment she looked worried, but then she saw his smile and smiled back.

"I know," she whispered. "You said it wasn't safe, but I was very careful. Do you want me to leave?"

"Yes," he whispered as he moved against her back. "But

not nearly as much as I want you to stay." He dug his hand into her hair and pulled her mouth to his, needing the taste of her more than air. As he kissed her, his hand brushed over her body. The proper Miss Norman was his, if only for a few minutes.

Abe held her tightly, not letting her turn to face him as he kissed her neck. "I'm starving for you. Do you mind?" His arm moved around her middle. "I like the feel of you against me."

"No, I don't mind," she answered, then let out a little sound of surprise as he gently tasted the side of her neck. His arm tightened just below her breasts and he felt her tremble.

He pulled away. "I don't want to leave a mark anyone would see. Unbutton your blouse, Sara."

He could feel her trembling. With shaking hands she opened her collar exposing her throat and the rise of her breasts above her undergarments. She'd done exactly what he'd told her to do.

For a moment he just watched her breathing, then he moved his fingers lightly down the curve of her neck. He touched the soft, pale skin just above her camisole. "I'll kiss you right here tonight." She drew in a quick breath and the cotton slipped just a fraction of an inch. Moving his fingers to the rise of her other breast, he added, "And maybe here as well."

She stood still, her eyes closed, her breathing shallow.

"Do you want this, Sara? Do you want my touch?" She'd come to him, but he had to make sure.

"Yes," she whispered. "More than anything."

He smiled and moved close once more. This time he didn't hesitate as he moved his hand over the cotton camisole. He heard her cry out softly, but he didn't stop. He felt of her breasts and the valley between them with only one layer of fabric between him and her.

Finally, he pulled away and saw tears sparkling in her eyes as he took her hand. They moved the few steps to the chair and he sat down as he had before, pulling her on top of him. Now the kisses turned tender with longing and his touch featherlight.

From this point on in his life, if anyone should ask him if he believed in miracles, he'd answer yes, for surely Miss Norman wanting him as dearly as he needed her was nothing short of miraculous.

He loved her as she was tonight, covering him with her body, relaxed as he moved his fingers over her. After a while she cuddled against his shoulder as if she'd done so a thousand times.

"I'm not sorry you came," he whispered, "but I don't want to talk. We can talk of whatever you want when we walk, but here, in this room, I only want to hold you."

He tugged her mouth open with his thumb and kissed her fully. When he finally let her breathe, he added, "You're mine, Sara. In this place there is no other world, no other people. Just me and you."

"Yes, dear," she answered as she stretched and kissed his cheek.

"Do that again," he ordered, loving the way she pressed her body against him while giving him an innocent kiss.

This time when she brushed his cheek, he turned and offered her his mouth. While she kissed him, he lifted her arm and set it on his shoulder. When she finished, she settled back against his chest.

"That was nice." He moved his hand in long strokes along her arm. For a while, he just held her, thinking what a treasure she was. He'd decided a few years back that his life would never change; he'd live the same days over and over until he died. Then a ghost gave him some advice and his world shifted. There would be no going back. Even if she never slipped into his study again, the memory of her would always be with him.

"Again," he ordered.

She straightened and kissed his cheek. A moment later, he dug his fingers into her hair and pulled her close as he whispered against her ear. "You'll do that every time I ask, won't you?"

His words were harsher than he'd intended, but she answered sweetly, "Yes, dear."

When she was completely relaxed in his arms, he leaned over her and kissed her long and deep, loving the way she'd learned to silently answer his kiss.

"I don't want this time to end," he finally said. "I love holding you like this, touching you, tasting the softness of flesh no one sees."

When he saw the blush in her face, he realized his words had embarrassed her. "I'll not speak of it again, dear."

She nodded and smiled up at him.

"But know," he added, "that I'll think of you like you are tonight always."

When he heard the clock tower chime, he knew their time was up. She pulled away and buttoned her blouse as he watched. She was only two feet from him, yet he could already feel the longing for her growing.

He stood, making himself move as far away from her as the room allowed. "I'll get my coat and hat. Once you're dressed we'll leave out the back. No one will see us. We can walk across to the side entrance to the little café at the Grand. I understand they serve a meal there until ten. We're having dinner tonight together."

"Oh no. It's too expensive."

He frowned at her. "We're having dinner there tonight, Miss Norman. Tonight and every Wednesday night from now on." He wanted to add "for the rest of our lives," but he didn't feel like she was ready to hear that yet.

"Yes, dear." She turned to pin up her hair.

He moved out into the storage room and smiled. He was stepping out with Miss Norman. Now it wouldn't be long before everyone knew they were courting. The hotel's café wasn't fancy, but he'd been there once and knew the food would be good. He'd take her to better places some nights. He could afford them.

Abe frowned. He probably should have asked and not ordered her to dinner. He really didn't know how to court.

"I'm ready," she said as she stepped from the study, looking like a very proper Miss Norman.

He stared at her. "You take my breath away, woman."

She smiled that tight little smile she allowed herself and he saw her blush with pleasure.

Abe picked up the cane he rarely used and they moved silently out of the store. He took her arm for support as they crossed the alley and walked around to the side door. The place was empty except for one waiter and a man reading by the windows.

Abe ordered for them, one plate of each of the two specials. Milk for her and coffee for him. When the waiter delivered the food, he let her choose which plate she wanted. They ate in silence. When the waiter served dessert, Abe said, "Was your food satisfactory, dear?"

"Yes." She looked down at her hands.

"You'll tell the boardinghouse you'll be having dinner with me on Wednesdays from now on?" It might sound like an order, but they both knew it was a question.

"I will if you like."

"I can think of nothing I'd like more." He lowered his voice and added, "Well, one thing maybe. The hour before we eat dinner was pleasant."

She didn't look up at him. He knew he'd crossed the line between what happened in the study and the real world. They didn't say another word as they finished. One more thing he didn't know how to do, he thought, he didn't know how to talk to a woman.

The rain had started by the time they walked to the front door. Abe ordered the hotel carriage to drive her home. While they waited, they watched the rain from just inside the front door. They laughed at the little streetcar rattling by with one mule pulling it along the line. Now and then the mule would pull the streetcar off the track and all the passengers would have to jump out and lift it back on.

"Looks like the passengers are doing more work than the mule tonight," Abe whispered.

She covered her mouth, trying not to laugh out loud.

He felt the magic of being in public with someone and still being very much in their own world.

Once they were inside the dark silence of the carriage, he took her hand. He thought of saying he was sorry, but he had a feeling she wouldn't want to hear it. He thought of telling her how he already ached to hold her again, but she might consider that too bold.

Finally, he decided not to even attempt to make small talk. The boardinghouse was only a few streets away. He didn't have time to pour out his heart, even if he knew how.

So he just held her hand, savoring the feel of her fingers between his. When the driver stopped, Abe climbed out and helped her down. Then he paid the driver and walked her to the bottom of the steps of her home. "Thank you for tonight," he managed, well aware that someone might be watching from the windows.

"Thank you for dinner," she answered.

"Good night, Miss Norman."

"Good night, Mr. Henderson."

He steadied himself on his cane and walked slowly away. With the mud and the rain, the street was dangerous for him. With great care he made it across to where the boardwalk started. Each small business was responsible for maintaining the section in front of their store. Some did a better job than others. As he stepped onto the walk in front of the post office he noticed someone had added a railing, making his steps more sure.

When he reached home, Abe sat in the study for a long while reliving every minute of the night. Finally, he closed his eyes, thinking he could still smell the hint of her perfume. He promised himself that if his Miss Norman would just give him time, he'd learn to be kind, to talk softly to her, to love her.

Footsteps from somewhere above the storage room drew him from his dreaming. For a second Abe tensed, then he realized it was only Killian's lady moving around in the apartment. He thought of calling up the stairs to see if Killian were there. Abe wanted to tell him that he'd eaten out with Miss Norman, but Abe figured O'Toole had his hands full of trouble right now.

Abe relaxed into his chair thinking about how he'd held her hand in the carriage ride home. In a strange way it had been as intimate as what they'd done in the study. He liked holding her hand. It gave his life a balance that had nothing to do with his weak leg.

CHAPTER 23

Main Street

When Killian O'Toole tried for the fourth time to see Rose, he was told she'd meet him in the café downstairs.

Killian frowned and walked back down to the little café off the lobby that served coffee, hot rolls, and a simple workman's plate for people who didn't want to go into the fancy dining room.

He'd been playing a game all day, acting like he was August's friend, acting like he was worried about Victoria Chamberlain, acting like he was helping in the search. So far they'd found nothing and August hadn't mentioned leaving Fort Worth, so Killian guessed he'd have to spend another day acting like he didn't know Victoria was only minutes away, probably talking to his dead brother.

He sat down in the shop and a tired waiter asked what he'd like without leaving his spot at the bar.

"Nothing," Killian said. "How about I just sit here and leave a two-bit tip for you not serving me?"

"Sounds good to me. I could completely ignore you for

four bits. For two bits I'll hover by now and then to make sure you still don't want anything."

"Four bits it is," Killian agreed.

While he waited, he glanced out the window and thought he saw his friend Abe Henderson climbing into a carriage. Of course, it couldn't be. Abe wouldn't hire a carriage to go around the corner, not even in the rain.

A middle-aged man in a tweed suit sat by the windows reading a book by candlelight. He must have paid his four bits too, for the waiter never bothered him either.

Rose wore a navy blue cape as she walked into the café even though Killian guessed she had no plans for leaving the building. Her hair was down for a change and streamed along her back like an ebony waterfall, beautiful and shining. The sight of her brought Killian back from his thoughts. Though Rose and Victoria were near the same height, Victoria was spring sunshine and Rose midnight calm.

He stood and held her chair. As she took her seat, her cape flared open for a moment and he saw a gun belt strapped low around her waist.

Killian had seen women wearing guns before and guessed if this lady felt the need to have one she had a good reason. He couldn't help but wonder if Victoria's disappearance hadn't somehow put Rose in danger, but he couldn't see how.

"Thank you for seeing me," he said as he sat across from her. They hadn't known one another long enough to be classified as friends, so he had no doubt she was seeing him simply because he'd been such a pest.

"I've only a few minutes, Mr. O'Toole. I presume you know there is to be no wedding, so I'll be leaving as soon as possible."

"I'm not here about the wedding . . . well, not directly anyway. I'm here to deliver a message from a friend of yours. She wanted me to tell you she's safe and exactly where she wants to be at the moment."

"You're the one Victoria eloped with? You're the one I thought I saw her with on the balcony?"

Killian's half smile seemed sad somehow. "You might have seen us on the balcony. But no, I didn't elope with her. I'm just a friend who offered help and she took it."

Both looked over toward the windows where the man in the tweed suit continued to read. He didn't move.

"I want to see her, but I'm needed here. Did you hear about the trial in Dallas?" Rose said.

"Everyone in town is talking about it. Jeb Tanner escaped and his brother seems to have been misplaced in the hospital."

Rose's eyes widened. "I hadn't heard about Owen, only Jeb."

Killian shrugged. "I also heard your cousin the ranger is out tracking them down. He's one of the best men Texas has. He'll find them."

For a blink, pain flickered in her pretty eyes. "No," she whispered. "They found him first. Duncan is fighting for his life. He's been shot."

Killian fought the urge to swear. "Men like Tanner have the advantage because they're willing to shoot a man in the back."

"I guess so. All I know is that he's hurt and I need to get him home as soon as possible. If the doctor thinks he can make the trip, tomorrow morning we'll be on the train. But before I go, if possible, I'd like to see Victoria."

"I'll take you to her before dawn. August, if he's still around, never gets up very early so it should be safe. We'll meet here. I promise to have you back in ten minutes."

Rose seemed surprised that her friend was so close, but she didn't argue. They shook hands and he stood as she left the café and hurried back up the stairs. He didn't have to ask where Duncan was—he knew—and the little lady was standing guard over him until she could get him home.

CHAPTER 24

When Rose returned, Hallie disappeared into the maid's quarters, saying she'd take the first shift in the morning. Stitch slipped out the balcony door, promising he'd be back by dawn. He'd checked the windows and doors twice, making sure Rose and her patient wouldn't be bothered. Rose wondered if he didn't sleep in sight of the balcony.

Finally, for the first time since she'd woke with Duncan beside her, Rose was alone with him. He'd mumbled a few times as if in pain, but the mixture of herbs and opium the doctor gave him allowed Duncan to rest so his body could begin to heal. He still looked so big and strong as he slept. Except for the slice of bandage covering his arm and shoulder, she found it hard to believe he was hurt.

For a while she sat by his bedside, keeping covers over his shoulder and checking to see that no fever had crept into his body. She thought of all the times he'd been hurt when he was growing up. Her papa would always tell her that he'd heal, but that didn't keep her from worrying about the boy. Once when he'd almost drowned trying to swim the river, she'd made a pallet on the floor by his bed so she could make sure he kept breathing all night.

Martha, their housekeeper, used to say that the Lord gave Duck to Rose so she'd have something to worry over and give the rest of the family some peace. Twenty years and nothing had changed.

"You're always such a worry to me," she whispered as she felt his forehead for the hundredth time. "Half the time I don't know what I'll do with you and the other half I wonder what I'd do without you."

As the night aged, she could no longer keep her eyes open, so she carefully lay down beside him, touching only his hand that rested outside the covers.

He'd rolled onto his good shoulder, so he faced her. She closed her eyes listening to his slow steady breathing for a while. Just how much he mattered to her settled against her heart. It was more than friend, more than family, a piece of him lived in her heart.

She was almost asleep when she heard him whisper, "Rose, are you safe?"

"I'm safe, Duncan." She brushed her hand over his. "And so are you. We're here together."

"Good," he answered, almost as if he were talking to a dream. "I love you, you know that, don't you?"

"Yes, I know that." She smiled. Even though they fought often and worried about each other always, deep down she knew he loved her. She'd seen it in his eyes whenever he'd come home. Even if the room would be full of McMurrays, he'd always search the crowd until he found her and then she swore she'd see him let out a long breath as if everything was right as long as she was there.

"How about we go home tomorrow?" she said as she smoothed his hair back from his eyes.

"I'll go if you'll go."

"Fair enough," she answered, realizing as she spoke just how much she wanted to leave. "I have to go check on Victoria at dawn to make sure she's all right, but then we'll book tickets for the trip. Stitch says he can fix you a bed that will be as gentle as a cradle on the train. You can sleep the day away and we'll be home long before dark."

Duncan shifted in pain. "I couldn't stop last night until I got to you. You're in danger, Rose. Beware."

"Stop talking and get some rest."

He laughed. "You know, I learned to talk just so I could talk to you and now you tell me to stop."

"I'm warning you." She grinned and used a threat she'd used for years. "Go to sleep or I'll tell Martha." The old housekeeper at the ranch had always frightened Duncan more than any of the strong powerful men.

"All right," he whispered. "Only stay close." He threaded his fingers through hers.

As his breathing slowed in sleep, Rose worried if she was making the right decision. On the train they'd be an easy target. Here, as long as no one knew Duncan was in her room, maybe they were safe. Only for her, and she guessed for him as well, there was never anywhere truly safe but Whispering Mountain. The ranch was like a fortress bordered by rivers and backing into a mountain. Anyone coming onto their land would have to come straight on in full view of the front of the ranch headquarters.

As Rose watched him sleep, it occurred to her that maybe she'd never married because no man she'd met had quite measured up to Duncan. He was smart and funny and brave. He believed in doing what was right and had no tolerance for men who prey on the weak.

She grinned. Only problem was, loving him was like loving a wild animal you knew could never be tamed. Still, she felt more alive when he was around and now and then almost believed she could be brave too. In a way, he was everything she wished she were. Reckless. Free. She knew she'd someday settle down and marry some sensible gentleman who'd be the perfect husband and father to their children, but when she dreamed, she'd dream of running free with Duncan by her side.

He might love her, but she'd never ask him to give up his freedom and settle down.

He tightened his grip on her hand. "You're safe," he whispered as if he were the one worrying about her even in his sleep.

"I'm safe," she answered, and almost added, *Until tomorrow.*

CHAPTER 25

Thursday
Second Avenue

An hour before dawn Stitch straightened from his cramped quarters behind the old door to the apartment. Through the slits in the wood he could see Victoria sleeping in her chair by the window with blankets wrapped around her.

The night had turned colder and he guessed she'd let the fire go out in the stove again. Icy rain tapped on the window but didn't wake her. Stitch felt cold all the way to the bone, but he'd have to bust through the boards blocking the door to light the fire, and that would surely wake the little lady. She might like talking to a ghost, but she wouldn't be too happy to see him in the flesh.

She'd cried a few times during the night and twice she'd called for Shawn. Each time, Stitch had leaned against the thin door and answered in what he hoped was a low ghost voice. He knew she just wanted to know that she wasn't alone, but it made him feel like he was truly helping to talk to her. Over and over again he'd say, "It's going to be all right, honey."

He grinned as he watched her sleeping. She reminded him of some kind of windup toy. Once she'd stopped crying, she'd tried on clothes in the other room until she'd found a black pair of riding trousers and a simple blue shirt.

"I'm going to be ready to run when Killian says it's time." She'd braided her light blond hair, talking all the while about how she'd survive on her own. "My father will go without me. If I don't cooperate, I'll be dead to him. So, I'll change my name and disappear among ordinary people. I can get a job. Surely there is something I can do."

Stitch wanted to tell her she'd make it fine on her own, but the poor girl didn't even know how to stock the stove. He felt sure cooking, cleaning, and sewing were skills she'd never acquired. If she and Killian did stay together, they'd be eating apples and scrambled eggs for the rest of their lives. If she had to make it on her own it would be a toss-up which got her first, starvation or cold.

In a few hours he'd have to make a decision. Miss Rose wanted him to go with her to take Duncan home, but he needed to stay here and help Killian get Victoria to safety. He had no doubt if the major or August Myers found her, they'd make her go through with the marriage and Stitch couldn't stand to see the beautiful little lady be any more unhappy.

But if he stayed here, that would leave Rose and Hallie to protect the ranger on the journey home. If the outlaws caught up with Duncan McMurray, he and both the women would end up dead. Rose might nurse Duncan back to health, but she wasn't a fighter even if she did think she was tough enough to wear a gun. Stitch figured most women wouldn't fire if the time came, so a gun around their waists might as well be a belt.

While Stitch worried, he heard footsteps on the main stairs that climbed the far wall. In the stillness, he listened and counted. Two people were coming up to the apartment.

Miss Victoria must have heard it also, for she jerked awake, fought her way out of the blankets, and stood so that she'd be behind the apartment door when it opened.

For a few heartbeats, neither of them breathed, but then Stitch heard Killian's voice whisper from the other side of the entrance. "Victoria? It's me. Is it all right if I come in?"

As she had the day before, Victoria was in his arms by the time he took two steps into the room.

It made Stitch smile to see Killian hug her wildly as if he'd counted the minutes as well since they'd last been together. The judge wasn't a man who smiled often, but he always seemed to smile at her.

Victoria let out a little squeal of joy as she noticed Rose behind Killian.

The two women hugged and both started talking at once. Stitch laughed so hard that he feared they might hear him. Killian looked lost in the flood of squeals and pats.

"I'm okay," Victoria said three times before Rose believed her. "I promise." She hugged the judge's arm. "He saved me."

Victoria kissed Killian's cheek and Rose did the same. As Rose pulled off her cape and moved to the table and chairs by the window, Victoria never stopped talking. "I didn't want to marry August Myers from the beginning and I told the major, but as always my father was talking and not listening. Myers was a war hero and that seemed to be the only requirement needed to marry his daughter and father the major's grandsons."

She offered Rose one of the blankets for her lap. "I let the talk of marrying Myers go on a month, thinking he'd forget about the crazy idea, but all at once the wedding was on. The major travels up here on business often and I thought if I moved the wedding to Fort Worth, I could see Killian and ask him what to do. Father agreed to having the wedding here. I think he was looking for a way to get out of Austin. He said we'd attract less attention than we would from the capital."

"Where is he planning to move?" Rose asked as she held

Victoria's shaking hand. Neither seemed to notice Killian banging about trying to relight the stove.

Victoria let out a little cry. "It's a big secret, but I guess it doesn't matter now. He'd planned to take me to Brazil. He and Myers have a plan to start a new colony there next to the Norris Settlement. They think with hard work and a great deal of money they'll build their own kingdom."

Killian moved to her side. "Surely they're not taking slaves."

Victoria shook her head. "No, they can hire cheap labor down there. They plan to get as much money here as possible and buy all they need once they are there."

"Lucky your father is rich," Rose said. "Most folks, even with land, are barely getting by. I've heard many of those who moved to South America after the war returned with even less than before."

"That's just it. The major ended the war with nothing. If I hadn't had a little trust fund from my mother's family we couldn't have kept our home in Austin. When this idea began to form, I noticed some of the men he called business partners didn't look like the kind who usually visited the house. Now, suddenly, he's been spending money. Wagonloads of goods are already at the dock in Galveston waiting for us."

Killian began to pace anxiously. On one round he checked the stove that was now offering some warmth in the room. "You need to keep the fire going," he snapped.

Victoria looked like she might start crying.

"I'm sorry," Killian said. "I just don't like you being cold up here."

She tossed her coat off. "I'm not cold and I'm dressed to travel. I thought we were leaving today."

Killian shook his head. "I don't see how. Your father is gone, but August is still hanging around the hotel. Word is he's got men out looking for you. One glance at that coat and they'd be on our tail."

She held out her beautiful black coat with the fur lining. "Rose will trade coats with me. It's too heavy for traveling anyway. With all the fur inside I feel like a snowman walking around and I won't need this heavy a coat if we move south."

Rose accepted the coat without question and Victoria turned to Killian. "See, problem solved. I'll take her cape, pull up the hood, and suddenly I'll be invisible."

No one in the room seemed to believe it would be that simple except Victoria. Rose pulled off her cape and gave it to Victoria, then slipped into the fur one. "We'll trade back when all this is over," she said as she buttoned the long row of pearl buttons down the front.

Victoria noticed the gun belt. "You're wearing a gun?"

"I'll explain later, but it has nothing to do with your problem." Rose shrugged. "Don't look so shocked. I wouldn't be a McMurray if I couldn't shoot.

A sound rattled from the stairwell. Then silence.

Killian stepped in front of the women. "It's probably only Abe bringing something to the steps."

No one moved. After a moment, Victoria whispered, "It might be your brother."

"What brother?" Rose asked, startled.

"Killian's brother is a ghost. He's been keeping me company."

"Ghosts don't stumble over steps," Killian offered.

"Maybe not, but Shawn snores. I heard him last night." Victoria giggled. "Maybe he stumbles too."

Before anyone could argue, the door popped open from a mighty blow and two men stood, guns pointed as if waiting to be invited in.

Stitch wanted to roar and frighten them away, but they'd only fire at the panel. Killian, if he was carrying a weapon, was smart enough not to try and pull it out. Rose kept her hands at her sides.

"Which one of you is Victoria Chamberlain?" the biggest of the two men yelled. He looked rough and weather worn with the dull eyes of a man who'd faced death many times.

"I am," Rose said before Victoria could speak. "Who are you?"

"No," Victoria corrected. "I'm Victoria Chamberlain."

The big man waved his weapon between them. "I'll ask one more time, which of you is Miss Chamberlain."

"I am." Rose stomped forward. "And I'm demanding both of you leave immediately."

The smaller man swore. "What do we do, Hargus?" Neither looked like leaving was an option they were considering. "Nobody told us what the woman looked like."

"We kill the man and take both of them," Hargus suggested. "Maybe there's a bonus for bringing an extra one along."

The shorter man shook his head. "We can't. We only got one extra horse and part of the deal was that the bride returns with her luggage." The stack of luggage, still locked, was piled in the corner. "We'll have enough trouble getting away with one, and all those bags."

The one called Hargus stared at both women as if it were some kind of puzzle he'd have to solve. "Her," he said, pointing to Rose. "She looks rich enough to be the major's daughter." He flicked the weapon toward Victoria. "She's probably the chore girl. Kill her."

Victoria let out a little sound and Killian put his arm around her to keep her from falling.

"No!" the second man said. "I told you before, I ain't into killing anyone unless I have to. They hang folks for doing that and I'm not dying just 'cause you give an order. Finding her is one thing. Dragging her back to her husband seems like the right thing to do, especially with the reward he's offering, but killing—that's not part of the deal."

"Fine." Hargus pouted. "Tie them up then. We'll be long gone with the reward before anyone finds them up here. If we got the wrong one, we'll circle back and trade out the women. How does that sound to you, Shorty?"

Victoria started crying, begging the men to let Rose go and take her, but they seemed to be finished listening. The smaller kidnapper gagged her first and shoved her in a chair. Hargus kept his gun pointed at Rose's head, warning Killian not to fight while the short man tied him.

Stitch fought to stay still. He wanted to do something, but he knew if he smashed through the wall, guns would go off, and the chances were good that a bullet would find someone in the room besides the strangers.

The short one pointed his pistol at Rose as he picked up a few of the locked bags. "We'll just take a few of these. That should be enough to get the reward."

The other kidnapper grabbed a small trunk. "Right. Now let's get out of here."

Stitch began making his way down the cluttered little steps, hoping to reach the bottom before they could get out of the store. If he could follow behind them in the rain, he could take them both before they had a chance to fire.

Stitch was one step from the bottom of the stairs when he saw Abe Henderson through the open door leading to the mercantile. If he walked to the back door of the bakery, there was a good chance Abe would see him and think he was an intruder. Stitch had never spoken to Abe, but he'd watched the man when he talked to Killian. If Abe saw him, he might shoot first, thinking he was protecting Miss Victoria, or worse, Stitch thought, Abe might attack him. If Abe did come after him, Stitch might hurt the man. He was almost twice Abe's weight and had the full use of both legs. The store owner wouldn't have a chance.

Stitch remained frozen, torn between helping Rose and fighting Abe. He rationalized his choice with the knowledge that the men were not planning to hurt Rose, only take her somewhere. Maybe they would bring her back when they found out she wasn't August Myers's bride. Even if Myers came with them, he wouldn't be likely to force Victoria into anything with the judge watching.

Stitch thought he heard the front door of the bakery open and close. They'd taken Rose.

Abe continued working in the storeroom. Stitch waited

only a few feet from freedom. Finally someone must have entered the front of Abe's store for he set the broom aside and went into the mercantile.

As silently as possible, Stitch made his break. He ran through the back door and out into the alley. Once there, the rain hit him full in the face.

He had no idea which way the two kidnappers had gone. Before he could get around to the front of Abe's store they'd be long gone, and on foot he'd have little chance of catching up with them. Carts and horses were passing like gray shadows and he couldn't make out any faces.

He figured he had two facts that would help him a great deal. One, they didn't know he was following them, and two, he knew where they were headed, or at least to whom. He guessed they'd deposit Rose somewhere, go get August Myers, and make sure he had the money with him before they told him where he could pick up his bride.

Stitch ran to his wagon and drove around the corner. He pulled to a stop where he could see the saloon where Killian and Myers drank. On a day like this August Myers would be in either the saloon or the hotel and from this point he could see both entrances. Though Stitch figured he wouldn't be welcome if he tried to walk in the front of either place, he had a good view of both. Once Myers came out with one of the kidnappers, then all he had to do was follow.

His mind was bubbling over with worries. Killian was tied up and probably going mad with worry. Hallie was upstairs alone in the hotel with Duncan and probably the young doctor Stitch still wasn't sure was old enough to be a real one. Hallie would do the best she could, but he doubted she was much of a nurse. Then there was Rose. Poor frightened Rose. Duncan had told Stitch to take care of her, to look out for her, to never let her leave the hotel alone, but she'd left with Killian when he wasn't looking.

Stitch had watched over Killian for three years now, but the judge never knew it. He'd lifted him out of the gutter a few times and kept him from being robbed once when he was too occupied to be on guard. Every week when Killian checked in at the Grand Hotel, Stitch watched. He was O'Toole's guardian angel and the judge didn't even know it.

Rain pounded on him, but Stitch paid it no mind. For a man who swore he'd never care about anyone including himself after he'd managed to stay alive through months in a prison hospital, Stitch suddenly had a full load of caring to carry around.

CHAPTER 26

Rose considered herself a woman of even temperament, but she was furious. The two bumbling kidnappers had pushed and poked her with their guns until they'd reached the horses, at which point they'd tied her to a saddle, pulled her hood down over her face, and ridden off with her between them.

After a few turns the man called Hargus reached over and grabbed her arm. "You be quiet now, miss, or I'll break your jaw." His low threat frightened her so badly she wasn't sure she could have made a sound even if she'd tried.

"We ain't supposed to hurt her," Shorty said in a whine. "Myers won't mind a few bruises in transport, but if you break her jaw he's liable to object."

Hargus snorted. "A broken jaw wouldn't hurt all that much unless she tried to talk. I don't reckon Myers would mind. He seems to like to be the one talking. A silent bride would probably fit him fine."

Rose tried to pick up sounds around her. She didn't know Fort Worth. Another block or two and she'd be completely lost. They moved on, splashing through mud puddles. She heard horses and wagons pass, but the thunder and rain muted all other sounds. Once, she thought she heard a woman's laugh and the sound of glass breaking. A few blocks later someone yelled, swearing about the weather.

"We're taking her to Yancy's place, right? I don't want to go all the way back to the dugout with her," Shorty piped up as if he just realized where they were headed. "Ain't nobody goes there since Yancy got shot but us anyway."

"Nobody would be there this time of day even if the old man could open up. I ain't dragging her all the way out of town to our place just to have to drag her back when we get the reward. Yancy's dive will be fine."

They made a few more turns and Rose realized there were fewer people around. She couldn't hear any wagons or buggies so they must be on one of the side streets. The smells around her reached her even through the rain. Rotting food and human waste.

Suddenly she knew where she was. The back streets of Hell's Half Acre. The smells hadn't been so bad near Hallie's house, but they were the same. The hood of her coat blew back just enough for her to see the road beneath her horse. She saw trash in the gutter and the rotting remains of a dog.

Another turn and they were out of the wind. Rose could hear what sounded like a child crying. Then a dog barked. Then silence.

Hargus stopped the horses. "I'll take her in. You go tell Myers we got his woman. Make him show you the money before you tell him where she is. Tell him if he shows up with a lawman, Myers will be the first one killed."

Shorty didn't seem to like the idea. "How about I stay here with her. You go tell Myers."

Hargus grabbed Rose's arm and yanked her off the horse. "Because you wouldn't guard her close enough. I know you, you'd get interested in that little tramp you sold to Yancy and leave your post."

"Oh, all right. I'll go, but don't you bother Epley while I'm gone."

"I wouldn't touch her if she was lying nude on the bar.

I'm glad you got rid of her. I hated listening to her sniffling every night in the dugout."

Rose tried to pull away, but Hargus wouldn't let her budge. She heard Shorty's horse moving on down the road as Hargus shoved her in the opposite direction.

They moved across uneven boards to the door of what looked like an old abandoned café. Hargus tried the knob, swore, then pounded hard enough to almost break the door in.

After a few minutes a young girl of about thirteen or fourteen answered. She opened the door and jumped back as if she expected Hargus to hit her.

"Is Yancy dead yet?" Hargus pulled Rose inside and re-locked the door.

The girl shook her head.

The kidnapper shoved Rose in a chair while still holding the end of the rope binding her hands as if it were a leash. "Get me some more rope, girl."

Rose leaned her head back and the hood slipped away from her face. "If you know what is good for you, you'll let me go right now. You can't just take a woman against her will. The law will see you in jail."

Hargus laughed. "You don't know nothing, lady." He pointed to the girl several feet away. "We just took Epley here. She was walking down the road last summer and Shorty took a liking to her. He just caught her up and we kept riding." Hargus laughed. "She yelled and fought for a while. We even had to tie her up at night or she'd run like a rabbit.

"A few days passed before her old man caught up to us and demanded her back. Shorty's funny about what he thinks is right and wrong. He don't like stealing and killing so he traded her papa two horses for the girl. Said he would have given three if she'd been fifteen. After that she quit screaming and went to crying. It took Shorty a week of slapping her every time she started bawling before she finally stopped. Hasn't said a word since. Just like a wild horse, he broke her, I guess."

Rose studied the girl. There were bruises on her bare arms and one of her eyes was black. Her limbs were bone thin and her hair matted. She reminded Rose of the stories her papa and uncles told about how Duncan had looked as a boy when they'd delivered him to the ranch. They said he'd looked more as if he'd been treated like an animal than a human. The girl looked like that now.

"Epley, hurry up with that rope or you'll be sorry you were so slow." He straightened as if proud. "I knock her around to teach her lessons, but I don't do to her what Shorty does."

Epley stepped forward with a two-foot length of rope. She held it out to Hargus with bony fingers.

"That's not long enough." He tossed it back in her face. "I swear I have to do all the work and all the thinking. I'm surrounded by idiots. And you, girl, if you get any dumber we'll let you go in the streets like you was nothing more than a stray dog. You're lucky old Yancy lets you work here for meals."

He shoved her aside and walked over to the shelves that looked like they must have once been where the dishes for the café were stored. He grabbed a long rope off the top shelf and handed it to the girl. "Tie that lady up good. I need a drink." As he walked across the room that had been part café, part saloon, he shouted, "You think about running, lady, I'll splatter your blood all over that pretty coat of yours. I could shoot you and leave you back in the alley of that fine hotel. Nobody would know I'd ever picked you up. They'd think you was just robbed and murdered like others have been lately."

The girl moved slowly, following orders. As she tied the rope around Rose's shoulders, Rose was shocked to see her slightly rounded belly beneath the cotton dress.

"How far along are you?" she whispered.

To her surprise, intelligent eyes focused. "I felt it move inside me a few days ago. Last time Shorty found out a babe was inside me, he beat me so bad the baby came. He said I'm too young to carry one till it's big enough to live." A tear washed down her dirty face. "He said he'd kill me if I got another baby in me, but I don't know how to stop it."

"Loosen my hands," Rose whispered. "We're both leaving this place."

The girl shook her head slightly. "I can't. I've tried. The last time Shorty tied me up and left me in the cellar so long I thought I'd die."

"I'll get you out, Epley. I promise. This may be our only chance."

Rose saw realization register in the girl's eyes. Either way she'd probably end up dead, but at least the nightmare would be over. Epley stopped in front of Rose and slipped the knot loose on her hands before she knelt and looped the rope around her skirts.

Hargus was back with a drink in one hand and a bottle in the other. "You want a drink, lady?" He offered the dirty glass. "In a few minutes you're going to be making me a lot of money, so we might as well start celebrating. That husband of yours wants you back bad. Half the town is looking for you."

"I want to go free. August Myers is not my husband. You have no right to keep me here." She looked around, guessing it wouldn't be to her advantage to make him mad. "What is this place?" If she could only stall for time, help would come.

Hargus took a drink and pulled up a chair as if he planned to visit. "It's always been old man Yancy's place for as long as anyone can remember. He served the cheapest whiskey on the acre and food most dogs won't eat. Drunks make this the last stop when they are low on money and too drunk to taste much of anything. Yancy lets them sleep on the floor if they pass out."

Rose looked at the floor covered with dirt.

"Shorty leaves Epley here so he can visit her regular. Don't want to go about with a kid in town and at the farm she's more trouble than help. Old Yancy lets her work here for her food and locks her in the back at night so we don't have to go looking for her come morning." He swatted at the girl's head. "You like it here, don't you, dummy? You got food to eat and the old man leaves you alone."

"What happened to Yancy?"

"One of his customers tried to kill him a few weeks ago. Claimed he caught him taking money from the drunks who passed out. Since then, Shorty and I have taken over the place. Old Yancy can't hold on much longer. He was more dead than alive when I checked on him three days ago."

"Why don't you take him to the doctor?"

Hargus shrugged. "It'd be a waste of money. I told the girl to look in on him a few times a day. Don't want him dying and smelling the place up."

"Once he's gone, Shorty and me think we might get the business going again with the reward. We heard you ran off and so we started watching for where you might have gone. Only clue we had was that you were staying in the Grand Hotel. Minute we saw a woman run out with the judge this morning, we figured it was worth a shot to follow."

Hargus liked to talk, Rose realized. He was mean to the core and didn't care about anyone, but as long as she could keep him talking he wasn't threatening to kill her.

He treated the girl as if she were some kind of bug he was pestering. He liked ordering her around and tripped her once when he got the chance, but Rose could tell that to this hard man, she was nothing. He hadn't been the one who'd caused the pregnancy. Shorty, the kidnapper who didn't believe in killing, had done that and then he'd blamed the girl.

Hargus was talking about the war when Shorty showed up again pulling a basket the size of a steamer trunk.

Rose didn't say a word as the two men moved behind the bar to talk. She couldn't hear everything, but apparently Myers wanted his bride wrapped in the basket and delivered directly to the train. They planned to knock her out, gag her, and lock her in a basket.

Swearing, Hargus yelled at Shorty, "How we going to carry that basket all the way to the train?"

Shorty grinned, almost making him look young. "Myers

paid a guy to drive me here and he's waiting to take us to the train."

Hargus didn't bother to tell Shorty he'd done well, he just looked up at Rose. "We'll take off her coat. It's worth something, along with any jewelry she has. I think we can consider that a bonus."

Rose fought panic. If they took off her bulky coat, they'd see the gun belt and the Colt folded into her skirts. They might also find the small gun in the hidden pocket. She was well armed now, but in a minute she might be defenseless and she couldn't let that happen. Not with these men.

"How about we strip her?" Shorty grinned. "We could give the girl her clothes and Myers won't mind if his bride comes to him naked." He smiled at Epley. "You'd like that, wouldn't you, girl?"

Epley didn't raise her head. She simply moved behind the bar like a frightened child.

"How we going to strip her if we're not supposed to touch her? She don't look like the type who'll just hand over her clothes."

"We could pour whiskey down her till she don't know what's going on. I've done that a few times to women. After half a bottle they don't know or care what's happening. You can do whatever you want to them and they don't even fight. One time down in El Paso, I had to use a full bottle on this big old girl. I finally had to hit her in the head to get her cooperation. Then I—"

"We don't have time for your stories, Shorty. I don't see any reason to waste whiskey on this one, we'll just hit her hard enough to knock her out and load her up. Her clothes stay on, but you're free to handle her anyway you like as long as you don't leave bruises."

Rose had heard enough. It was time to act. She could wait no longer hoping to be saved from these two idiots. Maybe she'd never be brave, but she could be smart and the only smart thing to do was end this now.

She slipped her hands free of the rope and moved them beneath her coat. Duncan's Colt was still strapped low on her hip. Barely moving, she pulled the gun from its holster and slowly stood shaking the ropes Epley had tied away from her shoulders and skirts.

Both men started toward her, yelling as if their words could trap her.

Rose straightened, squared her shoulders, and lifted the Colt. Over the years she'd learned to shoot, all the McMurrays had, and she didn't forget her lessons now. She drew in a breath and fired, her hand steady as stone.

Hargus fell first, a bullet passing through his left leg a few inches above his knee. Before he could yell, another hit his right arm, rendering it useless. The third shot hit the hand Shorty had held up as if to ward off gunfire. The fourth and fifth hit his legs and took him down as if there had been an ax blow at knee level.

The door exploded into splinters a moment later and Rose whirled the weapon toward the man storming in. One bullet. She'd have to take him down with her last bullet. There was no time to pull her second gun. No time to think. She raised the Colt and took aim at his head.

With one second to spare, she froze and eased her finger off the trigger. "Stitch?"

The big bull of a man didn't move. His body seemed to need a little time to recover from how close he came to being shot. Slowly, he looked around the room, then smiled. "I guess you didn't need my help as much as I thought you did, Miss Rose."

She felt her hand shake. Until now she hadn't had time to be afraid, she'd just done what had to be done. Rose stared at the two men on the floor. "I didn't kill them, but I think we need to have them arrested. They thought I was Victoria and kidnapped me."

Rose couldn't stop shaking. An ice storm seemed to be moving through her entire body. Without thought, she raised her arms to Stitch.

He hesitated, then swept her up in a big bear hug. "It's all right, little miss, you was as brave as you needed to be when it counted. You told me that first day you could take care of yourself, but I didn't believe you. I said I'd make sure you got out safe and back to the hotel and that's just what I plan to do."

The solidness of him steadied her. When he set her back down, she'd managed to gain back a bit of her composure. "I'm ready to go, Stitch." The dark ugliness of this place seemed to whirl around her.

The big man smiled. "Yes, miss."

Several strangers were at the door trying to volley for spots so that they could see in. One yelled that he'd run for the law while the others just stared at Hargus and Shorty jerking in their own blood like they were docked fish. Not one onlooker stepped inside to offer care.

Stitch moved to the two kidnappers, both crying for help. The scarred man just crossed between them and made sure all their weapons were removed. Then he stared down at them as if he saw only wounded snakes. "Where's the old man who owns the place?"

"He's dead," a small voice said from the corner of the room. "When he was shot, they left him in the back to die."

Rose wiped the Colt she'd borrowed from Duncan with her handkerchief and replaced it back in the holster. "Stitch, this is Epley. If she would like, she is welcome to come with us."

"Hargus said I'd be put in jail if the law finds me. He says I'm too young to be on my own so I'd go to jail unless I stayed with him."

Rose wasn't sure what would happen to a girl who was pregnant but not quite a woman. "I know a judge. We could ask him, but Epley, no one owns you. You're free to go or come."

The girl looked at Stitch and backed away.

Rose spoke softly to the girl. "Epley, this is Stitch, my friend. I swear he'll never lay a hand on you. No one will as long as you are with me."

"Or you'll shoot him?" The girl glanced over at the two wounded men. Hargus was cussing and Shorty had passed out.

When she looked up, Rose patted the handle of her gun. "Or I'll shoot him."

"Miss Rose," Stitch said politely, "we might want to be getting out of here before the sheriff shows up. You've got enough problems right now without spending the day explaining."

Rose raised an eyebrow. "You don't think we should stay around to get the facts of what happened straight?"

He shook his head. "Does it matter?"

"No. The girl and I are safe and that's all that is worth mattering about here." Rose straightened and removed Victoria's beautiful midnight coat. She draped it around the girl and walked her out while Stitch cleared a path with one sweep of his arm against the growing crowd.

The rain had slowed as he helped the girl and Rose into his wagon, then tossed the big basket in the back along with the few bags of Victoria's trousseau the kidnappers had brought along.

Ten minutes later the women were at the side door of the hotel. Stitch let them out, saying simply that he had something that needed doing but he'd return as soon as he could.

No one stopped Rose and the girl as they rushed up to her room.

They found Duncan propped up in bed eating and Hallie fussing over him. The young doctor was asleep in the chair next to the bed.

Rose set Epley down in a chair, grinned at Duncan, then stared at the doctor. "He looks exhausted," she said, thinking that Atamear looked worse than Duncan.

Hallie eyed the dirty, shoeless child then answered. "The doc's been snoring for an hour. Probably dreaming about being able to grow a beard." She pointed at the girl. "Who's she?"

"A friend who saved my life. I'll explain later." She motioned with her head for Hallie to move the tray of muffins closer to the girl. "How's Duncan?"

"He's—"

"I can answer for myself," Duncan interrupted with a frown. He turned his full attention to Rose. "Tell this woman to stop babying me like I was an invalid. I only got one little hole in me. Well, I would be fine, but someone stole my gun." He glared at her.

"Since you forgot to ask, Stitch and I are back safe and sound, but I think I need to talk to you about the fact that you missed your Colt more than me. Right now I need to get out of these wet clothes. If you even think of getting out of bed, I'll put another bullet in you and we'll have to wake up the doc." She motioned for Hallie and the girl to follow her into the bathing room.

Duncan looked like he was angry, but she saw the laughter in his eyes.

As soon as the women were alone, Rose asked the maid to run around to the Henderson Mercantile to buy Epley clothes she'd need for several days. While Hallie took the girl's measurements, Rose jotted down a note.

"This child is going to need everything from shoes to coat."

"I know." Rose handed over her purse. "Buy a traveling case and anything else she might need." .

Hallie stared at the purse. "You trust me with your money, miss?"

Rose laughed. "If you hadn't been honest, you could have picked my pocket days ago. Now hurry back, and as you leave the store, please hand this note to the man who owns the place and then disappear before he has time to open it."

Tugging on her raincoat, Hallie added as she left, "I'll order that cowboy another breakfast. That man eats more than a horse. You sure you want to keep him around, Miss Rose?"

Rose laughed as the maid disappeared. In truth, she could hardly wait to get back to Duncan and tell him all that had happened.

She showed Epley the bathing area and told her to stay

in the tub until the maid returned. The girl seemed suddenly shy, not comfortable pulling off the rags she wore while Rose was still in the room.

"You'll be back?" Epley whispered as Rose stepped to the door.

"When you're finished."

The girl nodded and smiled. "You are very brave, miss."

Rose wanted to tell her she'd never been brave. Then she reconsidered. Maybe just this once she had been. She'd been brave when it counted most.

CHAPTER 27

Second Avenue

Abe had worked for a half hour hearing something knocking away above him. He'd climbed the stairs to his rooms over the mercantile and found no window flapping open. Nothing in the apartment seemed to make the sound, but it still came as regular as a heartbeat. He checked the storage room and the old part of the bakery.

The knocking was coming from directly above the bakery.

Abe hesitated. Of course he knew Killian's lady was upstairs, though he'd never actually met her. He didn't want to frighten her, but something might be wrong.

He started up the stair. "Killian," he called, not wanting to surprise them.

The hammering started harder.

"Killian?" Abe reached the top of the stairs. "Are you in here?"

The door was open slightly. As he pushed it wider he saw them tied up in chairs by the window. Within seconds he was helping them get free. Killian was cussing mad, but the woman only cried.

After a moment Killian seem to realize that all the swearing was doing her no good.

Abe had no idea what to do or say. Asking questions didn't seem to help and he had little practice at calming hysterical females.

Finally, Killian pulled the woman under his arm and held her as she cried.

When she calmed a bit, he told Abe what had happened in short precise sentences. "They know where we are even if they didn't know which one was Victoria. This place is no longer safe, but our first concern has to be Rose."

Abe pulled a slip of paper from his apron pocket. "That explains this note some woman brought me a few minutes ago. I couldn't make sense of it. I thought it must have been meant for Henry."

Killian took the note and read it aloud. "Back at hotel. Safe. Have to stay with Duncan. You both should disappear. Rose."

Victoria stopped crying and took the note. "I almost got my one friend killed. Oh, Killian, I could have lost her. This is all my fault."

"Not you," Killian whispered as he kissed her forehead. "None of this is your fault."

"I should go to her."

Both men said no at the same time, but Killian added, "Not until we know you're safe. Trust me, any woman who can handle a Colt can take care of herself. You didn't send her out there, she wanted to go. She knew she was armed and would have a chance."

Abe nodded slowly. "Your friend is safe back at the hotel, but you're no longer safe here. If these two found this hiding place, so might someone else."

Killian agreed with Abe. "I'm not sure she's safe anywhere. I thought I was helping her, but I may have only made things worse." Killian shook his head. "August Myers seems to be willing to go to any length to marry her. She won't be safe until he's out of the country."

"Or one of them is dead," Abe added.

"Stop talking about me as if I'm not here listening." Victoria pouted. Now that she knew Rose was safe, the world could go back to revolving around her.

"I'm sorry," Killian offered, but Abe just stared. On a good day he couldn't handle even an ordinary woman and this wasn't a good day any more than Victoria Chamberlain was an ordinary woman. She talked to ghosts, had an imaginary staff who delivered a wagonload of luggage while everyone else slept last night, and had a judge so wrapped around her finger he was apologizing for talking.

"I should be getting back to the store." Abe said the first thing he could think of to escape.

"Wait," Killian stopped him. "We've got to figure something out. If Myers is willing to offer a reward to get Victoria back under any circumstance, he's willing to break a few laws."

"A lot of laws," Victoria stormed, suddenly angry. "I can't believe I ever even spoke to the man. My father is so taken in by Myers, he'll never take the time to hear the truth."

"Your father isn't here." Killian kept his words low. "He left with instructions for Myers to bring you with him no matter what. I heard a doorman say that even though it's been years since the war, Major Chamberlain gives the orders and expects them to be followed."

Abe watched the beautiful woman's face twist in rage. She knew she was trapped. Not even her father would help her. He'd passed responsibility for her off to another.

"There has to be a way out of this," Killian tried. "We've got to think of a safe place for her, Abe. Surely in a town this size there's somewhere."

"Myers isn't going to stop looking until he finds her and pulls her before a preacher." Abe had never met the man, but he'd heard about him.

"Or I'm married to someone else," Victoria whispered, an idea forming in her head as she spoke.

Both men were silent.

"Myers has probably figured out that Rose isn't me by now and the kidnappers are on their way back to get me." Victoria was a woman used to getting what she wanted when she wanted it. She shoved her tears aside and stared at the two men.

"All right. It's simple. Which of you two would like to marry me?"

Both hesitated.

She pouted. "Come on, gentlemen, it's not like either of you is courting anyone. You're both over thirty and bachelors. I'm not exactly without worth." She thought for a minute. "True, I do have a crazy father and a fiancé who's willing to go to extreme measures to win my hand, but on the upside, I have a small inheritance and I've already bought the wedding dress."

Abe spoke before he thought. "I am seeing someone. In fact, in the very near future, I hope to ask her to marry me."

Victoria looked at Killian. "That leaves you, Judge. You kissed me once, so you must have feelings for me."

"Of course I do. I'd die for you."

She smiled. "But, Killian, will you live with me?"

Abe could almost see Killian's logical mind working. He was a man who lived out of saddlebags. A man who bathed once a week. He had no family. No roots. No money. The judge was a loner who, until recently, had considered a grand evening one of drinking until he passed out.

But, Abe thought with a smile, Killian didn't see what he was. He was a good friend and a good man. He tried to do what was right. He kept his brother's memory alive in his thoughts, and most of all, Abe could see it in his eyes, Killian loved Victoria despite her perfect beauty.

CHAPTER 28

Main Street

LEANING AGAINST THE BEDROOM DOORFRAME, ROSE watched Duncan sleeping as she listened to Killian in the sitting room a few feet away. He'd explained the plan they'd come up with to save Victoria. It seemed a little extreme. Surely there must be a better way than sacrificing the judge.

When the judge took a breath, Rose asked, "Is this going to be a real marriage, Killian, or have you had time to think about that?"

He shook his head. "I haven't had much time to think about it. I think Victoria just wants to get out of this mess. I somehow can't see her wanting to put on an apron and set up housekeeping on what I make each month." He smiled a sad smile. "Me either."

"Do you love her?"

He nodded. "She's beautiful. I don't think I could ever tire of staring at her, but that's not why I love her. She's not like anyone I've ever met. She's unique."

Rose thought of asking if he'd ever really talked to Victoria, but she didn't see the point. If she knew Victoria, there would be other crises to fight as soon as this one was over. Maybe not as big, but just as demanding on his time. Killian O'Toole struck her as a dreamer. Maybe he didn't want anything real from Victoria any more than she wanted a real husband from him.

"I've got to go find someone I trust who'll marry us. Victoria still wants you to be her maid of honor. In fact, I think despite the change in grooms, she plans to continue all the other details. Thanks for loaning us your maid, Hallie. Victoria is going to need help. No one's seen that nutty maid of hers since she was fired."

With all that had been happening Rose hadn't given Betty Ann a thought. "Where's the wedding?"

"Nowhere sounds safe. I'll be on edge until it's done, then I'll worry about Myers making her a widow."

"How about here? I could be all packed up by dark. The doctor said as long as his stitches hold we can move Duncan tonight. We're not leaving until the midnight train."

Killian shook his head. "We'd have to move Victoria and all her stuff over here. I think she's safer across the alley. I used Duncan's name and got a couple of rangers willing to spend the day standing guard over there. It wouldn't surprise me if half the hotel staff is watching out for her, just hoping she'll show up so they can claim the reward."

He was probably right, Rose realized. Every time she stepped out her door someone asked her if Miss Chamberlain had returned.

Rose's mind began to do what she did best—organize. "What if just the two of you come over at dusk? You can use the garden stairs. I'll have Stitch move her luggage directly to the train. After you're married, you could leave with us at midnight and switch trains somewhere along the way then disappear for a few weeks."

Pacing, Rose added, "I'll have Duncan with me, and if we're careful no one will know you two have left the train until we reach our final stop."

"Might be a great plan. The midnight train wouldn't

have many passengers, and if we're in your private car no one would notice us."

Killian walked to the bedroom door and looked over at Duncan. "Your cousin going to be all right?"

"Sure. He's been complaining all afternoon that he's fine." She smiled. "He wants to get out of bed and go over to put a few more bullet holes in those two kidnappers."

"I know how he feels." Killian pointed to the young man sleeping in a chair in the far corner of the sitting room. "Who's he?"

"The doc. Seems he was up all night delivering a baby and stopped by this morning to check on Duncan. Hallie made the mistake of feeding him and he's been sleeping here ever since."

"And the girl sleeping in the maid's bed?"

"I'm just helping her find her way," Rose answered, knowing that Killian was just making sure all was safe for Victoria to return. "I told the girl if she'd like to come along, I thought she might want to stay with us on Whispering Mountain for a while."

"I heard you McMurrays take in strays."

Rose grinned. "We do. Once my papa took in my mother and three little girls. He says he didn't know what living was until he married."

Killian shrugged. "Who knows, I might feel the same way."

Without another word, he walked out. Rose didn't know whether to be happy for the judge or feel sorry for him. He was marrying Victoria, after all, and that seemed like a full-time job in itself.

She checked on Epley and then slipped into her bedroom, closing the door to the world beyond.

Without hesitating, she crawled in bed beside Duncan, needing him near even if he was hurt and asleep.

When she rolled to face him, his sleepy blue eyes focused on her. "I heard you were a hero," he whispered.

"Oh, you did? Well, you were probably misinformed. I've never been brave. I just did what had to be done."

"Rose, that's what heroes do." He reached and took her hand. "Why don't we get married tonight?"

"What?"

"I've been thinking. I'm comfortable with you. Both of us are over a quarter of a century old and haven't found anyone to marry. What are the chances we will? From now on it's a downhill slope. So here we are, stuck with each other. We might as well have two weddings tonight."

"Your proposal is very flattering, Duncan. I can't imagine why so many girls have turned you down over the years."

He ignored her comment. "Now think about this, Rose. You wouldn't even have to change names. I'd make a good husband to you and no matter where I traveled or how long I was gone, I'd always come home to you. That's what you are to me, dear, sweet Rose, you're my home."

When she didn't answer, he kissed her hand. "Don't answer me now. If you want to take an hour to mull it over, I understand. I don't want to rush you into anything. In fact, that's one thing I like so much about you. You put some thought into everything you do. You're great at all the things that make a wonderful wife. You can cook and run a house. Hell, you can run the ranch. Everyone loves you, and if you ask me, you're far better-looking than that glass princess friend of yours. You're always a lady and good at nursing the injured. That's important in my line of work. Hell, I'm never going to find a woman to measure up to you. Think about it."

Rose fought the urge to kick him. "I don't have to think about it. Good as you make it sound, the answer is no."

"But—"

"Let me put it in words you'll understand. Hell, no." She sat up so she could look down on him. "Duncan McMurray, I not only don't want you as a husband, I don't even want you in my family. From this day on, don't even tell people we're cousins. No blood runs between us, but now that I've shot a few men it doesn't seem all that hard. If you ever suggest marriage again, I'll use that last bullet on you."

"Now you're just being stubborn."

"Well, when did I stop being perfect?" She folded her arms to keep from thumping his head.

"About the time you turned me down. I was just being nice. You're going to grow old and spend your days baking and sewing and wishing you'd married me. Hell, woman, we both know you love sleeping with me. We might as well be in the same bed for the rest of our lives."

She scooted to the edge of the bed. "I'm getting the doctor. You must have been shot in the head and we didn't notice because of all that mess of hair. It's no wonder a woman doesn't step out with you. They're probably afraid of what might crawl out. Haven't you ever thought of getting a haircut?"

"All I did was ask a question!"

The doctor poked his head in the room. "Am I needed?"

Both the McMurrays yelled, "No!"

Before he could close the door, Rose added, "You might stand by, Dr. Atamear. As soon as I find a gun, Duncan is going to need another bullet removed."

The doctor closed the door mumbling something about waiting until he heard gunfire before he'd return.

She stormed around the room, throwing things.

"What is the matter with you?" Duncan leaned back. "You've never acted like this. Have you gone completely mad, Rose?"

"Well, maybe it's about time I did get mad. Really mad. If being efficient and calm gets me a marriage of convenience, maybe it's time I threw a few fits."

"You don't have to take my proposal like some kind of insult."

She stopped and glared at him. "I don't have to take it at all." She stepped out the balcony door onto the rainy little covered walkway. The thought crossed her mind that she should yell for Stitch to come toss Duncan off into the garden as he'd offered to do for August Myers. Maybe all men are good for is smashing the rosebushes below.

Looking down, she yelled, "I hate roses!"

Out of the corner of her eye she caught a movement from

the end of the balcony. When she turned, she saw Stitch walking toward her.

"You all right, miss?" he asked in his low, rich voice.

"No, I think I'm cracking up."

"Things will settle down," he offered. "They always, eventually, do."

She shoved wet hair out of her eyes. "Stitch, would you be able to buy me a gun belt that fits around my waist? I want one that has two holsters and two pistols. Not the huge ones, but something small that I can handle easily."

"I know a shop that could fix you up, but it'll cost you."

"I'll pay whatever. Just tell Hallie to give you what you think you'll need. When we move Duncan to the train tonight, I want to be well armed. Those two kidnappers were the dumbest outlaws in the world not to have opened my coat and checked for a gun. I won't be so lucky next time."

"You think there will be a next time, miss?"

"Yes."

"Me too. If all the folks who want to kill you people could vote, you could get elected governor."

Rose smiled. "You have a way about you, Stitch. You always manage to make me feel better. Promise you'll never ask me to marry you."

He laughed. "I'm too old for you, miss. You need a man who can fire those cheeks with passion, not anger."

"I fear he doesn't exist."

Stitch moved away, but she thought she heard him mumble something about such a man already being in her bed.

CHAPTER 29

Stitch moved, as always, unnoticed through the streets. He took care of plans for leaving even though he knew he wouldn't be going with them. Deep down he knew he should stay near Killian and that meant leaving, but there was no way he could travel with the judge and remain undetected. If the newly married couple did see him, they'd think he was hunting them. To them, he was nothing but a stranger.

He bought the tickets and moved boards into the train car so he could make a swinging bed for Duncan. He'd seen one once at the Yankee hospital he'd been shipped to. It was just ropes and boards, but it swayed with the movement of a train or wagon making it easier on someone who was hurt.

By the time he had it rigged up, it was almost dark. He needed to check on Victoria and Killian before he went back to his post on the balcony outside Rose's hotel room.

The bakery was dark. A ranger was watching the door, but he didn't see Stitch slip into the coal chute. From there, Stitch moved across the bakery kitchen knowing if he accidentally hit something, he'd be dead before he'd have time to explain.

Silently, he moved up the little stairs off the kitchen to the boarded-up door. Peeping through the cracks, he saw Killian sitting at the table. The exhaustion he wore on his face did not make him look like a man about to marry the woman he loved.

Maybe he was worried about Myers finding her. Maybe he'd changed his mind and didn't know how to back out. Killian wasn't a ladies' man. In the years Stitch had watched him he'd never seen the judge step out for the evening. He was polite to women, even the ones in saloons, but he never climbed the stairs with one.

Stitch felt helpless. For the first time there was nothing he could do to help. Killian had made his own bed here and a ghost of a brother couldn't even offer advice.

"I think we should talk about things, Victoria."

"What things?" She moved into the kitchen whirling around. "Do you think this dress is still too short? I could have Hallie take it down another half an inch. I wish I could get into my trousseau, but my father made me swear I wouldn't open a single trunk until after I was a married lady."

"I think the dress is fine," Killian said without bothering to notice what she was wearing. "Hallie, would you excuse us a minute?"

"Of course, Judge. I need to go downstairs for some thread anyway." The rather chubby maid left them alone.

Killian stood and waited until Hallie was gone, then said, "Victoria, we need to talk about important things. Things people about to be married discuss."

"Like what?" she said, still not giving him her full attention.

"Like money and kids and where we'll live. Like are we going to have a real marriage or is this just a show to get you out of this mess? I can handle it either way, but I have to know from the start."

She looked up at him and smiled. "A real marriage, I

think. Do you think Rose would let us have Hallie as a housekeeper? She's really wonderful. I think I could manage being a proper wife if I had someone who could help me."

Killian tried to get her back on track. "What do you think a real marriage is, Victoria?"

"You'll pick where we live. I'll decorate the house. You'll go to work and I'll run all that happens in the home as well as do all the shopping. At night you'll come home and sometimes we'll have dinner alone, but other times we'll go out. No matter where we live, we'll go out, promise me. I don't think I could live someplace where I didn't have a social life. And we'll have to travel to Austin now and then. I always want to visit my mother's grave."

"Who handles the money?"

"You will. When I marry, my trust goes to you. You'll give me a nice allowance and I'll do my best to spend it. I like spending money, but it's not something I have to do."

"Of course." He fought to ask what he wanted to know. "What if all the money disappears—will you leave me?"

"No," she answered. "I think I will like being married to you, Killian. Did you know that in the two years since we met at the cemetery you've never once yelled at me? I think that speaks well of the husband you'll be."

Killian tried again. "And will you sleep with me?"

She shook her head, giving his question little thought. "I don't think so, Killian. I've always slept alone. You'd probably keep me awake."

With that she walked out of the room. Stitch watched Killian pace for a minute, then take off down the stairs.

Victoria stepped back into the kitchen looking for him as if he were a necklace she'd misplaced. "Killian?"

She stomped her foot. "Why is that man always disappearing?"

"He's uncertain," Stitch answered.

Victoria looked around. "Shawn, is that you?"

Stitch didn't answer for a long while. It seemed far too odd to be pretending to be a ghost. Having Killian talk about his brother the ghost was one thing, but hanging around talking to people was quite another.

Finally he said the only thing he thought might help. "Killian doesn't want to sleep alone."

"Really," Victoria said, but footsteps sounded on the stairs before she could ask more.

Killian walked back in the little kitchen. "I shouldn't have left. That's no way to work things out. If we're going to have a prayer of making this work, we've got to talk about more than the hem on your dress."

Victoria moved up to him and put her hand on his shoulder. "Would you like me to sleep with you when we're married?"

Killian looked at her and smiled. "Yes, I think so. I think I'd like that very much."

She kissed his cheek. "Then I will."

He caught her hand and pulled her gently against him. "Do you know what sleeping with me means?"

"Of course."

He kissed her mouth before the words were completely out.

She settled into his kiss and Stitch decided he probably shouldn't be watching. As he began to move away he heard her whisper, "Promise to kiss me every night."

Stitch smiled, deciding Killian was too busy kissing her to answer.

As he moved down the stairs, he figured it might be time to give up his ghosting job. Killian was going to have his hands full and Stitch had a feeling there would be no more night drinking.

CHAPTER 30

Second Avenue

Abe used his umbrella as a cane as he moved across the street in late afternoon shadows. He'd used it enough that he'd learned to trust his weight every other step. Maybe he should think about buying one of those fancy canes with the gold knobs like Sam Houston always carried. No one called the man a cripple when he'd been shot fighting for Texas independence.

Out of breath, Abe made it to the door of the schoolhouse. He paused a minute, trying to think about what he planned to do. If he went inside, it would change things, maybe forever, and things seemed to be changing every day lately. He almost missed the days and weeks of calm sameness but not nearly as much as he'd miss Sara Norman if she was gone from his life.

Setting his jaw for whatever blow came, he opened the schoolhouse door without knocking. He figured his heart was doing enough pounding to be heard a half block away.

Miss Norman stood when she saw him, but she didn't move from behind the desk. "Mr. Henderson," she said more in the way of stating a fact than in greeting. She'd worn her gray suit today and seemed to blend in with her surroundings.

He walked halfway across the room and braced the umbrella against his bad leg. "Miss Norman, I've come to ask if you'd like to attend my friend's wedding tonight. It's nothing fancy, but I'd like you there with me if you're willing."

"I have papers to grade." She looked down at the stack of papers on her desk.

Abe didn't speak. He had no intention of asking again or begging. It wasn't his way. "Well, then," was all he could think of to say. He dreaded the walk back across the street.

She met his gaze before he had time to turn. "I'd be honored to accompany you, Mr. Henderson. I'll make an exception and not work tonight."

He nodded once and turned to leave. At the door, he stopped and looked back. "I don't know the time, but I'll pick you up at the boardinghouse."

He didn't wait for an answer. He closed the door and walked back to his store.

Once inside, he dried off and told himself the request went well. He could have made small talk, but he'd never been good at that. She'd said yes and that was all he'd gone across the street to hear.

Walking to the front of the store, he looked out at her working. He didn't like talking to her and he guessed she felt the same. Abe had never had much to say to anyone, including Killian. There were times when they spent an hour drinking coffee without saying much to each other.

Abe remembered back to his childhood. His parents rarely talked to each other, much less him. When he'd come home hurting and barely able to move, his mother would deliver his meal at night, then climb the stairs and eat hers alone. At first he'd spent the days in his study behind the shelves reading. Sometimes he could hear people talking, but his mother never said more than was necessary. She always believed visiting slowed the buying down. She'd come in with lunch not to talk but to explain the books while he ate. By the time he could stand, he knew every detail of the business and had taken over the daily book-work of ordering and accounts.

His mother never questioned him or thanked him. After all, he was just doing what was expected of him.

Abe watched Miss Norman as she stood and pulled on her coat. The need to hold her almost buckled his knees.

She closed up the schoolhouse and rushed across the street to his store. Abe was alone. No one had been in the store for two hours. Henry was out making a delivery, and Killian and the two rangers had taken Victoria back to the hotel.

Miss Norman blew in with the wind. For a moment he thought she'd changed her mind and was coming to tell him, but she was laughing as she shook the rain from her wool shawl.

"I'm glad you're still open, Mr. Henderson. I thought I'd buy a new scarf to wear tonight." She smiled at him with that tight little smile of hers.

He moved almost formally to the shelf that held all the scarves he carried. As she looked through them, he didn't say a word. He wanted to see her hair down, not up and covered.

"May we speak frankly, Miss Norman?"

"Of course, Mr. Henderson." She didn't look up at him. After all, here in the open, they were little more than strangers.

"The wedding we'll be attending will be small, but Killian is my best friend and I'm standing up as witness." He paused, thinking how he'd kissed her so tenderly, but now he hesitated to ask a favor. "I'm honored to do so. He's a fine man."

"Yes," she said, finally looking up at him.

Abe got to the point. "Would you be willing to help me pick out a wedding present?"

She smiled then. "Of course, Mr. Henderson. I'd love to."

A few minutes later the postman, a large fellow named Stanten, came in for his nightly cigar. Abe excused himself with a nod to Miss Norman and rang up the postman's purchase while she shopped for just the right gift.

Stanten seemed to want to visit, probably to have time to smoke his cigar before he made it home to the missus. There had been another woman murdered in the back alleys of Hell's Half Acre. "Third one," the postman said loud enough for Sara to overhear. "It's getting to where the streets aren't safe. They say whoever did it didn't even rob her, just beat her to death. No one knows who the poor thing was."

Abe didn't want Sara to hear the details so he tried to change the subject, but Stanten wanted to talk.

Five minutes passed before Sara put one of the quilts on the counter. Abe ordered them from a woman he thought was a real artist with a needle.

For a second, her eyes met Abe's and he nodded his approval. Then, without a word, she picked up her new scarf and handed him a dollar.

Abe wanted to tell her not to pay. He'd gladly give her it for a gift, but he guessed she wouldn't take it, not with Stanten watching. He gave her the change and wrapped the scarf in paper. "Thank you, Miss Norman."

"You're welcome," she said as she headed toward the door.

Henry was coming in and stopped to hold the door for her in a polite, impersonal kind of way.

"Miss Norman," the postman called. "Let me give you a lift to your boardinghouse. Tonight is not a night to be walking."

Abe didn't want her to go. He wanted to lock up and pull her back into his study, but he said nothing as she hesitated, then finally agreed to the lift.

He stood at the window on the far corner of his store and watched the buggy moving through the light rain. He didn't see her run up the steps, but as the buggy pulled away from her place, he saw the lamp come on in her room.

At least he knew she was safe and that she'd be waiting for him when he came to pick her up later. He had a wedding to get ready for and a gift to wrap.

Ten minutes later when he signed the card atop the boxed quilt, he wrote, *From Abe and Sara* without caring if it was the proper thing to do.

"Henry," he called.

"Yes, Mr. Henderson?" Henry said from behind the shoe counter.

"Run the store until I return. You know where everything is."

"Yes, sir."

Abe pulled on his coat. If he hurried, he'd make it the three doors down in time to buy a proper cane and maybe a new hat at the tailor. Abe grinned. He'd never bought anything from another merchant in town. All his life he'd made do with whatever his store carried.

Only tonight was special.

CHAPTER 31

Main Street

DUNCAN MCMURRAY SAT ON THE EDGE OF THE BED, trying to ignore the pain in his chest. The doc kept telling him how lucky he was, but right now he didn't feel very lucky. Bad luck seemed to be following him like a hungry dog. Losing the Tanner brothers was bad enough, but falling into a trap that had almost gotten him killed was worse. Then he'd made it back to Fort Worth, swearing all the way that he couldn't leave Rose alone only to find she seemed to be able to take care of herself just fine. She'd even refused to marry him, which didn't surprise Duncan. She'd refused to marry every man who asked her. Her road to the altar seemed destined to be paved with broken hearts.

In truth, he didn't count his among those broken. He loved her, of course, had since he was five, but proposing just because they were the only two people alive who could put up with each other didn't seem like a good reason to him after he had time to think about it.

"Looks like the wound is closed," the doctor said as he

began rolling a fresh bandage. "You're lucky it was your left arm."

"Stop saying I'm lucky, Doc, or I'll take a swing at you with my right. If I'd been lucky, the bastard who did this would have missed."

"Right," the doc agreed, and moved faster as if he thought he might be dealing with something that might explode at any moment.

"How many bullets did you say you'd dug out of people, Doc?"

"Twelve. I just forgot to say they were out of the same person. A bank robber the town used for target practice as he left the bank. He died before I got the first one pulled, but I went ahead and took out the others for practice."

"Glad you did," Duncan smiled. "You did a fine job. Now you can say you've operated and removed thirteen bullets and half your patients lived."

Rose walked in the bedroom like it was hers. "I've got everything arranged. The wedding will take place in the sitting room in one hour. Victoria is with Hallie getting ready and Killian went to his room to wash up. Stitch was sent to find a preacher and I've ordered food."

"Rose." Duncan hadn't been listening to the details. He didn't care. "Any chance you might forget I asked you to marry me?"

"I already have. You were obviously still under the fog of drugs."

"Obviously." He groaned thinking she was making him feel terrible, if that were possible. Being turned down was bad enough, but that she didn't take him seriously seemed worse. The doctor packed up his things and Duncan managed to say thanks as Dr. Atamear hurried away. For some reason the doctor didn't seem to like being in the same room with both of them.

Rose walked to the wardrobe and began unbuttoning her dress. "Turn your head, Duncan. I have nowhere else to change."

"Not a chance." He smiled and leaned back against the pillows.

She ignored him as she slipped out of her blouse and skirt. The sight of her well-rounded, petite body made him forget he was hurting. She turned her back as she changed her stockings, but he saw the curve of her calf for a second before she slid her petticoats back into place. Then she wiggled into a silk dress with buttons up the back. He liked the way the dress looked as it opened all the way to her bottom.

"I never realized how beautiful you are, Rose," he said, meaning every word.

She looked up as she tried to button her dress. "Drugs again?"

He played along. "It must be the drugs the doc gave me, but you have the nicest body. The kind of curves that make a man want to move his hands down your sides and nicely rounded hips, and those breasts must be something if you'd ever unbind them."

"Stop teasing me, Duncan. We don't have the time."

"Maybe I'm not teasing. I may be near death, but I still have eyes."

"Of course you're teasing and you are not near death. I've been told by more than one man who came to court that I'm the kind of woman men see as practical. A good choice in a wife because I can run the house and am not unpleasant to look at. None of them has quoted me poetry or claimed any passion for me." She straightened, raising her chin slightly. "It's all right. I don't need that kind of nonsense in my life."

"Oh no, dear Rose," Duncan whispered. "That is exactly what you need."

A tap on the balcony window kept her from answering. The frightening face of Stitch appeared behind the rain-streaked glass.

Duncan jerked at the sight a second before he recognized the man, but Rose simply rushed to let him in at the sitting room door. Grinning, Duncan added another beautiful thing about Rose. She saw people for who they truly were.

"I got your guns," Stitch said as he followed Rose back to the bedroom. "They're not as fine as I would have liked, but they'll serve you well if needed." He had a leather bag and a couple of pieces of expensive luggage.

"Thank you, Stitch. You're an angel." Rose took the leather bag. "If you two will excuse me, I need to finish getting ready."

She didn't wait for an answer but disappeared into the bathing area with the bag Stitch brought in one hand and her hairbrush in the other.

Stitch watched her go then took the chair next to the bed. "First I'm a ghost and now I'm an angel. You reckon I'm dead, Duncan, and don't know it?"

"You're doing better than me, Stitch. I usually only get called names that refer to my parentage, or lack of it. Rose thinks I'm an idiot and I've no reason to argue with her about the diagnosis."

Stitch still watched the door where Rose had disappeared. "That's one brave little woman," he said as if he hadn't been listening to Duncan. "You should have seen her standing there holding your gun. She made every shot count and the next one would have taken off my head if she hadn't recognized me."

"I'm glad I wasn't the one who broke in to save her. She's so mad at me right now she probably would've shot me." He groaned as he moved. "All my life I've been thinking I was looking out for her, and all of a sudden the world's turned upside down and I can tell you it don't feel right."

Stitch nodded. "I wouldn't worry about it. After being around her for almost a week now, near as I can tell, she stays mad at you. Maybe it's like an illness with her or maybe it's a religion." He set the luggage down. "Seems like I've been hauling Miss Victoria's luggage around for days."

"Forget about that, she's got a half dozen others that look the same." Duncan held his side. "You got any advice about helping me and Rose?"

"Nope. Fresh out. Figure I need to stop while I'm ahead."

"You going with us tonight, Stitch?"

"No, I can't, but I do have a favor. Any chance you could watch over Killian for me? The judge is a smart man, but since the war I've heard he don't even carry a weapon."

Duncan raised an eyebrow. "I didn't even know you knew Judge O'Toole."

Stitch wove his big, scarred hands together. "I know him, but he don't know me. I kind of watch over him from time to time."

"If it's important to you, I promise I'll do my best until they step off the train. After they're married we all plan to move down to the train station and board early. Rangers will be watching to make sure no one bothers us until we're under way. The bride and groom plan to get off at the first stop that has a good hotel. From then on I think we all should stay away and let them have a honeymoon."

Stitch smiled. "I think you're right."

Duncan leaned forward. "Would you help me get dressed, Stitch? I plan to make this wedding and I have no intention of asking Rose to help me."

"Miss Rose is not going to be happy you're moving around."

"I don't care," Duncan said as he pushed his good arm into the shirt Stitch offered. "I can't seem to make her happy. I might as well make her mad." He swore with pain as the other arm moved. "She thinks she's too good for me."

Stitch shrugged. "She's right."

"I know, but while I was almost dying I set my mind to the idea of always coming home to her. Only, can you believe it, she didn't take much to the idea."

"I'm not surprised." After Duncan swore again, Stitch added, "No woman just wants to be the place a man goes to when he's tired or hurt and ain't got no better place to go."

"Since when did you become a sage, Stitch?"

"I don't know. It just seemed to fall over me. Like some folks get religion, I guess. I've been trying to stop giving advice, but it ain't easy with so many of you lost folks to preach to." He laughed. "If I get any wiser I'll have to open up and start talking to the masses."

Duncan laughed through the pain as he tried to stand. "You want to come to the wedding we're having here?"

Stitch shook his head. "I think I'll just watch from the window."

"Will you help me to the other room? I'd like to be sitting in a chair when Rose comes back. That way if she takes a swing at me I'll be less likely to hit the floor."

Stitch stood by his side as they crossed the room.

"Did you get the basket delivered?" Duncan asked, fighting to keep his mind off the pain shooting through his body with each step.

"I did. It's on the midnight train in August Myers's private car. I put enough rope around it that Myers will be a while getting it open and, when he does, he's going to be real sorry."

They reached the chair and Duncan lowered slowly. "Does he know it's there?"

"Yeah, he watched from a carriage while I loaded it. Wouldn't even get out of the coach to help me lug it on, but he did pay me. Told me to take the money back to Hargus and Shorty, then gave me ten dollars in gold to forget I even hauled anything. I'm guessing he doesn't know his two partners in the kidnapping are in jail. The rangers had a doctor patch them up. He gave them so much opium to knock them out that I'll be surprised if they wake up before the middle of next week."

"Did Myers say anything else?"

"I heard him tell the driver to take him to the nearest gaming house. He laughed and said something about having a little fun to warm him up for a busy night."

Stitch laid the envelope of money on the table. "I thought you could give the money to Killian and the lady. Hargus and Shorty don't need it where they're going."

"I'll do that," Duncan promised.

Stitch hesitated and lowered his voice. "I heard talk among the haulers that Myers isn't very nice to the women he buys for the night. Heard he likes to hurt them enough to make them cry while he takes his satisfaction."

"I heard something to that effect in Dallas, but I could never get anyone to file a complaint."

Stitch shook his head. "I'm sure glad there's not a woman in that basket I delivered."

"So am I." Duncan leaned back in his chair and vowed, "When this is all over, I plan to find Myers and have a little talk with him."

"I'll go with you, Ranger. Just to see you're not disturbed while you and him are visiting."

Stitch moved out onto the balcony as someone tapped on the door. A moment later waiters from the fine restaurant delivered Champagne and little sandwiches not big enough to be a full bite. They made another trip bringing in glasses and a small cake.

Duncan had finished off half the tray of sandwiches when Rose came in. She took one glance at the tray and gave him one of her looks that said she thought he was a few levels below the family dog. He tried to look innocent, but being the only one in the room, it wasn't easy.

Suddenly the place was full of people. Killian, all dressed up in a new black suit, which looked about the same as his other one, came in with his best friend, Abe Henderson, and Abe's lady, a Miss Norman. She looked shy and Duncan didn't miss that Henderson never let go of her arm. Henderson was tall and might have been handsome but for his hard-set features. The only thing that didn't appear chiseled in stone about the man was his gentle hold on the shy lady.

Hallie entered with the girl Rose had picked up at the kidnapping. Hallie had changed from her maid's uniform into a black traveling suit with a short black cape. Epley's clothes were almost identical except they were brown. A man who claimed to be a preacher and who looked like he'd been sobered and scrubbed for the occasion walked in and stood by the fire.

Last came Victoria looking, as always, as beautiful and

fragile as a porcelain doll. Her wedding dress, with matching floor-length coat, was ivory. Everyone froze as she walked the length of the small room as gracefully as if she were in a cathedral.

Finally, Killian stepped forward and took her hand. "You sure you want to do this?"

She nodded.

"Then we begin."

Ten minutes later the ceremony was over and they all toasted the couple. Rose had everything organized, down to the carriages waiting at the north door. This late in the evening no one would notice them leaving, and even if one of the staff did see Victoria, they wouldn't have time to notify Myers.

Duncan tried to smile, but the throbbing in his shoulder was pounding all the way to his head. He let the others go first so no one would see Stitch help him down the back stairs. The fewer people who knew he was hurt, the better.

"I don't know if I can keep my senses about me enough to guard the train."

"Don't worry. I'll be there watching out for you until you're out of the station. I know what to do. Did you tell Miss Rose that Myers rented the last car?"

"No. I'm hoping we'll all be boarded before he arrives."

"I gave his driver the ten dollars to make sure that happens." Stitch laughed. "He almost didn't take my money. He said it wouldn't be fair because he's taken Myers around long enough to know that the man will be out whoring until the last minute."

Duncan didn't want to think about what would have happened if Victoria or Rose had actually been delivered to Myers, but anger seemed to help him focus.

"Myers has been spending money like a madman all day, the driver said. He told someone that after tonight he'll be a rich man." They'd reached the side door and Stitch helped Duncan into a bed made for him in the back of Stitch's wagon. Duncan could feel the wooden sides of a stretcher against his shoulders as he lay down.

Once Duncan was in, Stitch covered him with a tarp. "I'll take it as easy as I can."

Duncan was too near passing out to answer. He knew Rose would have everything ready when they pulled up beside the train. Porters would be waiting to help him inside, and as always, Stitch would disappear into the shadows.

CHAPTER 32

With steam from the engine whirling around them, Stitch watched men lift the stretcher from his wagon and carry the ranger into a private car. The curtains were all down, but he knew Duncan would be the last to arrive. No one would see him being placed on the special sling of a bed. No one would know how the ranger had disappeared.

Silently, Stitch moved to the end of the platform and waited. Miss Rose and all her people were safe, but he wasn't finished with his job yet.

In the quiet night, he listened. The rain had finally stopped, but the air was thick, so damp it seemed to push against his skin. As he stared at the train car he couldn't help but smile. Killian O'Toole was married. Something Stitch thought he'd never see. In a few hours he and his bride would be safely away from all this trouble and the others would be headed for a ranch some claimed was a fortress.

A slight sound tapped just behind him. Every muscle in Stitch's big body tightened.

Then he smelled a familiar perfume and a hand touched his arm.

"You should be on the train, Hallie," Stitch whispered as she moved in front of him.

"I wanted to say good-bye. I'm going with the McMurrays and I don't know how long it will be before I get back."

Stitch didn't know what to say. "Good-bye, Hallie. It was real nice knowing you."

She let out a huff. "If you'll lean down a little, I'll kiss you good-bye. I don't know if I'll ever see you again, but you're a good man and I've decided maybe you're a man I wouldn't mind having as a friend."

He leaned down, glad it was dark. His face would be hard enough to touch without having to look at it as well.

She placed her hand on his cheek and touched her lips to his. He took the feel of her like a blow, but he didn't move. No woman, including his mother, had ever kissed him.

She stepped closer letting her body press lightly against his and, to his surprise, continued to kiss him. The woman acted like she hadn't even noticed the scars cutting up his face and her body seemed every bit as soft as he'd imagined it might be.

When she finally pulled away, she patted his cheek. "That wasn't so bad, was it?"

He smiled, wishing he could see her better. "No. It wasn't."

"Well, I'd best get back to the train. I don't really know where I'm going or where I'll end up but for the first time in a long time I'm looking forward to seeing what tomorrow brings. I have a feeling that wherever I settle is where I'll want to be."

He reached out and took her hand. "Hallie, if you decide to work for O'Toole, I think the new missus could really use your help."

"She's already offered me a position, but I don't know. Miss Rose has been good to me and she says she'll help me find something."

"If you work for the O'Tooles, I'll find you."

"And what would you be doing that for?"

"Maybe just to look up a friend, or maybe I'd come after

you hoping for another kiss." Stitch couldn't believe what he was saying.

"Well, if you did find me, you just might get what you were hoping for." She tugged away from him and ran back to the train before he had time to say another word.

His thoughts were full of Hallie when he noticed a coach pulling up to the station. August Myers stumbled out, a bottle in one hand and a carpetbag in the other. As he moved to the last car Stitch ran behind the train and took his place.

He watched as August stepped into the dark private car, tumbling over a few pieces of luggage before heading straight to the basket. "Hello, bride. I see you and your things have arrived," he said, setting the bottle on a table. His rented car looked ragged and worn even in the poor light, not freshly cleaned like the one Rose had insisted on.

August kept up a steady stream of conversation as if there were someone inside the basket listening. "I hope you don't mind if I double-lock all the doors tonight. We wouldn't want to be disturbed, would we? By the time we reach Galveston we'll know one another well and I'm positive you'll have no comment about our marriage. Your father had full confidence in me. He told me to do whatever it took to make sure you and all your things make it to Galveston on time." August laughed. "With any luck, by the time we get there you'll already be pregnant. I think you'd make him very happy if a child were to come nine months from tonight."

While Myers worked the knots, Stitch slipped between the two cars. Once he disconnected the last car, he stood next to August's door and listened.

He heard the man swearing as he drank and tried to untie all the knots. Just as the train whistle blew and the engine began to roll away from the last car, Myers threw the lid open. "It's time to come out, my—"

Amid the noise of the train leaving as it picked up speed and the long whistle blowing, no one but Stitch heard the rage of a wild boar roaring out of the basket or the screams of a drunk.

Stitch felt the car rock first to one side and then another as the animal fought to escape, but no one in the empty train yard noticed that August Myers's private car remained while the rest of the train headed south.

As he slipped away Stitch's only regret was that he couldn't get a full-grown wild pig in the basket and had to settle for one that weighed a mere hundred and fifty pounds.

He laughed. "I doubt Myers will be impregnating anyone tonight."

CHAPTER 33

After midnight
Fort Worth train station

ABE AND SARA SAT IN THE BUGGY HE'D RENTED AND watched the newlyweds run for the train. He knew he probably should have taken Miss Norman home, but Abe didn't want the night to end.

"I'm so happy for them," Sara said. "They looked right together."

"They did," Abe answered, wondering if he'd see Killian again. He knew Fort Worth was as much home as anywhere to O'Toole, but now the new wife would have something to say.

Miss Norman curled back into the buggy, trying to stay out of the wind. She sat so straight, even in the shadows she didn't touch him.

"It's late, I'll take you home."

He turned the horse toward the lights of town. "Thank you for accompanying me tonight."

"Thank you for inviting me." She hesitated. "If you

wouldn't mind, Mr. Henderson, would you stop by your store? I think I left my wool shawl there."

"Of course."

He pulled to the back of his store and tied the horse before helping her down and unlocking the door.

She didn't look at him as she walked through the storage room to where he'd left a low lamp burning between his desk and the study.

The schoolteacher stood perfectly still as if on the edge of a ledge. He moved around her. He'd seen her like this before and he knew what to do.

Abe didn't say a word as he opened the door to the study and waited for her to enter. It crossed his mind that she might have simply left her shawl, but the need to hold her was too great to allow reason to prevail.

Passing him without looking at him, she moved into the study and took off her coat and new scarf. Then, she crossed to the washstand and slowly took down her beautiful hair. As she combed through the waves, Abe felt his heart relax. He hadn't said a word. He hadn't touched her all evening, but she'd known what he wanted and maybe, just maybe, she wanted the same thing.

He moved behind her and took the brush from her hand. As he turned her to face him her body brushed against his. Without a word, he kissed her, loving the way she gently placed her arms on his shoulders and closed the distance between them.

When he finished one long kiss, he took her hand and led her to the big old leather chair. Sitting down, he watched her standing above him still too shy to meet his stare.

His hands circled her waist then slid over her skirt and along the sides of her legs.

She remained perfectly still as he moved his hand across her middle, feeling her breathe. He pulled her to him and buried his face against her blouse, loving the smell of her and the warmth of her beneath the layers of starched cotton.

With one tug she settled onto his knee.

He placed his hand low against her waist as he kissed his

way along her throat. "It is time to unbutton your blouse, dear."

This time her hands didn't shake.

When she finished the third button, he said, "One more tonight."

She did as he ordered and the dress gave free revealing the valley between her breasts. He leaned her back against the arm of the chair and kissed her tenderly. When he straightened she'd relaxed against him, her eyes closed. Without a word, he slid his hand beneath the lace of her undergarment and cupped her breast. She let out a little cry of surprise as she bowed as if to meet his touch. He waited, but she didn't try to pull away. He moved his fingers over her soft flesh and saw a tear escape from her closed eyes. One silent tear.

Removing his hand, Abe pulled her close against his heart and tried to think when all he wanted to do was touch her. Kissing her softly, he rocked her in his arms. Had she liked his touch or was she just enduring it? He wished he could tell her how much he needed her and how dearly he wanted her, but if one touch frightened her, his words might terrify her completely. He wanted her to know how being with her like this had become the center of his world.

Moving his hand along her back he waited for her to relax once more and finally she did. "Are you all right, Sara?" he whispered against her ear as he played with her hair.

"Yes, dear," she answered.

"Did I frighten you?" His hand smoothed over her cheek.

"No, dear."

"Then kiss me like you did before."

She stretched to his cheek and kissed him lightly.

"Again," he whispered, loving the way her body pressed against him as she moved. The second kiss moved from his cheek to his lips but was still featherlight.

"That one was better," he said as he moved his hand along her side. "Now, tell me why my touching you made you cry?" He had to know what he'd done wrong.

She didn't answer for a while and he continued to brush his hand along her back. Finally, she answered, "I didn't expect to like it so much."

Abe laughed and hugged her wildly. "You almost gave me a heart attack, woman. Don't do that again."

"No, dear," she barely managed as he kissed her hard on the mouth.

When he finally allowed her to rest back against the arm of the chair, his fingers began to play along the valley between her breasts once more. He knew he had to say something. He had to let her know how much she meant to him. "You bring me great pleasure, Sara. When I'm not with you, I think of touching you like this." He pushed the lace aside so he could feel more of the fullness of her. "I'll play your proper game when we're in public. You'll be Miss Norman and I'll not touch you or speak of how I feel, but know that every moment, every second that you are being so polite and proper, I'm thinking of you like this. I'll be wanting to hold you and touch you like this." He shoved the blouse away another inch so that he could see more. "I'm living for the few minutes we spend in here alone and away from the world."

She was so still, he added, "Do you understand?"

She nodded and arched again as his fingers slid over her breast once again.

He tried to be gentle, but the knowledge that she wanted this between them pounded through his brain. Taking his time, he learned the curve of her and loved the soft sounds of pleasure she made. When she cuddled close so he could kiss her, Abe smiled.

"You'll come here when you like." He kissed her between words. "I'll be waiting, but when you're here, you're mine if only for an hour."

"No," she said surprising him. "You're mine."

She straightened and kissed him lightly. "You're mine, Abraham."

He laughed and kissed her back, thinking of arguing but knowing that she was right.

CHAPTER 34

ROSE PACED THE LENGTH OF THE TRAIN'S PRIVATE CAR trying to shake the feeling that something was about to happen. Since her dawn kidnapping, her nerves hadn't settled. Her insides seemed to be spinning around beneath her skin. Nothing, not filling the day with work, or worry over Duncan, or any of the hundreds of other things she'd done seemed to help. Rose felt it all the way to her bones. Trouble was barreling toward her. It might not get here tonight or tomorrow, but it was coming at full speed.

They'd been racing through the night for an hour. Duncan was sleeping like a baby in the swinging bed Stitch had made for him. Killian and his new bride were talking quietly in the far corner. Hallie had stretched out on the settee and was snoring away. Epley sat beside her, her brows knitted with worry.

Passing the girl, Rose patted her shoulder. "Everything is going to be all right, Epley, you'll see."

"What if Hargus and Shorty come after me? Shorty said he'd let me die tied up if I ever tried to run again."

"How long had you been at Yancy's place?"

"A few months. The old guy was never mean to me, but

he'd lock me in the back room every night. Sometimes he'd tell me I'd done a good job of working and he'd be sure Shorty had a few extra drinks when he came in next." The girl looked up at Rose. "I didn't mind the work except on Friday nights when Hargus and Shorty came to town. Hargus is solid mean. He'd hit me just for the fun of it, but it was Shorty I hated. He'd watch me while he drank, then come find me." She lowered her head. "I hated what he did, but he kept telling me it was my fault and I'd better get used to it."

"It wasn't your fault," Rose said as she put her arm around the girl. "I wish I'd killed them both."

"I do too, miss, 'cause they'll come after me and you too. I watched Hargus beat a dog to death right after I got to their dugout so I know what's waiting for me."

Rose brushed the handle of her Colt. Funny how the feel of a weapon could bring a kind of comfort. If anything happened she had to be prepared. As far as she knew Killian didn't carry a gun and Duncan might not wake up in time to be helpful. "Do you trust me, Epley?"

The girl nodded.

"Then believe me. No one is going to hurt you while I'm around, but I'll need your help until we're safe on Whispering Mountain land. Promise me if trouble comes you won't hesitate, you'll run and keep running until you know you're safe."

The girl nodded and Rose moved away.

She began to count the hours until they'd be home. Her papa and a few of his men would be at the Anderson Glen Station to pick them up. Once they were on Whispering Mountain land they'd be safe. It seemed impossible that she'd been gone a week, but once she made it back home Rose swore she'd never leave again.

The train's whistle blew through the night as they rolled on.

Rose moved beside Duncan and was surprised to find him awake.

"Hello, beautiful," he whispered. "There's something

about a woman wearing a gun belt that makes my heart race."

She laughed. "You probably need more opium."

He shook his head. "No more. I hate what that stuff does to my head. I'd rather put up with the pain."

She leaned close. "Get well quick, Duncan. I don't know if I can handle much more."

"You, Rose?" He moved over a few inches on the swing so she could join him. "I'm beginning to believe you can handle anything, baby."

"What's with the names?" she asked as she lowered beside him. The platform rocked slightly as she cuddled against him.

"I'm trying to find one that fits you."

"How about just using my name?"

"I'll explain later, honey, just get some sleep." His good arm pulled her close and she felt his breathing slow.

For the moment they were safe and she could close her eyes. She could rest.

In what felt like minutes, Rose awoke to the jolting of the train pulled into the first of four stops before she was home. She slipped from Duncan's side and crossed to the window. The stop shouldn't take long to take on water, but as all inside slept, time passed and the train didn't continue.

Finally, she could stand the wait no longer. She climbed off the train and walked beside the track to where the conductor and a porter stood. This time of night there were no stands open for burritos or fruit. Looking out at the flat land, the whole world seemed lonely.

"Is there a problem?" Rose asked the conductor.

The chubby man, with the smell of cigar and coal about him, smiled at her. "No, miss, just a delay. We got a wire that there was a broken rail up ahead and men are checking it out."

"This time of night?"

He looked at her as if he considered her simple. "Yes, miss. No trains run until it's safe. We wouldn't want to lose any paying customers."

The porter grinned. "Appears we already lost one."

The conductor frowned and Rose glanced at the train. When she'd boarded, she thought she remembered the engine, their private car, two general passenger cars that were empty, and an old private car on the back. "What happened to the last car?"

The conductor shrugged. "He booked at the last minute. Guys on the yard were fighting to get him hooked on. I guess he changed his mind."

The uneasy feeling hit Rose again. Something was definitely wrong. "How much longer?"

"If the break is only a few miles out we should be under way in another half hour. If not, they run the track on a handcar until they find the break or reach the next water station."

Rose looked at the scattered buildings that seemed to be a struggling town. From the layout she guessed it must have been a stagecoach station years back. "Is there a hotel here?"

The porter shook his head.

Killian had already told her as much. He'd planned to take Victoria at least one more stop down the rail.

"Is there a place where I could rent wagons?"

Both men looked as if they thought her mad. "You wouldn't want to do that, miss, not in the middle of the night. You and your hurt man I seen delivered would be far safer on the train."

The porter added his advice. "Even if the repair takes till morning, we'll be on our way before you could drive a wagon anywhere."

Rose thanked them and walked away. She could almost hear a clock ticking in her head. Time was running out. Someone was on their way to get them and when they did people would die.

She wasn't surprised to find the judge waiting for her on the steps of their private car. He looked even more worried than she felt, if that were even possible.

When she explained the problem to Killian, he didn't

tell her she was being foolish. In fact, he agreed with her. "I've had the same uneasiness since we left. There's a pack of wolves chasing us and it's a gamble which one will get to us first. "I'm not sure where Myers is, but he won't just quit when he finds the note I left him at the hotel saying I married Victoria. The man may not be in love with her, but he's in love with power."

"Duncan's got the Tanner brothers after him. If those two had any sense they'd lie low then crawl farther west and change their names." Killian shook his head. "But they won't. Their hatred is too deep. Duncan and his men killed two of their brothers during an attempted train robbery last year and I hear Jeb and Owen blamed it all on Duncan."

Rose had heard the stories before. "From the way Duncan talks they spent every waking minute after he caught them telling him how they were going to kill him."

Killian shook his head. "Funny, they're not the ones I'm worried about most. I wouldn't be surprised if Victoria's father doesn't come after us. I'm sure the thought that his daughter married me will send him over the edge."

"Why?" Rose asked. "You're a good man, Killian."

"I'm not a war hero. August told me one night when he was drunk that the major almost didn't let him use me as the best man because he'd heard rumors that I'd been a coward in battle. Myers laughed and said the major wanted a hero to breed with his daughter. Myers claimed the old guy told him to keep her pregnant until she'd birthed a dozen sons."

In the still night air Rose whispered, "Were you a coward, Killian?"

He looked straight at her. "Yes. I'd been a soldier for about four months when I caught up with my older brother. We went into a battle together. We'd worked manning a cannon for hours amid noise that sounded like what I think hell must sound like. Then we were hit or the cannon blew—I don't know which. I fell face-first into the mud and must have been knocked out. When I came to, all the men around me were dead. My brother was covered in blood. I started screaming and running. I don't know how long I ran over the battleground with bodies everywhere, but at some point I fell over a man who was still alive. I carried him to the road and waved down an ambulance wagon. The driver was hurt, so I took over driving the team. I worked two days helping out until I finally collapsed."

"You saved many lives," Rose whispered.

Killian shook his head. "I couldn't save my brother. When I got back to where he'd fallen, the Union soldiers had combed the place. His body had been taken away and put in an unmarked grave along with hundreds of others."

"I'm so sorry, Killian."

"I worked the rest of the war driving the hospital wagon, but I never carried a gun after that. All my family was dead and I didn't much care if I lived or died, but now I have Victoria depending on me. I'll do what I have to, to keep her alive."

"Then help me come up with a plan. To my way of thinking, staying on this train is not an option."

To her surprise, Killian agreed. "I'll go into that cluster of buildings and see if I can't wake up the blacksmith. Maybe he'll sell us horses and wagons. We'll probably need three—Victoria says she never goes anywhere without her luggage."

Rose thought of the dozen matching bags Victoria had bought and had her maid pack with new clothes. They'd fill a wagon.

"Where do we head?" she asked.

"I ran this circuit when I was training. It'll take us two hard days of travel, but we could go across the back country and be at another train station by tomorrow night."

"It sounds better than waiting here."

"I agree." Killian took a step off the train. "Tell Victoria, if she wakes, that I'll be right back."

Rose leaned down so she could whisper. "Do you have enough money?"

Killian smiled. "Yeah, we got a wedding present left in

an envelope. Duncan said a man dropped it off, saying only that the money was for Victoria."

An hour later they were packed into three wagons. Rose drove the first team with Duncan settled in between boxes of supplies Killian had bought. Killian and Victoria were in the second wagon along with all her luggage.

Epley and Hattie brought up the third wagon with bedding and weapons. They were a strange-looking caravan pulling out of a no-name town in the middle of the night. Reason told Rose they could have made do with two wagons, but they'd travel faster with three not so loaded.

The conductor had asked Rose what he was supposed to tell folks when he pulled into Glen Station and they were gone. Rose didn't mince words. "Anyone who asks," she said, her voice hard, "tell them we vanished."

CHAPTER 35

For a while, Stitch watched the old private car sitting alone on the tracks. The wild boar must have settled down after he ate any food in the compartment. August Myers was nowhere in sight. Stitch figured he was locked in the tiny water cooler or he'd swung up in one of the luggage racks. Stitch didn't really care as long as the man wasn't following Killian and Victoria.

A night watchman passed by about one. He waved his lantern once toward Stitch, then shouted. "You're a little early to hire out. The next train won't be here until five."

"I didn't want to miss a fare," Stitch answered. "Thought I'd sleep here. The yard is always quiet this time a night."

The watchman agreed. "It may be pretty quiet come morning. Word is we got a break somewhere down the line. Last train out is stopped a little over an hour out and is waiting for an okay to move on. Don't look like it'll happen before daylight. Workmen can't seem to find anything."

Stitch waited for the watchman to move along, then silently crossed over to Myers's car. He looked into each slit in the curtains. There was no sign of him or the boar. Finally, he saw the wild pig in the corner with what looked like a Bowie knife run completely through him.

Myers must have killed the pig and disappeared out the back of the car without anyone seeing him. Stitch had been watching an empty car for an hour, patting himself on the back for having delayed Myers.

He'd doubted Myers was sober enough to act quickly, and from what he'd seen of the man, Myers wasn't the type to carry a huge knife. He was more the kind who carried a thin blade in his boot or maybe a little gun in his vest pocket but Myers had surprised him.

Stitch moved in the shadows, picking up information from carriage drivers and livery stable boys who worked the night shifts. Once, he'd helped out a man named Pip whose wagon had broken down. Pip had been in charge of delivering stacks of paper to every major corner of town before dawn. Stitch had refused money, knowing he'd be taking a man's pay if he did. Now he found Pip in the basement of the newspaper office and asked for the favor back.

Two hours later, Pip delivered. Myers had dropped by the city desk just as the editor was putting the latest edition to bed. He'd asked for his wages and a loan. He'd gotten only what he earned. Then Pip said he was seen leaving with two men. Rough types, one of the printers claimed. Men who'd cut your throat for a halfpenny.

Stitch thanked Pip and said they were even. The next favor would be on him. Pip nodded and both men knew they could count on the other when they needed a friend.

As Stitch moved through the streets he knew he couldn't just stay here and do nothing. He had to try and help. Only here, on the back streets of Fort Worth, he did fine. He moved among bellmen and night watchmen and even policemen who knew him, but if he went on the road, he'd be alone. He'd be a freak who frightened anyone he saw. No one would help him.

As he drove toward Second Avenue, he worried and planned. Somehow he had to help Killian O'Toole.

With no other option, he broke into Abe Henderson's mercantile. Silently, he climbed the stairs to Abe's apartment, but the man wasn't there. As he slipped back down the stairs, he saw a light burning in a little room off the storage area.

Abe's long legs were stretched out in front of him as he slept in an old leather chair. A book rested on his lap and the scarf Stitch had seen on Miss Norman at the wedding was wrapped around Abe's hand.

Stitch had seen the shop owner many times talking with Killian, trying to walk without limping when he had to go out. Stitch knew he was a fair man. No one ever claimed he cheated them when they hauled orders from the train. Stitch had even been in the store a few times after dark. He'd always kept his hat low when he'd needed something. Abe had been polite but never particularly friendly.

His only hope was that Abe would be reasonable now.

Stitch blew out the light and took a deep breath. He had no choice. He had to talk to Abe. In the total blackness of the windowless room, Stitch shoved one of the long shelves from the storage room down across Abe's chest, pinning his arms below the arms of the chair.

Abe came awake with a start. "What?" he yelled more angry than frightened.

"Henderson, I'm not here to rob you or hurt you. I just got to talk to you."

"Let me up!" Abe said, struggling with the board Stitch was leaning his weight down onto.

"When we've talked, I'll let you up but not before. I need your help and I must be sure you hear me out."

"Who in the hell are you?" Now Abe was getting angry and Stitch couldn't blame him. If he'd been sitting up straight in the chair, he might have had a chance at breaking free, but slouched down like he was, he couldn't get any leverage from his arms or his legs.

"I'm Shawn," Stitch said. "Killian's brother."

Henderson stopped struggling. "The devil you are.

Shawn's been dead for years and don't bother telling me you're a ghost. No spirit has the strength to hold me down."

"I'm Shawn O'Toole," Stitch said again. "And I need your help. Killian and Victoria are in trouble and they don't know it. I've got to get to them."

Abe stopped struggling. "Light the lamp. Ghost or man, I'll see your face. I remember Killian's older brother. He had thin scars on his face."

Stitch let go of the board and struck a match. "The thin lines are still there along with other deeper ones I got when a cannon blew up in my face. The Yanks didn't see much use in being careful when they stitched me up."

To Henderson's credit, he didn't turn away when Stitch turned into the lamplight. "I was maybe four or five when you left home, but I remember the thin scars. Folks said your old man put them there."

"He did."

"Why didn't you just run away?"

"I thought about it, but my mother had a baby. I knew if I ran, Killian would be the one he'd start cutting on next. So I killed him, then I stayed around till Mother could manage. I was thirteen when I left to earn a man's wages. Killian couldn't have been more than four." Stitch smiled. "You know, I don't think he ever noticed the scars. They were just part of me and he followed me around like a pup."

Abe leaned forward. "Does he know you're alive?"

Stitch shook his head. "I thought he was dead too for a long time. I recovered in prison and got offered a chance to fight on the frontier for the rest of the war. It took me four years to get back, but I settled here because it was home. I stayed in the shadows. Then one day I was hauling produce just before dawn and I seen Killian sitting on your front porch. He was older, of course, than the boy who followed me to war but still thin. He laughed just as I passed and I swear I recognized him before I even looked his direction."

Abe finished Stitch's thought. "So you became Killian's own private ghost."

"Something like that. I didn't know he'd been talking to me for years, trying to keep me alive in his mind, until I heard him tell you about it. He thinks I died a hero. I couldn't just come up and tell him I'm no more than an alley rat."

Abe was silent for a while before he said, "You're his family, Shawn. He needs to know you're alive. You were his big brother, his hero."

"I ain't much of a hero. Most folks around here wouldn't talk to me if they knew I wore blue even if it was on the frontier. They call men like me Galvanized Yankees, like we had a choice." Stitch straightened. "I'm not here to tell you my sad story. I'm here to ask you to help me get to Killian before Myers does."

"I can't walk without a cane or crutch," Abe admitted. "I can't sit a horse for more than a few hours." He limped to the little stove and watered down coffee that had been thickening all day.

Stitch nodded. "Can you drive a wagon?"

"If I need to." Abe handed Stitch a cup.

"How are you with a rifle or pistol?"

"Fair but out of practice."

Stitch nodded. "I can scout, but I can't walk into businesses and train stations and ask questions or make any inquiries. Last time I was outside these few blocks I found places that wouldn't even serve me food because they couldn't stand to look at me."

Abe took a drink letting the old coffee shock him full awake. "You are one frightening-looking man, Shawn."

"Call me Stitch. It's the only name I've used in years." He smiled down into his cup thinking of one woman who hadn't minded the scars when she'd kissed him. Hallie was with Killian. Another reason he had to leave.

"All right, Stitch, tell me what is so important that you had to frighten a year off my life to wake me and why the newly married couple isn't safe."

Halfway through Stitch's story, Abe began to pack. By the time they'd talked it over, Stitch's wagon was loaded with a box of supplies, bedrolls, and rifles from Abe's store.

"We can pick up fresh horses along the way," Stitch said as he tied down the cover on the wagon bed. "With a few extras, I figure we can take turns driving and make twice as many miles a day."

Abe stepped up on the bench and said, "I have to make one stop before we go."

"We don't have the time."

"We make time."

Stitch didn't bother to ask. He turned the wagon toward the boardinghouse. Then he waited in the shadows as Abe, one step at a time, climbed the steps to the door.

He had to knock several times before the owner answered, but without much protest she said she'd fetch Miss Norman.

Abe stood on the porch waiting. The boardinghouse owner had closed the door in his face, making sure he wouldn't be inclined to follow her inside. A nearby streetlight reflected in the gold-colored knob of his cane.

"What do I say?" Abe whispered to Stitch. "She's going to think I've lost my mind. I rarely leave the store much less the town."

Stitch swore. "Do you love her?"

Abe shook his head. "I don't know anything about love. It's not a word I've ever used. I admire her. I want her. I need her."

"If you've got the symptoms, you got the disease. Tell her you love her. Tell her to wait for you and then tell her good-bye. We need to be on the road."

Stitch watched as a frightened Miss Norman appeared at the door wrapped in a long gray blanket. "What is it, Mr. Henderson? What's wrong?"

"Close the door behind you," he said. "I've something to say."

She did as ordered, but she didn't look happy about it.

He handed her back her scarf reluctantly. "You left this."

"You woke me up to bring back my scarf, Mr. Henderson. That was kind but not practical."

He looked down, not wanting her irritation to be the

memory he took with him. "I'm leaving to go help a friend. I don't know when I'll be back and I doubt I'll have time to write, so don't expect a letter."

Stitch coughed.

Abe continued, "I left Henry a note. He'll be running the place until I get back. If you need anything while I'm gone, tell him to start you a credit. I told him if he had a question he should ask you and whatever you say is the same as me saying it."

Another cough.

"I don't want you to worry about me. I wouldn't be going if it wasn't a matter of life—"

Stitch's next cough was even louder.

Abe frowned at him and took Miss Norman by her shoulders. "I have to go, but I want you to wait for me to come back. Promise."

She had stopped looking frightened and started looking angry. Stitch refrained from coughing again.

"Why?" she whispered.

"Because, Sara Norman, I love you," Abe said as if someone had tortured the confession out of him.

Miss Norman nodded. "All right then. I'll wait."

Abe let her shoulders go. "You'd better get back inside. It's cold out here. I'd hate for you to catch a cold."

"Yes, dear."

She vanished and Abe made his way down the steps. When he was back on the wagon bench, he said, "There, I said it. I figure I won't have to say such a foolish thing again for several years. She should know how I feel."

Stitch made a slight sound and the horses started moving. "You forgot to kiss her, Henderson. You should have kissed her."

Abe frowned. "It was hard to think with all your coughing."

Stitch laughed. "Maybe it's good you're leaving town. You don't know how to talk to a woman. She looked more like you'd come to tell her the school was on fire than anything else. You got to stop ordering her around. Women don't like that kind of thing. In fact, I'm surprised she didn't just step out and slap you now that I'm thinking about it."

"Oh, and you know women?"

"I know enough to stay away from them." Stitch picked up speed as they moved onto the deserted main road. "Or at least I did until lately."

CHAPTER 36

Rose had no idea where she was going or how far the next town might be. Killian had mentioned two hard days in a wagon, but he hadn't named a town. She only knew she was headed south. The storm had been lighter in this part of the country and the roads were easy to travel. Though clouds threatened, the stars offered enough light to see the dark inky ditches on either side of the road.

About an hour out they caught up with some teamsters delivering supplies to the smaller towns the railroad couldn't service. The men were half-asleep and letting their tired horses set the pace. Rose guessed the teams of horses made the trip at least once a week and knew the way. She could have moved faster if she'd passed them, but it was safer to follow.

When the teamsters stopped to water their horses, one of the boys riding with them offered to drive Rose's wagon so she could sleep in the back with her husband. Rose had made up a story that he'd been thrown from a horse, but she wasn't sure the men believed her.

She was so tired she couldn't think of a better lie. She just crawled in the back and slept beside Duncan. His breathing was easier and the movement of the wagon didn't wake him.

When she wiggled in beside him, he moved his arm over her and mumbled something she didn't understand. "About time you made it home."

An hour before dawn, when she woke, she was surprised to find him sitting on the bench with the kid. Duncan must have been telling him stories about the Texas Rangers because the kid said, "Your wife's awake, Ranger."

She didn't correct the boy.

Duncan looked around at her and said, "Morning, pumpkin. How's my sweet apple pie this morning?"

Rose didn't answer, but she guessed Duncan must be hungry.

On a flat plain near the road they circled the wagons and watched the sun come up. The teamsters made a fire and everyone but Hallie and the girl relaxed on the tall grass. The haulers were used to the road. They slept on their hats and covered up with blankets caked in mud.

Hallie, who'd slept while Epley drove most of the way, made biscuits and fried up slices of ham. Two hours later the sun warmed the air a few degrees and the smell of fresh coffee woke everyone up. They ate and talked like old friends, and Rose did her best to try not to notice how the teamsters and the mules they worked smelled about the same.

The men were polite but didn't seem comfortable talking to the ladies. They preferred to talk to Killian and Duncan. She could almost imagine them telling in days to come about the time they'd spent with a Texas Ranger and a judge.

Rose walked among the wagons and found Epley asleep. Her open palm showed places where the reins had cut into her hand. Rose removed her gloves and tucked them into the girl's pocket.

When she stood, she saw Hallie watching from a few feet away. "Make sure she uses them," Rose said.

"I will," Hallie answered.

"Did she eat?"

"Not much, but I saved a few biscuits for her. I'll watch

over her. She reminds me of a wounded bird too young to fly."

"Me too, but we've got to give her a chance."

Hallie grinned. "You sound just like your uncle."

Rose shook her head. Her uncle Travis was a great man who helped make the world a better place. She'd never done anything. "He changes lives."

"Well," Hallie whispered, "you changed this one and I figure that is a start."

When they finished loading up, the young teamster moved back to Hallie and the girl's wagon, saying he'd drive for them for a while since Hallie cooked breakfast.

Duncan slowly pulled himself onto the bench and took the reins.

"You need to rest," Rose objected.

"I've been resting for days. I need to stretch my muscles."

When she opened her mouth to correct him, he said simply, "I can handle it, Rose, darling. Stop mothering me."

"Fine."

The wagons moved back onto the road. After fifteen minutes Duncan said, "You going to pout all day?"

"No, and I don't want to be your mother, or your sister, or your cousin. I don't want to spend the rest of my life worrying about you."

"Fair enough, Rose, what do you want to be?"

"We're both twenty-five years old. Don't you think it's about time we became just friends."

"Nope." Duncan passed her the reins while he looked for a cigar in his coat pocket. "I think we should be, at the very least, best friends, sweetheart."

"I'd like that, but can a man and a woman be best friends?"

"Why not? Seems to me like we already are. Only problem I see is that at some point one or the other wants more."

She thought about that. "Oh," she finally said, "like the woman wants to get married and the man just wants to go to bed."

Duncan shook his head. "I'm afraid it's the other way

around. Think about it, Rose, that's the way it is with us. I, under the smoke of drugs, asked you to marry me and every time you get the chance you crawl into bed with me. I'm trying to do the honorable thing here, Rose, but you're not making it easy."

She opened her mouth to argue, then realized he was teasing her.

As they moved across open country they talked as they'd never talked before. Most of the time others were around or they seemed to just want the silent companionship they'd had as children, but today both had too much to say.

When they stopped to rest the horses, Duncan went down the list of supplies with Rose, making sure they had enough guns and ammo as well as food. "I don't want to frighten you, but we've got to be prepared. When we stop to rest the horses next time, I want you to take Hallie, Epley, and Victoria a half mile away and practice firing every weapon."

Rose had never seen him like this. He was as organized in this world of danger as she was in her world back at the ranch. He had a quick mind and an easy way of talking to people. Duncan was a natural leader and, to her surprise, far more understanding of Victoria's problems and of Epley's fears than she thought he might be.

When they stopped the second time, he gathered the group and said, "Killian and I will watch the wagons while you practice shooting."

None of the women looked happy about going, but they all carried weapons and headed up the hill.

Rose did the best she could to show each one how to load and fire both a rifle and a pistol. Hallie already knew. Epley didn't want to touch the guns, but Victoria took to the new experience with gusto.

By the time they got back Killian and Duncan had made coffee. While everyone drank, Duncan explained, "The teamsters are moving on ahead and they'll be turning northeast. I think we should go southeast at the fork. We'll still be heading in the general direction of Whispering

Mountain, but that road will be flatter, and the best Killian and I can remember is there's a train station several hours south of a town the kid told me about. We should reach the settlement long before nightfall. We need to stop and send telegrams."

As they climbed back on the wagons Rose continued to help him plan. For the first time she truly saw the ranger in Duncan. He wasn't just a thrill-seeking boy who refused to grow up—he knew his job. He told her a little about the Tanner brothers. When he mentioned that they seemed to have nothing to show for two years of robbing, she suggested that maybe they were stockpiling money for a reason. A big reason.

"They're too dumb to plan past one change of clothes," Duncan said as he thought out loud. "But they could be following orders. Maybe they've been promised something grand, something so big it would be worth the risk, something so important that it would even be worth killing for."

"You're starting to sound like the major and August Myers," Rose said. "They want to start a new world and rule it like kings."

"The Tanner brothers wouldn't go along as foot soldiers," Duncan said, "but they might go along thinking that at some point they could rob the kings. That would explain why they got so furious at me when I caught them. I interrupted a two-year plan. They were on their way to rob the major."

"Your theory doesn't hold up, Duncan. Why would the major have all his wealth in Fort Worth? And even if he did have it there, why would he leave without taking it? Hallie searched his room. Nothing was there, and when he walked out of the hotel he wasn't even carrying a carpetbag. Two years' worth of loot from train robberies couldn't be carried in his pockets."

"You're right, but it was an interesting theory. I can't see a man like the major sitting around drinking with the Tanners. Now Myers might. The major had the brains to plan the robberies, Myers traveled enough to tip a gang off on which train to rob, and the Tanners were ruthless enough to pull it off." He shook his head. "It seems like we got the pieces, we just can't get them to fit together."

She smiled at him.

"What?" He frowned.

"We've been talking for an hour and haven't had an argument."

"Impossible." He grinned. "Must be a leftover effect from the drugs."

CHAPTER 37

THE SUN WAS JUST SETTING WHEN THE THREE-WAGON caravan pulled into a small German settlement. Duncan stayed with the women and the supplies while Killian called on a friend he knew there. Along the main street of the town were small houses the Germans called Sunday houses. They were built by farm families to use when they came in for Sunday services that sometimes lasted all day. Only this time of year many of the homes were empty even on Sunday.

Killian came back with a key to one of the homes. He said his friend loaned it to him because the owners had gone to take their son back east to school. The little square house was sparsely furnished but neat and clean.

Duncan insisted Killian and his new bride take the main bedroom. The women took the one with small beds lining three of the walls and Duncan swore he'd be comfortable on the floor in the living space.

Everyone helped carry in the supplies needed for the night, but Victoria's luggage was left in the wagon. Though officially married, she could now open everything, but by the time they made beds and cooked a stew she said she was too tired to look for the keys so there was no sense in hauling in luggage.

Right after they ate, Victoria unpacked her nightgown and a hairbrush from her small traveling bag and said she was going to sleep. To Duncan's surprise, the princess didn't complain much, but she ate little and that bothered him. Killian told him that she thought this mess was all her fault, but Duncan knew he'd have to take a share of the blame. Until they knew who followed, no one in the group would feel safe.

Killian paced the floor for a while trying to talk to everyone until finally he disappeared into the bedroom as well.

Hallie, Epley, and Rose said good night a few minutes later and suddenly Duncan was alone.

For a while he watched the fire and thought how nice the silence was. It seemed like he'd been listening to people talk every waking moment for days.

The women had insisted on giving him so many blankets his bed on the floor was way too soft to be comfortable. The pain in his arm and shoulder was only a dull ache now. If he could have had a few drinks of whiskey the pain would be completely gone. Duncan found it hard to believe that when Killian rounded up the box of supplies, he'd forgotten whiskey.

He leaned back and tried to figure out who would be the first of several bad guys to come at them. For tonight, at least, they were safe. The horses had been stabled in a community barn just behind where they were. There had been plenty of room for the wagons to be rolled in as well so everything was out of sight if someone did pass by. The doors were locked. No one knew where they were. For tonight all could sleep in peace.

But come tomorrow they'd be out in the open again. Killian's friend had told him they could reach the train station in about eight hours, but it usually didn't stop at the station until after six in the evening, so they'd have an easy day of driving to reach the train in time.

He finally fell asleep. The fire in the fireplace had burned low when he felt Rose slide against his side.

"What do you think you're doing?" he whispered.

"I couldn't sleep in there. Hallie snores."

"What makes you think you can sleep with me, darlin'?"

"I always have. Shut up and go back to sleep."

He moved closer. "First kiss me good night."

"No. Stop teasing me."

"I'm not teasing you. You're not sleeping with me anymore, Rose, unless you kiss me good night. Half the time I figure you're so mad at me you might kill me in my sleep. If we're best friends, kiss me good night."

"Oh, all right." She rose to her elbow and kissed him on the cheek. "Now go to sleep."

"As soon as I kiss you back." Still half-asleep, he rolled against her and covered her mouth.

Duncan wasn't sure what he expected. Maybe she'd hit him or yell at him, but what he hadn't expected was for her to kiss him back. He felt like he'd stepped off into a raging waterfall and all his senses were exploding. She tasted like heaven and felt warm beneath him.

The kiss was great, but he shuddered suddenly as he realized she knew what she was doing. This was no innocent kiss. She'd practiced!

The flood of emotions flowing over him pulled him down until all reason, all thought stopped and the world revolved only for them.

When her tongue slid into his mouth, Duncan pulled back. "What in the hell do you think you're doing?" he said, more angry at himself than her.

"Me? I'm trying to go to sleep. What do you think you're doing?"

"Best friends don't kiss like that."

"Well, apparently they do, Duncan, because you just kissed me like that."

"No, I was just following your lead. You were the one doing the kissing." Duncan didn't know whether to be angry or pleased. This was Rose he was still leaning on, and she felt so good beneath him. This was logical, sweet, never-exciting Rose.

"Go to sleep," was all he could say as he turned away. He wasn't about to tell her that after maybe a hundred samplings of girls' kisses, he'd never had a reaction like the one he'd just had. If she'd gone any further, he might have self-combusted.

He was wide awake as she cuddled against his back. As always, she pulled the covers, wiggled for a while like a windmill spinning down, and finally went to sleep. Apparently the kiss hadn't rocked her world as much as it had his. For all he knew she kissed every guy who came along that way. No, he corrected. If she did there would be men hanging out on the porch at Whispering Mountain.

Duncan wasn't around women much, but he considered himself a man of the world. He'd fallen in love a few times, at least with the idea of love. He had spent some interesting evenings with the ladies.

But never, never, had anyone kissed him like Rose just did. Hell, he felt like a virgin who'd just been touched.

He spent the next hour wondering where Rose, who never went anywhere or did much of anything, would have learned to kiss like that. It didn't seem to be something that a young lady would learn at finishing school, but she'd sure learned it somewhere.

Maybe he should go back and have a little talk with every man he'd sent to meet her. He should strangle whoever it was who taught her to do that kind of thing with her tongue.

Duncan swore. He could still taste her on his mouth. He'd probably starve before morning for another taste but there was little doubt in his mind that she'd shoot him if he rolled over and woke her for another sample.

He lay awake thinking that he'd have to kiss her again just to make sure it wasn't the lingering drugs in his blood that had made him have the reaction. Slowly, he rolled over and studied her in the firelight. Sleeping a few inches away was the same practical Rose he'd known for twenty years.

She'd bossed him around until he'd been half-grown and she'd worried about him every day since he'd signed on with the rangers. If she was his best friend, why'd she have to kiss him like that? Now friend wasn't the first word that came to mind when he looked at her.

She took care of the family. She went to church every Sunday. She visited anyone in town who was sick and always baked for any fund-raiser. She didn't have one bad habit. And, he now added to his mental list, she kissed with a passion that made a man forget to breathe.

CHAPTER 38

Killian lay in bed a few inches away from Victoria and waited. He knew neither of them could sleep, but he didn't know what to say and he guessed she didn't either. Finally, he whispered, "Are you sorry we married?"

"Are you?" she answered.

"No."

"Me neither. I am sorry I got you into such a mess."

"I'm not. If all this hadn't happened I probably wouldn't have gotten around to kissing you for years and you wouldn't have asked me to marry you."

She laughed. "Don't tell our grandchildren that I asked you. They'll think I was a very forward woman."

Killian wanted to say they wouldn't have to worry about that problem unless one of them got brave enough to move over six inches. He didn't know if he could do it. She'd said she knew what went on between a husband and a wife, but he doubted she had any idea about the details. Somehow scaring her to death on their wedding night didn't seem like a good plan.

He didn't know much more about it, in truth. A few times, more out of curiosity than anything else, he'd visited a lady of the evening. Not a saloon girl who turned several men an hour in business but a nice place where the women were all dressed like ladies when they answered the door.

He'd paid a half month's pay to go in such a place in Houston while he was studying to be a lawyer. A woman ten years older than him had taken him into a parlor and talked to him real nice while she brushed her hand along his leg. Then, after he'd finished off a few drinks, she'd taken him upstairs and, without turning up a lamp, told him to remove his clothes. When he'd done what she'd asked, he turned and found her in bed waiting.

What happened next had been so fast he wasn't sure he could remember it all. She'd pretty much done all the work and he'd cooperated. When he finished, she said, "That was nice," like he'd just kissed her cheek.

He lay there among all her pillows and lacy sheets while she slipped out of bed and dressed. She did it slow, letting him watch, letting him see all of her. Maybe she wanted to make sure he got his money's worth. He remembered thinking that she'd had a nice body and he'd wished he had thought to feel of it, but once she dressed she left him alone.

Killian thought of that time in Houston. It had been nice, he still thought, but it hadn't been what he wanted. He'd wanted more, much more than he could get from a woman that he paid by the hour.

Victoria had given him that in a way. Not physical but mental. She'd made him laugh and think and dream. He knew she was spoiled, but there was a tenderness about her. She made him think that he was worth something. She made him want to try harder and learn more.

"Are you asleep?" She broke into his thoughts.

"No." He smiled, thinking how strange it was to lie so close to her in the dark.

"You want to play a game?"

"Sure."

"Okay, close your eyes."

"Victoria, it's pitch black in here."

"Close your eyes."

"All right. They're closed."

"Hold your hand up."

He lifted his hand off the covers, having no idea what she was doing, but he knew she loved games. Once, when they'd walked in the cemetery, she'd tried out every name on headstones to see how each fit with Victoria. They'd made a game of trying to find the best one.

He jerked slightly when he felt her hand touch his.

"What do you feel, Killian?"

"Your hand." He closed his hand around her slender fingers. "It's a very nice hand."

She replaced her hand with her hair. "And now?"

"The end of your braid."

He waited. After the bed shifted a few times, he felt her put her bare arm in his hand. "I'm guessing that must be your elbow, Victoria."

"Brilliant. You've now touched the prettiest part of me and the ugliest. All the rest is somewhere in between my terribly wrinkly elbow and my beautiful hair."

"What are you saying, Victoria? I don't understand the game."

"What did you touch, Killian?"

"Your hand, your—"

"No. Who did you touch, Killian?"

"You."

"And, who am I?"

"Victoria." He stopped, suddenly understanding. "My wife."

She laughed. "That's right. I'm your wife. Now that you've touched the prettiest part of me and the ugliest, might you be interested in touching the rest?"

He grinned. "I'd like that very much."

With one simple game, Killian began a journey of knowing his wife, which he figured would take him a lifetime to complete.

CHAPTER 39

ABE HENDERSON AND STITCH TOOK UNTIL MIDAFTER-
noon to reach the first stop on the train's route, but they
knew they'd caught their first break.

The train that had pulled out of Fort Worth at midnight
was sitting on the tracks, still waiting for a report from the
team of workers sent out to fix a broken spot on the rails.

Stitch stayed back with the wagon while Abe visited
with the conductor.

"What's the problem?" Abe asked as he offered his flask
of whiskey to the conductor.

"Thanks," the chubby man said. "It's been one hell of a
night. We thought we'd only have a few hours' delay, but
something must be wrong. The crew searched all night and
couldn't find a thing broken on the tracks. They're running
one final check now. We should be under way soon."

"What made you think there was a break?" Abe acted
like he took a drink and passed the flask back.

"Had a telegram waiting for us when we stopped here.
Now the office in Fort Worth thinks it might have been a
false report, though why anyone would want to stop an
empty train in the middle of nowhere is beyond me."

"Guess someone just wanted to waste your time."

"I guess. Last night I thought those people who rented wagons and headed out were crazy, but now it seems they may have been smart."

Abe raised an eyebrow as if he didn't believe the conductor. "Folks left a perfectly good train and took wagons?"

"Sure, a couple of men and four women. We helped them load everything up and they headed south like they thought they could make it by wagon before we'd get to the next stop."

He looked down the tracks. "Who knows, maybe they will. Until we get permission to move we ain't even in the race."

Abe spent a few more minutes talking as he watched Stitch drive over to the livery and trade for fresh horses. When he joined the big man, Stitch grinned. "You did good, shopkeeper. I don't think a detective could have done it any smoother."

"I read a lot of books." Abe shrugged. "And my favorites are mysteries."

Stitch headed south. "The boy at the livery told me his boss woke him up last night to hitch up three wagons. He said one of the men crawled in the back of the first wagon like he was hurt."

Looking out over the endless land, Abe shook his head. "How are we ever going to find them in time? Whoever delayed this train will be on the next one rolling through and they'll have horses that can travel much faster."

"But they won't have me," Stitch said as he slowed the team at the first fork, surveyed the ground, and then slapped them into a fast pace. "I ever tell you what I did on the frontier? I was a tracker. I picked out the markings on the last wheels to roll out of the barn and I'll follow them true."

By nightfall Stitch found a camp where the three wagons had pulled off along with several others. A few hours later, he spotted another site where they'd stopped to rest. While Abe watered the horses, Stitch brushed the place where the three wagons turned south and left the trail where tracks led off to the north. It wouldn't fool an expert tracker, but maybe it would fool men riding fast on horseback.

They didn't take time to build a fire but instead just ate the jerky Abe had packed along with apples and mason jars of water.

"Why'd you pack the whiskey, Henderson? I didn't know you to be a drinker."

"You been watching me?" Abe asked.

"No more than I watch everyone," Stitch answered.

Abe accepted his answer. "You're right, I'm not a drinker. Always saw it as a waste of money. I brought the whiskey 'cause I thought it might help with the pain in my leg. I'm used to standing on my feet but not moving around without something to brace my bad leg on. I figured it'd start giving me problems within a few hours."

"Does it?"

"Haven't had to use it yet. Funny, the worry about how it might hurt was worse than the ache."

Stitch nodded but didn't say more. Like Abe, he wasn't a man used to conversations. As soon as the horses were rested, Stitch moved on with tumbleweeds tied onto the back of his wagon to dust away any hint of what direction they were traveling.

Through the night both men took turns resting in the back. The sun was up when they pulled into a small German settlement. The tracks they'd been following since yesterday blended with others on the wide road into town.

"I've heard the Germans build their main roads wide enough to turn a team, but I've never seen it."

"You don't travel much?" Stitch asked.

"I don't travel at all."

As they moved closer to the stores, Stitch added, "Might want to think about marrying that little teacher and spending some time seeing the country."

Abe nodded, but he didn't seem to be listening. He was looking for a business that was open early. He spotted one and pointed.

Stitch pulled the team to a stop.

"I'll go see what I can find out," Abe said as he lifted his cane from the side of the wagon and walked toward the neat row of stores.

"I'll stay out of sight. Maybe I'll go over to the barn and see if I can't buy enough feed for the horses. They could use a rubdown and some rest before we push on." Stitch didn't wait for Abe to answer. He wasn't asking permission, just stating a fact.

The day was still early and the nearest barn he saw was over by a beautiful little church. He pulled his wagon around to the back and found all he needed on a workbench near the corral. Even though his bones ached from the endless ride, he wanted to take care of the horses first. No one seemed around, so he turned the horses loose in the corral and went to work on them one at a time.

Twenty minutes later he was cleaning one of the hooves when he heard the front door of the barn open. From the length of the shadowy barn he saw a woman slip in and move over to where several wagons looked like they'd been stored.

One at a time she began to look under heavy tarps.

Stitch set down the tools he'd been using and moved into the shadows. He didn't want her to spy him standing in the sun. He was frightening enough in poor light.

With a little squeal, she pulled one trunk out of a wagon and tumbled backward from the load.

Stitch ran to help. "You all right?" he shouted halfway to her.

The woman scrambled to her feet and reached in the wagon. Stitch stopped as she swung a rifle at him.

"Get back or I'll shoot," she said in a shaking voice. "I know how to use this."

Stitch kept his head low. "I wasn't going to attack you, honey, just making sure you weren't hurt."

"Shawn?" she whispered, sounding even more frightened than before. "Now am I seeing a ghost? I must be going mad."

He didn't know what to say. The truth seemed his only

option. "I'm no ghost. I just followed you and Killian to make sure you were safe. A man named Myers and two lowlife men who look real mean are on your trail. If they reach you, I plan to be here to help. I swear, honey, I didn't come to hurt you."

She lowered the rifle. "Who are you, really?"

"I'm Killian's brother. That much is true, but I'm not a ghost."

"Why don't you look at me? Why didn't you tell Killian you were still alive? How could you let him believe you were dead?"

Stitch felt her questions hit him like blows. She was right, he should have told Killian. He used the only defense he could use. "I'm not that easy to look at, honey. I'd frighten you if you saw my face. I thought it would be easier for Killian if I just stayed in the shadows where I belong."

He didn't look up, but he heard her moving toward him. She was the most beautiful woman he'd ever seen and she was about to see just how ugly he was.

Stitch turned to move away, but she caught his hand. He could have shoved her back. He could have run, but something deep inside him told him it was time to stop running.

"Shawn?" She whispered his real name as her free hand cupped the side of his face. "Shawn, my ghost, my friend, my husband's brother."

He looked up and met her stare. She wasn't shocked or frightened. He felt her fingers move along his cheek.

"So many canyons, so many cuts. I can almost feel the pain you must have had to bear."

Stitch closed his eyes, forcing himself to let her touch him when all he wanted to do in this world was hide away. Only he couldn't. They were in danger, and deep down he knew if they died, he'd die inside.

Finally, she let her hand drop. "I'm glad you're not a ghost. Killian will be very happy. He never let you go, you know, not even when everyone told him over and over that you were dead."

"I know."

Like a butterfly, her mind flew on. "Oh, Shawn, I'm glad you're here. Can you help me carry this trunk? It seems to have broken open when I fell. I want to wear a new dress today. After all, I'm a married lady. I know just the one I have to put on this morning. Nothing too frilly, we're still on the road, you know, but something in yellow. Killian's favorite color is yellow."

Stitch smiled. "I didn't know." He helped her pack up her things. When he picked up the trunk and lifted it on his shoulder, he thought it far heavier than a normal case. No wonder it had broken the lock and come open, she'd packed far too much inside.

"That's odd," Victoria said as if he'd missed something important in life. "What's your favorite color, Shawn?"

He didn't answer. In almost forty years of life he'd never thought about it.

Victoria tugged his free arm along toward a little house. "You know, Shawn, what color do you look best in? That's usually what people think of as their favorite."

"Shadows," he finally answered.

Victoria laughed. "That's not a color. I'll have to think about it, but I'll let you know. It's important for a man to wear a touch of color."

Stitch smiled. He could see why Killian loved this woman. There was something childlike about her and wise at the same time. Five minutes after meeting him she was more concerned about what color he wore than about how he'd frighten most of the people he met half to death. They'd talked about his scarred face and now it was time to talk about something else.

CHAPTER 40

Saturday

Duncan pulled Rose out the front door when she passed through the parlor. He'd tried to talk to her since she'd stepped out of the little bedroom at dawn, but there was never a time when people weren't surrounding them.

"Duncan, stop this. I have to help with breakfast or we'll never get out of here."

"We need to talk," he whispered, then yelled back at Hallie. "Rose and I will get that coffee you said we might need."

Rose let him guide her along, but she wasn't happy about it. "We don't have to have the coffee right now. We've plenty for breakfast and we can make it to the train without a cup." She looked suddenly worried. "How are you today, Duncan? Are you in pain? Did the stitches break loose?"

"Forget the stitches and forget the coffee." He pulled her into an arbor next to the church. A cluster of winter morning glory vines blocked them from anyone passing. He figured it was as near as he would get to being able to talk to her alone.

She looked confused when he leaned close and said, "Where in the hell did you learn to kiss like that?"

With a flash of lightning in her eyes, she stormed, "I don't think that is any of your business."

"Damned if it's not. You're family."

"Stop swearing at me, Duncan McMurray, and I think we've already established we're not family. Maybe I just felt like kissing you and I don't remember you objecting at the time."

Duncan dug his fingers through his hair and forced himself to calm. He wasn't going at this right. For once he didn't want to argue with Rose. They'd always been honest with each other, and he might as well be now. "I've never been kissed like that, Rose."

The anger in her gaze melted into surprise. "Never?"

"Never."

She smiled the way women always smile when they understand something and know it would be a waste of time even trying to explain it to a man. "I won't tell you where I learned to kiss, but I will say that I insisted on practicing until I got it just right."

He opened his mouth, but she added before he could get a word out, "Don't bother to ask who."

"Fine, Rose. How about I ask when?"

"When what?"

"When will you kiss me like that again?"

She moved out of the arbor. "Not now. We have to go get coffee. There is simply no time."

"When?"

"Maybe tonight. Maybe never."

Duncan followed thinking that getting coffee must have moved up ahead of kissing on her to-do list. As he walked across the wide road to the general store, he wondered if the kiss could have possibly been as great as he remembered. Rose never did anything wild in her life, how could she have kissed him like that. Just thinking about it made his head hurt.

As he walked past a man sitting in a rocker on the porch

of the store, he said, "Morning, Abe," before it dawned on him that Abe Henderson shouldn't have been within miles of this place.

Abe grinned.

Rose turned and recognized the man who'd served as Killian's best man. "Why, Mr. Henderson, how on earth did you get here?"

Duncan brushed his hand over his Colt. "Something's wrong, isn't it?"

Abe nodded as he stood. "Stitch and I got here as fast as we could. We had to warn you. Myers and two men we think might be the Tanner brothers are riding hard to overtake you. We're guessing you've got three, maybe four, hours before all of you need to vanish."

Duncan forgot all about the coffee and the need to kiss Rose. Right now his mind only had room to think about one thing—survival.

He grabbed Rose's hand and started back to the little house.

Abe fell into step beside him, limping as fast as he could.

Rose tugged so hard, Duncan finally slowed. He turned to Abe. "How many men do you think they'll have with them?"

"Stitch said he saw a few hanging around the hotel who looked like they were waiting for orders. If the Tanners had their men with them, I'm guessing a dozen at the most. From what I've heard of Myers, he's not the type to come after you unless he thinks he's got the advantage. He won't know Stitch and I are with you, but he knows even wounded a ranger's not an easy target."

"He's coming after me?"

Abe Henderson shook his head. "He's coming after Victoria. You and, I'm guessing, Killian are just two he plans to knock out of the way. If he gets the chance he'll kill everyone except Victoria. She's worth a fortune alive. The way I figure it, he's only got a few days to get her back to her father in Galveston or he'll lose this fortune he's been telling everyone is going to fall into his hands. Once he gets the money, my guess is Victoria won't live long, or if she lives with Myers she'll wish she were dead. Stitch said they found Victoria's maid beat near to death. She claimed Myers did it because she didn't keep up with Victoria like she should have."

Rose moved in between the two men. "Both of you have to calm down before we go inside. I don't want Victoria frightened out of her mind."

"We also need to get somewhere where we can defend ourselves. If they hit us here, people in town would die and I don't want that. This town is too small to even have a sheriff, so everyone here would probably get involved if a gunfight breaks out on the streets."

"Out in the open we'll be sitting ducks."

"We'll load up and race for the train station," Duncan said. "I'll need a horse so I can ride drag. If I see them coming I'll fire off a shot so you'll have time to make ready."

"I'll go find Stitch and meet you at the house," Abe said.

Duncan pointed out where they'd be and Abe turned off toward the road leading to the barn.

CHAPTER 41

KILLIAN STOOD AT THE BACK DOOR OF THE LITTLE house, watching Victoria walk in from the barn. He hadn't noticed when she'd slipped out, but Hallie told him she'd gone to find a new dress to wear among the luggage they'd been hauling around. After last night, he could barely focus enough to answer. They'd talked and touched most of the night until slowly they'd grown used to each other.

He felt like sometime during the evening they'd traded hearts. They'd become a part of each other. They'd become one. If anything ever happened to her, he knew his heart would stop beating.

For a minute he just watched her come near with her arm looped around some man's free arm. The stranger carried a trunk on his shoulder. Killian couldn't see the man's face, but he didn't like the way he strolled with Victoria as if they were old friends.

When Killian stepped out on the porch, Victoria saw him and waved. She was smiling and Killian swore he could feel the sunshine from her smile.

Hallie walked from the kitchen and also spotted Victoria. "Who's that big fellow?" she asked.

"I don't know, but I plan to find out." Jealousy was something new to Killian and he didn't like the fit.

Suddenly, Hallie screamed and almost knocked him down running off the porch.

Killian watched as the big man lowered the trunk and caught Hallie in midflight. He swung the woman around like she was no more than a willowy girl.

Victoria smiled and rushed to join Killian. "Isn't it wonderful?"

"Isn't what wonderful?" Killian didn't see anything to be happy about. "Who is that holding Hallie?"

Victoria laughed. "It's Shawn, your brother. He's come to help."

Memories whirled in Killian's mind. The big brother he remembered when he'd been four. A body on the battlefield covered in blood. The ghost who'd picked him up once when he was drunk and carried him home. The man before him, muscular and scarred.

"Shawn?" Killian said the name low, but the big man must have heard him.

He set Hallie down and walked alone to Killian. He didn't seem to know what to say, but he raised his face and stared directly.

"Is it really you, Shawn?" Killian was afraid to hope.

The stranger nodded and Killian saw a tear fight its way down the scarred face. "What's left of me."

Killian took one step toward his big brother and then they were locked in a hug so tight it crossed all the years they'd been apart.

"How you doing, little fella?" Shawn asked as if the six-foot judge were no more than a small boy.

When they finally separated, everyone laughed and hugged. Killian felt like a fool introducing his brother to Victoria, who seemed to be Shawn's good friend. In fact, Shawn called her honey as if they'd known each other forever.

Hallie called his brother Stitch. As soon as the hugs were over she began complaining that now she'd have to cook up a half dozen more eggs, but Killian didn't think she'd mind. "I'll put pepper on yours like you like them, but I think it's an insult to the chicken to do so."

Stitch put his arm around Hallie and squeezed just to hear her squeal as they all moved inside.

They'd just gotten settled at the kitchen table when Duncan and Rose came through the front door with Abe Henderson in tow.

To Killian's surprise, Abe knew his brother too. They'd been traveling together to catch up with everyone. Abe said when Stitch asked him to come along and help, "no" wasn't one of the choices he offered.

Killian stopped the rapid-fire conversations all around him with a sudden yell. As soon as all were silent, he asked, "Does everyone here know my brother but me?"

"Yes," they all said at once, and went back to talking.

Frustrated and confused, Killian looked at his wife for help and he found it. Her warm smile said it all. No matter what else was going on in the world today, at this moment in time he was the luckiest man alive.

She moved near and put her arm around his waist. "I told you I've been talking to Shawn."

"You did." He kissed the top of her head and noticed no one in the room was paying any attention to them so he kissed her cheek. "Are you all right about last night?"

She didn't look up, but she whispered, "I don't know, Killian." She moved an inch away. "Maybe we could do it again tonight before I decide."

Killian laughed, loving her humor. "We can do it as many times as you like. Take all the time you need to make up your mind."

She moved back beneath his arm. "It could take years."

"I'll try to hold up."

CHAPTER 42

AN HOUR LATER, DUNCAN MCMURRAY CLIMBED IN the lead wagon. "I don't understand it," he mumbled more to himself than Rose. "For years, when I wake, it takes maybe five or ten minutes to be in the saddle and heading out. How come it takes us an hour? Seems like with all the help it should take less time, not more."

"We had to load and pack a meal. Stitch had to make sure he could board his wagon, though heaven knows when he'll be back by this way to pick it up. Victoria always has trouble with her hair in the morning and everyone had to use the same privy."

"I'm sorry I asked," Duncan said. At least they were on the way and would make great time, or so he thought. Within an hour Stitch signaled for a stop because Hallie had to run to the trees. Fifteen minutes later, Killian stopped them all so Victoria and Epley could make a visit.

Duncan declared there would be no more stops, but when Rose tugged on his sleeve an hour later, he pulled up without a word.

By noon he turned the reins over to Rose and untied his saddled horse. Stitch took the lead with Killian and Victoria on the bench with him. Duncan knew Stitch would up the pace and Killian said he was familiar with the road from here on. By traveling across open country, they'd cut some time off the trip.

"Be careful," Rose whispered as he slowly climbed up on a horse. "You're not completely healed, Duncan."

"If I promise, what do I get?"

"To live," she said, smiling sweetly as if she had no idea what he was hinting he wanted. "Otherwise you'll probably bleed to death."

Duncan rode back over the trail they'd just traveled and stopped his horse on a ridge where he could see the land stretch for miles. If Myers and his men were following, they'd be kicking up dust and he'd see them in plenty of time to warn the others.

He smiled at the silence around him. This was what he loved. The wildness. The solitude. The stillness as if he were the only man between heaven and hell. Reason told him that someday he'd get too old to be a ranger and he'd have to settle down, but he figured when that happened he'd miss this life for the rest of his days. He'd probably get used to sleeping in a bed and eating three meals a day on a regular basis, but he'd never get over the adventure. The feeling of always needing to be fully alive.

After a half hour, he turned his horse and rode back toward the wagons, scanning the landscape for a new place to serve as lookout. He never rode near enough to the wagons for them to know he was there, but now and then he'd catch sight of them winding through the rolling hills.

By midafternoon and still no sign of horses riding toward him, Duncan knew they were safe. If trouble came now, they'd have a good chance of outrunning it. Unless the kid with the teamsters had been wrong, they were within an hour of the station. From there it would only be a two-hour trip to Anderson Glen Station. Even though they were a day later than planned, it would still be good to be close to Whispering Mountain.

He backtracked once more and looked north. The road

was still clear and to the south he could see the outline of a water tower. Low on the horizon, dark clouds were brewing and Duncan had the feeling that one way or the other they were heading into a storm.

Watching for another fifteen minutes, Duncan smiled. They were going to make it. This odd little mixture of people had outrun trouble. He turned his horse and rode hard toward the wagons.

They were already pulling the wagons alongside the station before he reached them. If possible, this stop for water was more desolate than the one at the last station. Not even an old stagecoach house marked the beginnings of a town, just a small four-foot-wide shack of a ticket office and corrals with chutes built for loading cattle. A quarter mile from the water tanks was what looked to be the remains of a mission and Duncan could make out a small cemetery just beyond.

He stared at the weathered crosses, thinking that cemeteries sprang up faster than towns in this part of the country. Life since the war had been hard, but he could feel things finally settling down. Thanks to the railroad and cattle drives, brighter days were coming.

The train was nowhere in sight. Small runs like this one were often late and never early. Duncan's only worry was that someone might find them before the train made it in.

No one in the wagons felt safe. All seemed on guard. Stitch and Killian paced the platform, keeping watch. All the women sat with a gun nearby. Abe stayed in the wagon even though they'd moved the horses to one of the corrals. No one talked except in short sentences. They all just waited, needing the silence to feel safe.

Finally, they heard the low whistle of a train and all moved into action. By the time the train pulled in to take on water, everything and everyone was ready to be loaded. They took the horses but left the wagons. Victoria, in her funny way, left little notes on each of the wagon benches that said, *Take me, I'm yours.* She signed each note, *The wagon.*

Duncan bought tickets for Anderson Glen and they all moved into the first of three passenger cars. It was crowded, and they moved slowly. He couldn't help but study the people. Families mostly. One group of men, who looked like gamblers heading for greener pickings, sat in the back. A half dozen young Harvey girls were traveling down the line to one of Fred Harvey's many cafés.

"We're safe," Rose said as she took the seat next to Hallie. "In a few hours we'll be in Anderson Glen. If no one is there to meet us, we can spend the night at the hotel and drive to Whispering Mountain in the morning. There's nothing more beautiful than crossing onto our land with the morning sun."

Hallie frowned. "I don't like the country. Never have. I grew up on the plains. Nothing but grass and buffalo chips."

Rose smiled. "How do you like towns?"

"Not much. Too many people."

Duncan grinned at Hallie's words. Sometimes he felt the same way. No matter where he was, he was wishing for the other. He patted Rose on the shoulder and followed Stitch to the platform out back, thinking he'd feel safe when he made it back to Whispering Mountain too.

"Did you check the other passenger cars?" he asked the big man.

Stitch shook his head. "The guy who took my ticket said they were full except for the last one. He said some cowboys had blocked it off so they could smoke. Wouldn't even let the gamblers come in."

"I might take a walk through." Duncan had seen cars claimed by groups before. Most of the time it wasn't worth causing trouble over. Men who didn't like to travel with the masses were usually the same men the masses didn't want, so it worked out well. "You mind staying here on the platform and standing guard until I get back?" He felt movement and knew they were rolling.

"I was already planning on it," Stitch said. "Killian told me he'd be at the other end."

"Good." Duncan moved away, jumping to the next platform as the train rattled into action.

In the last rays of the setting sun, he saw two riders step from their horses onto the far end of the train. Both looked well armed. From habit, Duncan checked his guns. Maybe they were just men running late, he thought, or they could be train robbers joining their gang. When he'd investigated a few of the Tanner robberies, witnesses had said half the men were already on the train when the other half rode up on horseback. One witness even commented that the train had slowed just before the robbery, but nothing was ever proven that connected the robbers with the conductor.

Something didn't feel right and Duncan hadn't lived for years as a ranger without trusting his feelings.

He took his time moving down the aisle of the second passenger car. There were several hard men on this one and not as many families. The atmosphere was louder, rougher. He heard swearing and arguing. He took note of every man wearing a gun.

When he stepped out on the third platform, he took a deep breath of fresh air and leaned down to pass through the next car.

Out of nowhere, something slammed against the side of his head and Duncan crumbled.

His last thought before he blacked out was that he had to get to Rose. He had to get home.

He felt like he was swimming in inky waters as someone lifted him roughly and shoved him into a dark place. His hands were bound so tightly he couldn't feel his fingers and a bag that smelled of dirt was shoved over his head.

After a while the pounding eased in his skull and he could make out voices swearing. One he recognized as Jeb Tanner. "I say we kill him now," Tanner kept repeating.

Another man kept ordering in a low tone, "No. We stick with the plan."

Duncan struggled, trying to kick anything close by. Once, he connected and heard someone scream in pain. A moment later blow after blow began to slam against his chest and ribs. Whoever was retaliating planned to do as much damage as possible. Duncan felt something damp on his shoulder and knew stitches had pulled free. He was bleeding again.

A hard kick to his head landed him back in the inky water and he stopped worrying about anything for a while.

When he came around again, another body lay partly over his legs. Jeb's whiny voice was begging for the kill. "We can kill this one, can't we? He's the reason your wife ran off. He stole her from you."

The low tone of another man came again. "No. You can't kill him. He's a judge. All hell breaks loose when you kill a judge or a ranger, so stop asking."

Duncan listened, but he didn't hear Killian speak. Either they'd knocked him out cold, or he was smart enough to know that no matter what he said, it wouldn't matter.

The train rattled on as Duncan remained still and tried to figure out how many voices he heard.

Five, six, a dozen, he couldn't be sure.

All he could figure out was these outlaws were collecting the men in his party one at a time and soon all that would be left were the women. Also, it made no sense for even a dozen men to pick this train to rob. There wasn't even a mail car among the passenger cars and he counted two dozen men traveling in the first few cars who were well armed and would return fire if the outlaws started shooting.

He tried to concentrate. An old ranger, who'd managed to stay alive until retirement, had told him once that no matter how bad things get, the devil always gives a man one chance.

One chance, Duncan thought. He'd be ready when it came. If it came.

CHAPTER 43

Rose watched the others. Epley was two rows ahead with Victoria. They were both asleep with Victoria's luggage scattered around them. Hallie stared out the window next to Rose and Abe sat a few seats up as if he were on guard. She hadn't seen Stitch or Killian in a half hour and Duncan had disappeared completely.

As quietly as she could, she slipped from her seat and moved to the front of the car. She'd expected to find Killian on guard, but he wasn't there. The platform was empty.

A few minutes later when she passed Abe, he whispered, "Where's Killian?"

Rose slowly shook her head.

Abe stood and followed her through the car to the far end. When they stepped out in the cold wind, no one was there to greet them. Lightning flashed, blinking daylight for a moment before blackness returned. After a second of panic, they saw Stitch sitting on the steps, his feet hanging off the train, his head low.

Rose knelt and lifted the man's hand from his head. "Are you hurt?"

"Just a dent in my head," Stitch complained. "Almost

knocked me out. I've been sitting here trying to figure out if my brains are dribbling out or if it's just blood."

"What happened?" Abe asked as he handed Rose his handkerchief to use as a bandage.

"Someone must have been up top when I stepped out. He hit me hard with what felt like a railroad spike."

"What happened to him?" Abe looked around. "He's got some explaining to do."

Stitch shrugged. "Sorry. I don't think he'll be talking. I reacted without much thought. I grabbed his shirt and tossed him off before I took the time to question why. He's a few miles back, probably still rolling."

Abe moved away from the door. "Stitch, we'd better get you inside."

As the big man moved into the car, Rose whispered to Abe, "That still doesn't explain where Killian and Duncan are."

"Wherever they are, my guess is they're in trouble. We've got to be very careful from here on out."

Rose pulled her gun and tried to fight down panic. "How long until we stop?"

"Another half hour or so." Abe leaned close. "They couldn't have just vanished. My guess is they are somewhere still on the train."

Before she could think of an answer a man stepped from the other passenger car and joined them on the rattling platforms. She knew who he was even before she saw his face. "August Myers," she whispered.

The man straightened as if in uniform. "At your service, Miss McMurray. You seem to have lost something. Perhaps I can help you find it . . . or should I say 'them.'"

"What have you done with the ranger?"

"Oh dear." Myers smiled as if still in casual conversation. "Don't forget the judge. There was to be a third man missing but my man failed in his mission." He shrugged as if it wasn't important. "I assure you they are both in good hands. The ranger may have a headache, but Killian was smart enough to cooperate when he felt a gun pushed into his back. The ranger must have a death wish because, even hurt, he took on two of my men and almost won before they finally beat him down."

"Where are they?" She pointed her gun at his middle. This time, she swore she'd shoot to kill if she had to.

"Do put that away, woman. I know you have no intention of shooting me, for you see, I'm here to help. I think I can ensure the safe return of both men, who so bravely protected you, if you'll only allow me to take my wife with me. We'll let you all go on along your way and we'll continue on to Galveston after the next stop. You'll all be home safe for I understand the Anderson Glen Station is near your family ranch, and my wife and I will be on our way to a new life."

"You're mad," Rose said simply. "Victoria wouldn't go with you and she's not your wife."

"If she doesn't, she'll be a widow before this train stops. The judge will be killed and tossed off. Within hours the wild animals will eat enough of his flesh so that no one will recognize him."

Rose looked up to see Victoria standing at the door. She'd heard every word. She braced herself against the door and looked like she might faint at any moment.

"Good evening, Victoria," Myers said. "I hope you'll consider carefully going with me. A wrong choice will get two good men killed tonight."

"I'll stay on the train if you'll let everyone else off at Glen Station," she said almost calmly. "You must promise not to hurt anyone, August."

"They are of no importance to me." Myers gave her a little bow. "I promise, my dear. Your friends will be safe, but you have to know that this little game you're playing is over. I said I'd deliver you, trousseau and all, to your father before we sail and I always keep my word."

Rose didn't know what to do, and when she looked at Abe he didn't seem to have any idea either. They couldn't let Myers win so easily, but fighting now might mean lives lost.

Myers pulled out his watch. "We'll be stopping soon. You'll see all your friends put off with most of these other worthless farmers and merchants, if you'll swear to me that you'll make no scene either here tonight or later when we board the ship at Galveston. Otherwise, you'll see them all dead."

Victoria nodded. "I'll make no scene."

"Then come with me. You're finished with these people."

She moved out of his reach. "I'd like to hug Rose good-bye. I fear I'll never see her again."

"You're right," Myers said with a smile. "You won't."

On the windy platform, Victoria hugged Rose, whispering words that made no sense. She was gone before Rose could ask what she'd meant.

Abe and Rose moved back inside the first passenger car. "We can't get to them," Abe said. "None of us can climb over the top, and to go straight down the aisle would be walking into fire. Our only hope is that Duncan and Killian can get loose and fight from their end."

"We have to get ready. The train will be slowing down soon." Rose whispered what Victoria had said to her in Abe's ear and he agreed to go along with it.

"I don't see what difference it makes, but if that's what she wants . . ."

Doctoring Stitch took up most of the time left. By the time he had a tight bandage around his head, the train was slowing. There had been no opportunity to tell him what had happened on the platform.

When the train stopped at a busy station, everyone scrambled off. Rose handed each of her group one of Victoria's bags and hurried them off with the crowd. "Move near the ticket office and place the bags out of sight."

Hallie frowned when Rose handed Stitch a small trunk. "Can you carry this, Stitch?"

"I can."

"Then move off fast with all the others."

Rose shoved two of the small bags in Hallie's hands. "It's important. Once we're off make sure you set the bags out of the way, out of sight, and no matter what we should not stand together."

Hallie's bright eyes showed that she knew something was up, but she'd wait to question.

Abe, with his cane, was the last to climb down the steps. He caught the attention of a porter as he ordered three pieces hauled down the steps and delivered to the depot. When he joined the others on the platform, the last of Victoria's bags were being loaded on a cart to be transferred inside. A light rain muffled the sounds of a storm coming in.

They waited without speaking, knowing that the train would only be paused by the platform for a few more minutes before it flew off south again into the night. Finally, two bound men, their faces covered with grain bags, were shoved off the last car. They both hit the platform hard.

For a few heartbeats all the world seemed silent, then thunder rolled and lightning flashed. One man, dressed in buckskin, jumped off the train and kicked Duncan, making him roll along the wood leaving a trail of blood.

Someone yelled an alarm from inside the train. The outlaw gave a final kick before the crowd on the platform could reach him.

"Come on, Tanner," the same voice shouted again from the last car.

The attacker jumped back up the steps and yelled one last death threat at Duncan as the train rushed away.

With the smoke still swirling around them, everyone ran to the men and began untying them. Killian came up fighting mad, but Duncan remained curled in a ball.

Killian ran the platform as if he could somehow catch the disappearing train.

"You shouldn't have let her go," Duncan whispered to Abe. "You shouldn't have traded us for her."

"I didn't," Abe said calmly. "She made the trade. She said she'd go if you were turned loose alive."

"But we've lost her!" Duncan seemed to be fighting to stay conscious. "There's no way to catch her in time. I heard Myers say they'd go straight from the train to the dock and board."

"No," Abe reasoned. "I've already thought ahead. We can send a telegram and have the law stop him."

Duncan closed his eyes as he shook his head. "Myers took great pleasure in telling me that men all along the line were cutting wires tonight. They'll never have the telegraph lines up and running by morning. Once they're out to sea we'll have no way to reach them. She's his."

Rose had been trying to wipe enough blood off of Duncan to see how badly he was hurt, but it wasn't easy with him twisting away with each touch.

She finally caught Killian's attention. "Why were Victoria's last words to me to take the luggage? She loves her clothes. It makes no sense for her to leave everything."

Stitch's low voice cut through the night air. "She'll be back." He laughed, then yelled in the direction the train had gone. "You got them, honey. You figured it out."

"How can you know that? Myers won't let her just turn around and come back for her luggage, no matter how much she wants it." Killian looked at his brother as if he had lost his mind. "I've lost her."

Stitch grinned. "She's not the one who wants those bags. It's Myers and her father. Back in the barn when I first saw her, she'd just dropped one of the trunks. Her case fell open and I helped her cram everything back in. I thought the trunk was heavy, but I didn't figure it out until I went back in the barn to get the wagons."

He pulled a gold coin from his pocket. "All those bags are stuffed not just with her trousseau but with her father's gold. My guess is Victoria didn't know until the case broke open, but then there was little time to tell anyone or examine the luggage."

"She wanted it left with us because she knows it's the one thing Myers will come back for. Not her things but the money. I'll bet right about now she's filling him in on that fact so we'd better scatter."

"Why didn't the major take it with him? After all, it's his

gold." Killian asked as they began moving all their belongings to two old wagons for hire parked at the edge of the platform, "Why leave it with Victoria? I don't care about the gold, I only want her."

"Neither does your wife, little brother, but she wants these men caught even if it means risking her life." Stitch had figured it out. "Her father has spent the past two years dealing with thieves and men who would kill for worn boots. There's nothing they wouldn't do for a fortune in gold. He may have figured out that the only way he'd get out of the country alive and with the money was if he packed it with her. I'm guessing that was why he agreed to come to Fort Worth. It may have been hidden near there."

Killian nodded following the logic. "He left Austin with one bag. Came to Fort Worth and bought his daughter all the clothes. My guess is with each day of shopping and each new trunk, he packed away another load of gold."

"Stolen gold," Stitch added as two men came running up from the end of the platform. One held a doctor's bag and the other identified himself as the acting town marshal. The doctor was old but went to work on Duncan, and the marshal started asking questions in rapid fire.

Killian paid them no mind as he yelled over the thunder. "I don't care about the gold. I want my wife back."

Rose knelt beside the doctor as he checked Duncan. The ranger didn't respond. He'd finally passed out. "We need to get this man out of the storm." She turned to Killian. "I'll take care of him. You get your wife back." Killian nodded but she saw little hope in his eyes.

"When the train returns, they'll be coming for the gold. I'm guessing they'll leave Victoria on the train under guard."

Killian followed her logic. "Stitch and I will stay here and get her out. You take care of Duncan somewhere safe."

They all helped load Duncan in the second wagon. When Hallie started to climb in, Rose stopped her. "The outlaws will come after us. We'll make no secret of where we're going with Duncan. You and Epley would be safer . . ."

"I'm going with you, Miss Rose, and I'm sitting on that

luggage with a rifle over my lap. You can help doctor your ranger, but it's my turn to stand guard. I told Miss Victoria that I'd work for her, so the way I see it, I'm starting right now."

Rose didn't have time to argue. Abe helped her into the wagon with Duncan.

"I have to stand with my friend," Abe said, nodding toward the judge. "He's the only one I have and I can't afford to lose him. Will you be all right, Rose?"

"We'll be fine. Just get Victoria back."

The marshal walked beside the wagon. "I'll stay here. We might as well stop trouble before it gets off the platform. If that train comes back, every man on it will be in my jail within no time. You don't need to worry about that, Miss McMurray."

Rose didn't know the deputy well, but she'd seen him before when she'd come to town. "Thanks, we'll be at the little house. If even one slips past you, we'll be ready for him."

Everyone in Anderson Glenn knew where the little McMurray house was, but the outlaws probably wouldn't know.

At least Rose prayed that would be true.

CHAPTER 44

Anderson Glen

THE WOMEN AND THE DOCTOR CARRIED DUNCAN INTO a little house built between the school and the church. For twenty years it had served as a second home for many of the McMurrays. On cold winter days the children often stayed over at the house so they wouldn't have to make the long drive back and forth from the ranch to school. The place belonged to no one member of the family, it belonged to them all. The big McMurray men often called it the Dollhouse because it was so small, with one bedroom downstairs and a loft for any children.

The doctor set to work on Duncan while Rose lit the fires and put water on to boil. Hallie and Epley carried in all of Victoria's luggage and the one remaining box of supplies they'd packed for the road.

"If they'd just bring Miss Victoria back, I'd hand over these bags," Hallie promised. "I'm tired of moving them around."

Rose smiled from the kitchen. "I feel the same. How could one woman wear all those dresses?"

Though they tried to keep their conversation light, all three were listening for shots to be fired. With the thunder and the lightning, their nerves were on edge. Epley walked around the house examining everything.

"This is a house no one lives in?" she asked.

"It's like a guesthouse. Lots of people live here for short spans of time."

"I never seen a house so beautiful."

Hallie agreed. "I'm going to buy me a house like this someday. You can come live with me if you want, girl. We'll be snug as bugs in a rug."

Epley smiled. "I'd like that."

Rose looked around at the place. She'd always thought of it as plain and simple. Her mother had added touches here and there but nothing special, she'd thought, until now.

True to her word, Hallie picked up one of the rifles and planted herself in front of the luggage.

Rose disappeared back into the bedroom to check on Duncan. He'd always been so strong and alive. She couldn't stand to see him hurt. To her relief, she found him sitting up while the doc wrapped his ribs.

"How is he?" Rose asked.

Duncan looked up with one swollen black eye and several bruises turning dark purple. "I think the patient died," he mumbled around a swollen lip.

The doc laughed. "It must feel like that, Ranger, but I assure you, you'll live to fight another day. You got more bruises than anyone I've ever seen, but near as I can tell, except for a few cracked ribs, nothing is broken."

Rose touched the fresh bandage on his arm. "The stitches over his wound didn't hold?"

"The wound opened back up, but most of the blood loss was from his nose and mouth. That lip will probably give him more trouble than the new stitches." He winked at Rose. "Last doc must not have known he was dealing with a ranger or he would have double-knotted every stitch."

Duncan tried to laugh but stopped when blood started dripping from his lip.

The doc handed him a cold, damp towel. "Press that on the cut. Try not to talk for a few days, don't eat anything but soup, and no kissing—otherwise you'll be dripping blood forever from that gash you got just inside your lower lip."

The doc stood and washed his hands. "Keep him quiet for a few days. He's had a few hard hits to the head. If you can, keep him in bed."

"I'll try," she said as she walked the doctor out, "but if I know him, we'll be moving to the ranch as soon as we know Victoria is safe."

As soon as the doctor was gone, she locked all the doors and turned down the lights. Chances were low that one of the outlaws would make it past Killian and the others, and then find this place. But if they did, she planned to be ready.

When she went back to Duncan, he was lying back in bed with his eyes closed. Without saying a word, she slipped his Colt next to his hand.

"Thanks," he whispered.

"Don't talk," she answered as she took her gun belt off and placed it on the bedpost. She wanted it in easy reach but was tired of wearing it.

With her back against the wall, she lined three rifles up beside her. One way or the other this would all be over tonight.

CHAPTER 45

Killian stood in the shadows of a pile of lumber on the opposite side of the tracks from the depot and waited. He hadn't carried a gun since the war. Twelve long years he'd believed there was nothing worth fighting over and now there was. He would save his wife or die trying.

In the stillness, he remembered every detail of their night together and somehow it kept him warm. If all he had to remember was one perfect night it would be enough, more in fact than he thought he'd ever have.

"Killian?" Abe whispered from a few feet away. "Did you ever think about settling down and hanging out a shingle? Fort Worth is finally growing like crazy, and with all the drunks and gamblers you'd probably have a good law practice."

"Why are you thinking about this now when we're fixing to go into a fight as soon as the train arrives?"

"I was thinking I was cold and that made me think of coffee, which made me think about you and me talking, and then I thought, maybe if you bought the bakery from me, you and Victoria could live above it and you could turn the first floor into a law office."

"Strange," Killian answered. "I was thinking about getting killed."

"If I think about getting killed, all I worry about is making you promise to tell Miss Norman one more time that I love her. I think she'd like to hear that."

"I don't," Killian answered, "since I'd be the one telling it to her right after I tell her you're dead. And when did you have time to tell Miss Norman you loved her?"

"Your brother told me to tell her before we left town. He said it was the right thing to do."

"Abe, you got to quit listening to a ghost."

"I'm not a ghost," Stitch yelled from five feet away. "If it wasn't for this storm, I'd come over there and knock both your heads together. Neither one of you knows a thing about women. I can't believe either of you found a woman who'd even speak to you much less let you get close enough to talk to."

"And you do?"

"Sure, I'm the only one of us who was smart enough to pick me a chubby one. She'll keep me warm and happy while you two are freezing and trying to figure out what to say."

Killian laughed. "It was so peaceful when you were a ghost, Shawn."

"You'd better listen to me, little brother. You're going to need to settle down. Abe's right, you can make a lot more money defending crooks than you will as a judge. Plus you got to come home every night or your missus will starve to death in a cold house."

"All right, if we get out of this mess alive, I'll buy the bakery and make a lot of dough." Killian was the only one who laughed at his joke.

The faraway sound of a train whistle cut through the dense, stormy air. They all got ready to move. The plan was simple. They would wait until the outlaws left the train. The marshal and his men would capture them between the depot and town. A hundred yards of pens and open ground seemed the best place. The lawmen planned to wait until the outlaws were midway between, too far to make it to town or back to the station, and then they'd step out from hiding with guns ready and arrest them.

While that was going on, Killian and Stitch would slip into the car holding Victoria. With luck they'd have her safe and away before anyone made it back to the train.

When the train pulled in, Killian couldn't seem to take a deep breath. The windows in the first car were open and the lamps were burning. All other passenger cars were empty. If there had been any other passengers making the next leg of the journey tonight, they must have been let out when the train stopped before reversing direction.

He saw Victoria sitting perfectly still by the window in the middle of the car. All but one man slid off the train and hit the platform. Myers, taller than most, was in the lead, motioning orders with his raised gun. The lights of the station were out for the night. As the men moved away from the glow of the lanterns from the car, they disappeared like smoke.

The lone man remaining in the car with Victoria moved along the aisle, blowing out one lamp after another until the only light made a circle around her.

Killian knew what the guard was doing. He was waiting in the darkness of the car, using her for bait should anyone want to try and take her.

"Ready?" Killian whispered.

Abe stood slowly and braced himself against the lumber. He raised his rifle. He'd offer the O'Tooles cover and, if necessary, draw fire to act as a diversion so they could get Victoria out.

Killian watched his brother move to the far end of the car. Stitch would be going in from the south door. Killian knew it was time for him to move, but he stood frozen in place. The gun felt wrong in his hand. It seemed to pull him backward in time to a day when the whole world fell into hell.

All the noise. The fires. The sounds of men dying. The sight of his dead brother.

Killian blinked. His brother wasn't dead. Shawn was alive. He'd made it through the war. And now he might be shot if Killian didn't act fast. He focused on his wife sitting frozen in the center of the car, as he began to run for the north door.

Just as Killian reached the door to the passenger car, a shot rang out inside. He shoved his way in yelling like a single warrior fighting the gods.

A flash of lightning blinked the car into full light, and for a second Killian saw a man standing over Shawn ready to fire another round.

Killian screamed again and threw his body at the guard.

For a moment the guard hesitated, and that was all Stitch needed. He swept his strong arm against the shooter's legs and buckled them.

The shot went wild, and before he could fire another both O'Tooles were on top of him.

Killian hit the guard hard one time before he could rein in all his anger, and then he helped Stitch pull the man up and search him for other weapons.

"Are you hit?" he asked Shawn.

"No, but I felt the bullet fly by and part my hair."

When Killian turned and saw Victoria's frightened eyes, he calmed. Leaving the man to Stitch, he ran to her and knelt beside her seat. "Are you all right, Victoria?"

She shook her head. "My hands are tied to the seat," she whispered. "They were afraid I'd warn you." He slipped his hands down to hers and freed the rope. "I knew you'd come for me."

"I would have come for you even if I'd had to go all the way to South America. I'd never stop looking for you. You're a part of me."

Killian tossed the ropes to his brother. "How about we get out of here?"

She smiled. "I'd like that."

She stood and hugged her favorite ghost, then took Killian's arm. As they walked off the train, Abe met them, his rifle on his shoulder.

"Good job, Killian."

"I didn't do much," Killian said, thinking that fear controlled most of his actions. Not fear of dying but fear of losing his family, Shawn and Victoria.

"You saved my life, little brother," Stitch said. "You're a real hero."

Killian wanted to argue, but he was too happy. He didn't care about being a hero, he just wanted them safe.

They walked down toward the depot as the marshal and his men herded the rest of the outlaws together. The men had given up without a fight.

Victoria gripped Killian's arm so hard she drew his full attention.

"What is it?" he asked as Stitch moved to the other side of her as if sensing he needed to protect her.

Abe voiced her fear before she could. "Myers is missing."

CHAPTER 46

Duncan drifted in and out of sleep. He'd been beaten up in fights worse, he decided, as if that were the bright side. Every time he got up the strength to open his one good eye, he saw Rose sleeping in the chair like some kind of guardian angel.

Maybe she was. She always had been. He could remember a time years ago when he heard everyone else talking around him, but he couldn't say a word. No one had ever taught him how. He didn't know how to act or what to do. He'd been five when Travis McMurray found him in a campsite tied to a rope like a dog. For weeks people tried to make him do things he didn't understand and all he could think about was running and hiding.

Everyone tried to tell him what to do, except Rose. She'd just walked up to him, taken him by the hand, and shown him how to act.

He grinned, then groaned in pain. She was still bossing him around half the time, but tonight when he was getting what little brains he had kicked out of him, all he could think about was that she might be hurt. No matter how many times he was hit, she was the one thing on his mind.

She was the one person he couldn't live without. Rose McMurray was simply the center of his world, like it or not, there was nothing he could do to change that fact and he knew he wouldn't want to even if he could.

He forced his one good eye open again and looked at her one more time before he fell asleep.

"My sweet Rose," he whispered.

The wind from an open window brushed across his cheek as he dozed off.

In what seemed like hours later, he awoke to the sound of someone talking. On instinct, he reached for his Colt that Rose had left an inch from his hand.

It was gone.

A dry laugh came from a few feet away. Duncan forced his eye open.

Myers stood behind Rose, his hand on her shoulder keeping her still in the chair. "Good evening, Ranger. I hope you slept well. I would have been here sooner, but I had a little trouble beating your location out of the wagon driver. Finally, he decided to cooperate."

Myers's voice was so calm it didn't seem to fit with what Duncan saw. He fought to clear his mind enough to think. With the broken ribs, he'd have little chance jumping forward to attack, though he might have tried it if Rose hadn't had a gun pointed at her head.

"You're a sound sleeper, Ranger McMurray. I got everything I need loaded in the wagon while I was waiting around to tell you good-bye. Even decided to take the two women you had in the parlor along with me. At least part of the way." He smiled. "You see, once Victoria told me what was in her bags, I understood her father's plan and I figured something out. I didn't need her or the major. All I needed was the money. I thought of killing my bothersome ex-bride, but it would be a waste of effort. Better to use her as a diversion at the station while I slip away from the others. Let her new husband have her. When I get to Galveston, I'll hire my own ship and make my own way. The major's spent so much time rattling on about his grand plan that I know every step."

"You can have the gold, Myers. Leave the women here."

Myers laughed. "They're not important to you, Ranger. They're only a runaway and a maid. Only this one matters to you." He tapped the barrel of his gun against the side of Rose's head. "I'm not taking them to hurt you. I'm taking them for my own entertainment. As long as they are useful, they'll stay alive. Once they are no longer needed, well, let's just say I've found it very interesting to watch a woman die. Most don't fight, they just cry or beg. I'm guessing the older one will beg and swear and give me hours of pleasure as she dies an inch at a time. The young one will cry. I don't like that as much so I'll probably kill her fast."

Duncan couldn't believe how Myers could have fooled so many people. His insides must be rotted to the core. "You won't get away with it."

Myers laughed. "I have for years. No one ever suspects a war hero. As a newspaperman, I move easily from town to town. No one connects the murders of a few worthless women with me. I don't even bother to bury them, I just leave the bodies in the alley."

Duncan stole a glance at Rose's face, fearing that Myers's words might be frightening her to death, but she only sat quietly as if waiting for the men to finish talking so she could serve tea.

Myers patted her shoulder. "Only I can't take this one with me, much as I'd like to." He laughed and moved the gun against her midnight hair. "I've even been telling her about the fun we might have, but this one belongs to you and you'd never stop looking for me if you thought I had her. So, you see, I have no other choice but to kill you both."

Duncan fought from using every bit of the energy he had left in his body to charge Myers. He might die trying, but in that moment Rose would have a chance to run. He'd give his life to give her that one chance.

"Be prepared to watch her die, Ranger. It's the least I

can do to you for causing me so much trouble. Who knows, you might find it fascinating to see how easily they die. Women are such frail creatures and they make such a show." Myers laughed suddenly. "Or, maybe I should shoot you first and let her screams be the last thing you hear."

Duncan closed his eyes trying to make his brain think of something, anything, fast.

"Kill me first," Rose said simply, her words echoing around the silent room.

When Myers didn't move, she demanded, "Kill me first, I said. I can't bear to see him die. It would be too painful."

Duncan wanted to stop her words. How could she tell a man who loved watching women in pain that the worst thing in the world for her would be to see him die? Myers would probably kill him and make Rose watch him bleed out.

He opened his eyes just as she wiggled in the chair, turning toward the gun. "Kill me first. I demand it."

Myers grinned as if suddenly having fun. "You don't demand anything. It's not your choice. You have nothing to say."

He raised the gun from her head to point it toward Duncan. He took his hand off her shoulder and dug his fingers into her hair. "I don't want you to miss this. So watch close."

A gun fired and Duncan drew in a quick breath, waiting for the pain to hit him.

Nothing.

He forced his eyes open, fearing what he would see. Rose, the center of his world, dead. The pain was far greater than any bullet could have ever caused.

Only Rose wasn't dead. She was standing up from her chair as gracefully as ever. He saw the blood on her face and across her hand that closed around a small gun.

For a moment Myers seemed to have disappeared, but then Duncan spotted him lying against the wall with what looked like a bullet hole just beneath his chin.

"You killed him?" Duncan was having a hard time believing what he was seeing.

Rose stepped to the washbasin and began scrubbing

away the blood. "I know. I had to. I thought he would never turn loose of my shoulder so I could reach the gun Uncle Travis insisted I carry in my pocket. It's been bothersome this past week, but every morning I did what he told me. Even though I had the gun belt, I kept the other. It wouldn't be polite not to have listened to my uncle's advice."

Her words were conversational, but Duncan noticed she was washing her hands over and over and over. Slowly, he forced himself to move out of bed. In a few steps he was behind her, touching her with his good arm. "It's all right, Rose. You did what you had to do."

She turned into him and finally stopped talking.

Someone must have heard the shot. There were shouts and men running and then Stitch came flying through the door. He rolled across the floor, then jumped to his feet, his fists balled and ready for a fight.

"Evening, Stitch," Duncan said, without loosening his grip on Rose.

The big man relaxed slowly as he looked around.

Duncan knew what he was looking for. "She's in the wagon all tied up. My guess is she's going to be mighty glad to see you."

Stitch nodded once and stepped over the door.

Duncan let Rose help him back to bed as men flooded the house. Stitch let out a yell when he found Hallie and Epley out in the wagon. Everyone was shouting and crying and laughing. When Victoria came in the room, she hugged everyone, even the deputies.

Rose, on the other hand, remained calm. She told her story exactly as it had happened. How she planned out what she'd say and just how she'd wanted to sound. How she'd waited for her chance and then pulled the trigger knowing the bullet would travel up into Myers's brain.

The deputies removed the body and took all of Victoria's bags into custody. She made each man promise to bring her clothes back after they'd taken out the gold.

Finally all settled down. Since no one wanted to sleep in the loft above, Killian suggested they move to the hotel for the night now that it was safe. Hallie said she would stay and help Rose with Duncan, but she had a feeling Rose could take care of him all by herself.

Epley didn't say a word, she just walked out with Hallie. Rose might have saved her in Yancy's bar, but Hallie had become her mother.

When all were gone, Rose made Duncan a cup of tea, which he tried his best to drink. "We're here alone, darlin', and I can't even kiss you," he complained.

"It's all right. I'll just sleep with you. If you don't mind, I'm exhausted."

As he had before, he watched her undress down to her petticoats and camisole before crawling into bed with him.

For once she didn't want to talk. She just curled up beside him.

After a while he heard her crying softly. He rolled over and put his good arm around her, but he didn't tell her to stop. Other women might have been hysterical if they'd gone through what she went through, but not Rose.

He gently kissed the top of her head. "You know, Rose, if you ever let yourself go, you're going to be one wild woman."

"You think so?"

"I'm hoping so, and when you do, I hope I'm around."

CHAPTER 47

Sunday morning
Anderson Glen

THE NEXT MORNING ABE FOUND STITCH DOWN IN THE dining room of the small hotel, eating two breakfasts at the same time.

"Mind if I join you?"

"Wish you would. I managed to keep my hat on and my head down until I started eating. The waitress almost tossed my food at me and ran when she got her first good look. Maybe you can get her to come back and bring my coffee."

Abe waved at a girl hiding behind the swing door that probably led to the kitchen. "Coffee," he called. "For two." After a few minutes, she brought it out, but she didn't look at Stitch.

Before the coffee had cooled enough to drink, Killian and Victoria joined them. Victoria leaned down and kissed Stitch's cheek as she passed him.

Abe didn't miss the squeal of fright coming from the kitchen. Suddenly the scarred man became very interesting. Each time the waitress came out she braved getting a little closer to him.

Everyone at the table tried not to notice the waitress who kept circling. They no longer saw the scars on Stitch's face. He was simply their family and friend. Killian took Victoria's hand as he looked at his brother and Abe. "We think we're going to head back today once we give our statements to the town marshal and collect Victoria's things."

"I was thinking that too." Abe smiled. "I've been worried about the store. No telling what Henry has given away while I've been gone. What about you, Stitch? Going home or after your wagon?"

The big man shrugged. Before he could explain, Hallie and Epley came into the dining room and another table was pulled up. Everyone ordered and settled into an easy way of talking only good friends can manage.

The marshal dropped by and asked each of them to stay another day until all was settled. The Tanner brothers had already been picked up by the rangers and were on their way back to Dallas. They both claimed Myers was the brains behind all the robberies. Jeb Tanner sent Duncan a personal message that said he'd kill him if he ever got out, but the threat wasn't taken too seriously from a man in chains.

Abe excused himself and dropped by to see Duncan at what everyone called the McMurray little house.

Abe was relieved to find him improved enough to be complaining. Rose had arranged for one of the McMurray wagons to take him back to the ranch, but Duncan didn't want to leave town until every one of the outlaws had been put away.

When Abe walked in the kitchen to get Duncan a cup of coffee, the ranger yelled, "Where's your cane?"

Abe looked down, realizing he'd forgotten it. In fact, all morning he hadn't thought about his leg at all. He'd never pushed himself as he had the past few days, and to his surprise his leg seemed stronger.

"Where'd you leave it?" Duncan asked as he nodded a thank-you for the coffee.

"I'm not sure. I think on the pile of lumber behind the train. I was so worried about Killian and Stitch being hurt, I didn't even think about it."

"You could have fallen."

Abe grinned. "Yeah and I probably will. I guess if I do, I'll just have to get up. It's not the end of the world."

"I don't know, when you're looking at the world through one bloodshot eyeball, it looks pretty near the end." He smiled, then swore at the pain. "I think I'll go home and recover."

"Good," Rose said as she walked in to join the men. "I'll make the arrangements, but I'm afraid I won't be going with you. Victoria has asked me to go back to Fort Worth to help set up her new place and I think it will be great fun."

Abe grinned. The pretty little lady had just added a new level of misery to Duncan's life.

CHAPTER 48

Sunday
Anderson Glen Hotel

STITCH WAITED FOR HALLIE TO COME ONTO THE PORCH of the hotel. He hadn't been able to speak to her alone since all the trouble started.

She walked out and sat in one of the rockers as if she didn't notice him standing there.

"When you heading home?" he asked.

"Epley and I thought we'd go when Killian and Victoria do. I've got my work cut out for me helping them."

"That's the truth," Stitch said, taking one step toward her.

"When you going back?"

He didn't look at her. "Whenever you are."

Hallie laughed. "You think since I let you touch my chest and I kissed you once that I'll just let you follow me home?"

Stitch frowned. "Something like that."

Hallie stood up. "And what would I do with a man like you once I got you home and housebroke?"

"Keep me." Stitch smiled.

Hallie moved up close and locked her arms around him. "I might just do that." Then, in bright daylight, she kissed him. When she finally pulled away, her cheeks were red and her breath quick. "You do have a way with words, Shawn O'Toole."

"I'll not settle for a sample, Hallie."

"I always figured you wouldn't."

"So, we go home together?"

"Together."

CHAPTER 49

Wednesday evening
Second Street, Fort Worth

A FEW DAYS AFTER THE TROUBLE AT ANDERSON GLEN, at exactly six o'clock, Abe Henderson walked across the street to the schoolhouse and informed Miss Norman that in one hour they had a dinner engagement.

She stood and nodded, showing none of the surprise at seeing him reappear in her life that he'd expected.

"Would you like me to pick you up here or at the boardinghouse?"

"Here," she said. "I have papers to finish, Mr. Henderson."

He returned one hour later and waited while she collected her things.

She was wearing her Sunday dress and the shawl she wrapped around her looked new. Abe knew without asking that she'd been waiting for him to return. Henry had told him that she'd stopped by the store twice a day, but never asked a direct question about his return.

They walked to the café at the Grand and he told her all that had happened while he'd been gone. She listened, then told him of how she checked on the store and Henry had been very helpful.

He took her arm on their way home.

"Mr. Henderson, it seems your leg is better," she said as they walked.

"I'll always limp." He turned toward his store and not the boardinghouse. "But I no longer consider myself a cripple."

She smiled that tight little smile of hers. "Mr. Henderson, you were never a cripple. You were only a man with a limp." She waited as he unlocked the store door and held it for her.

She walked past him and all the way back to the storeroom.

"I'll leave you to get ready, Sara." He'd said her name slowly as if it were a caress.

She moved into the little study while he stood just outside the open doorway and watched her take off her coat and pull the pins from her hair. He watched her in the mirror as she unbuttoned her dress, just the exact number of buttons he'd told her he liked unbuttoned.

When she turned, she smiled. "I missed you," she whispered.

"I missed you."

He moved close and circled her in his arms. "I've been thinking that we could save money if you moved upstairs. You wouldn't have as far to walk to school and there is plenty of storage up there that we could turn into more space."

She stiffened.

"No, Sara, don't say a word. I've made up my mind. I want you with me. We can be married Sunday." He moved his hands over her body. "I plan to have you in my bed until the day one of us dies. If you want a house, I can afford one, but I'm thinking the apartment will serve us well until the children begin to come."

She pulled away. "I'll hear the words, Abraham."

He was tugging the lace off her beautiful breast. "What words?"

"The words you said to me when you left."

He had trouble thinking much less remembering, but finally he managed, "I love you, Sara."

She smiled. "I'll hear them every day we're married."

She met his gaze, standing firm on her demand.

"All right. I promise."

"And, we'll still close at lunch just like you do now. Some days we'll come in here and do what we like.

He moved his fingers lightly over the rise of her breasts. "I'll agree to that.

"And you'll ask me to marry you, not tell me."

"I thought I was asking . . ."

She shook her head.

"All right, Miss Norman, will you marry me?"

"Yes," she said, and neither felt the need to say another word.

CHAPTER 50

Main Street

Duncan hadn't seen Rose for almost a week and he'd been in a bad mood since the morning he'd watched her step on the train.

He was still hurting, but he had to go to Fort Worth and tell her it was about time she came home.

When he got to the Grand, she wasn't in her room. He searched the café and the dining room, then walked across to Second Avenue and checked with Abe. No one had seen her all morning.

Crossing back to the garden of the hotel, he let himself in the balcony door of her bedroom. Exhausted, he spread out on the bed and fell asleep. He might be healing, but he wasn't running at full speed yet.

An hour later when he woke, he felt her at his side. Without saying a word, he rolled over and kissed her.

She melted into his arms and gave him back a kiss better than he'd dreamed about. A deep ever-after kind of kiss he'd longed for.

When he finally pulled away, he brushed her beautiful

hair back and said, "You're my home, Rose. You're where I belong."

"And you, Duncan, are my one love. You always have been. It just took us both a while to realize it."

He kissed her again with a passion that shocked him. His wild Texas Rose was in his arms and he never planned to let her go.

When she finally pulled away, he whispered, "Where have you been all my life?"

She laughed. "I've been right here waiting for you."

Read on for a special preview of the next
novel in Jodi Thomas's heartwarming
HARMONY series

CHANCE OF A LIFETIME

CHAPTER 1

February 3, 2012
Harmony Public Library

HUNDRED-YEAR-OLD ELMS CAST SPIDERWEB SHADOWS from a dry creek bed to the brick corners of Harmony Public Library as Emily Tomlinson closed the blind over the back window of her office. Night was coming. Time for her to move to the front desk. Grabbing the black sweater that always hung on a hook beside her desk, she pulled it over her plain cotton blouse and charcoal trousers.

From now until closing, she'd feel wind blow in every time the library doors opened. Before she could settle, winter's frosty breath reached her. Emily didn't look up. Though she wondered who might be coming in just before closing, she didn't want to see the night beyond the doors. She might be in her early thirties, but the child in her still feared that the night just might look back.

Sam Perkins leaned on his broom and whispered, "You didn't make it out before dark, Miss Tomlinson. You want me to walk you to your car when you lock up? Ain't no other staff here on Friday night, and that wind is liable to carry a slim little thing like you away."

The janitor's voice sounded rusty in daylight, but at night it turned haunting. Sam Perkins missed his calling as a narrator for ghost tales on a midnight radio show.

Emily didn't like the possibility that everyone who worked at the Harmony Public Library knew of her fears, even the janitor. "No, I'll be fine. Who just came in? I was too busy to notice."

Sam shrugged. "Some guy in muddy boots and a cowboy hat worn low."

Emily laughed. "That describes half the men in this town."

The janitor moved on, having used up his ration of conversation for the evening. He wasn't friendly, smelled of cigarettes most of the time, and had never read a single book as far as she knew, but he was the best janitor they'd had in the ten years since she'd accepted the post of head librarian. The others had been drifters or drunks, staying only long enough to collect wages to move on, but Sam never missed a day's work.

Emily closed her log and locked the cash drawer for the night. She had a pretty good idea who the cowboy with dirty boots was, as he'd come in on Fridays for as long as she could remember. Most of the time he didn't say a word to anyone, but she knew he was there.

Walking around the worn mahogany desk, she crossed to the beautiful old curved staircase that climbed the north wall. Cradled beneath the arch of the stairs were all the new magazines and day-old newspapers from big towns across the state.

Emily had bought comfortable leather chairs from an estate sale so the area looked inviting, even though few visited. Most days, the wall of computers drew all the attention.

Sure enough, Tannon Parker was there. His big frame filled the chair, and his long legs blocked half the walk space. His worn, gray Stetson was pushed back atop black hair in need of cutting.

"Evening, Tannon," Emily said with a grin. "How's your mother?"

"About the same," he said as he looked up slowly. "She didn't know me. She called me by my dad's name tonight."

For a second, he reminded her of a little boy and not the man before her.

Emily wished they'd been close enough for her to brush his shoulder in comfort. He might be a tall, powerful man in his prime, but he seemed to carry the weight of the world tonight.

Only she couldn't touch him. They weren't friends anymore. She'd known him all her life, could name every member of his family, but one lie, one night, had passed between them years ago, and neither knew how to build a bridge over it.

"I'm sorry," Emily managed to whisper, "about your mom. I'll never forget those great cookies she used to make." A memory from fifteen years past drifted back. She and Tannon had both been seniors on the high school newspaper staff. The night before the paper came out everyone always worked late. Mrs. Parker would tap on the school window and hold up a tray of cookies. Kids knocked each other down to open the door for her.

"Yeah." Tannon lifted his paper as if he didn't know what else to say.

Or maybe he was remembering another memory neither would ever forget. A memory that had more to do with pain and blood than cookies.

She straightened, feeling a little like she'd been dismissed. "We'll be closing in twenty minutes. I'll let you know when I have to lock up."

He didn't answer as she moved away and began collecting books left scattered on tables. When she climbed the stairs to where walls in a once-huge, old home had been removed to allow for long aisles of books, she saw a shadow leaning against the corner window.

"Franky, you still here?"

A girl's giggle reached her before a boy of about fifteen

stepped out tugging his partner-in-crime by the hand. "Is my dad here for me?" she asked.

Emily noticed the girl had pink lipstick smeared across her mouth, but she didn't seem to care. She just stared at Franky like he was a rock star.

"If you two want to check out anything, you might hurry."

"Yes, ma'am." Franky winked at the girl. "We've already checked out."

The girl giggled and ran down the stairs, joining her friends who were clustered around one of the computers. When she was too far away to hear, Emily whispered to Franky, "How long until you get a car?"

"Fourteen more months," he said with a grin. "I can't wait."

"Me neither." She laughed. "Did you get your homework done?"

"It's Friday, Miss Tomlinson. No one would ever do homework on Friday. What if the end of the world came or something and you'd wasted your last few hours doing math or English. Monday morning I could be out fighting zombies or aliens for the last food on the planet and I'd be thinking, great! at least I got my homework done."

Emily saw his logic. "I hadn't considered that," she said as she walked with him down the stairs.

"Don't people like you worry about that kind of stuff?"

"People like me?"

"You know, older people." Franky shook his shaggy hair. "You should. Tomorrow you could just open your front door and find yourself in a fight for your life." He looked around. "Come to think of it, nobody would probably come in here. No food, or weapons, or medicine. That's what we'll all be fighting over when the end comes."

She played along. To the boy she must have seemed as old as this building. "Zombies don't read?"

He shook his head as if she were beyond dumb. "Miss Tomlinson, I fear you're a goner. Zombies don't do nothing but run around looking for live people to eat. They'll rip your arm off, beat you to death, and then have you for dinner. Maybe you should think about getting a gun or a man to protect you."

When they reached the desk, she handed him a book on the life and works of Hemingway. "Thanks for the advice, Franky. Here's a book that might help with that English assignment that's due Monday. Just in case the world doesn't end."

He looked at her with raised eyebrows. "How'd you know about that?"

Emily winked. "A zombie told me."

Before he could ask more, a horn honked and he darted for the door. "Thanks," he yelled back. "That's my dad."

The girls over by the computer wall all giggled and waved at him. Then, like a gaggle of geese, they all hurried out.

The library was suddenly silent. Emily began turning off the computers and closing doors. It had been a long twelve-hour day, but she had nowhere else to be. Friday nights were like every night for her. She'd go home, eat supper, and read.

As she tugged on her coat and reached for her keys, she noticed Tannon waiting.

He held the door as always for her, and she thanked him as he checked to make sure the lock clicked solid. She thought of walking on to her car, but waited. He might not be much for company, but Tannon was steady and safe. Whatever waited in the darkness wouldn't appear if he walked beside her.

For once, he broke the silence. "The zombies wouldn't come after you if the end came like the kid said."

"You heard."

"I couldn't help it. You two were standing right above me. But you'd be safe if they were looking for people to eat. They'd go straight to the bakery across the street. The Edison sisters would keep them in food for weeks. Last month, I heard they had to move the counter out a foot because the sisters could no longer get behind it to wait on customers."

Emily laughed. "That's not a nice thing to say."

"Just stating a fact. By the time the zombies finished with the third sister, they'd all be diabetic."

"Then they'd cross the street to the library and eat me. Maybe I should buy a gun to fight them off. I'm not sure I'd want them in the library even if they were just looking for a snack. I've heard they often have limbs fall off as they walk."

"I'd come get you long before then if there was trouble."

She glanced up at him, almost firing back that once there had been trouble and he hadn't come, only the memory of that night fifteen years ago was too painful to speak of. With a quick nervous move, she pulled her car door open and jumped in. The thank-you was lost in the slam of her door.

A few seconds later, she looked back at him in her rear-view mirror. He was standing in the empty parking lot. He looked solid as an oak with his feet wide apart and his hands shoved deep into his Western-cut leather jacket. The stoplight caught her at the corner. She watched him as he turned and walked across the street to where he'd parked his pickup in front of the bakery.

It was Friday night and Tannon Parker was headed the same place she was.

Home alone.

CHAPTER 2

A FEW BLOCKS AWAY FROM THE HARMONY LIBRARY, Beau Yates finished the last song in his first set at Buffalo's Bar and Grill. He ended with an old Gordon Lightfoot song from the seventies called "Sundown."

Beau didn't know why he loved the song. Some of it didn't even make sense to him, but it had a special kind of magic that made folks who heard it stop and sing along. When he finished the final chord, the crowd went wild with applause.

"You did it again." His partner, Border Biggs, laughed. "I swear, man, you're getting better and better and all these drunks know it."

Beau shook his head. He couldn't see the gift everyone kept telling him he had. He just followed where the music took him. He knew he was good and liked to perform, but in truth, he played more for himself than the people beyond the caged stage.

Six months ago, when his dad heard that he was playing at a bar, the old man waited in the parking lot one night and preached at full volume about how his only son was wasting his life and shaming his upbringing. At one point he even thanked the Lord for taking Beau's mother so early so she wouldn't feel the humiliation.

Beau might have cared if he remembered his mother. He wasn't even sure she was dead; his dad had a way of stating wishes as if they were facts. But he just stood there as he had all his life and listened to the preaching as if his old man were a carnival barker pulling souls in for the next show.

Border Biggs, true friend that he was, had stood beside Beau until his old man had gotten tired and driven off. Then, as if they'd just been delayed a minute, Border had said, "How about one of them steaks at the truck stop? I've been hungry for so long my stomach is starting to gnaw on my ribs. Now that my brother is spending all his time over at his girlfriend's house we may starve to death."

"Maybe Big thinks we should feed ourselves. Maybe even buy the food. After all, we're old enough to vote and almost old enough to drink."

Border shook his shaved head. "I was afraid something like this would happen if he ever found a female who smiled at him. I knew it wasn't likely, but I guess I'd better get used to the idea. Last time he came home all he brought was a gallon of milk and Fruit Loops. I hate Fruit Loops. If you ask me, only clowns should eat them things."

Beau yelled over his shoulder as he led Border to the car. "I love Fruit Loops. It's like a Hawaiian vacation for your mouth."

"You must have loved them. You ate them while you watched me starve."

"All right, I'll buy the steaks." They stored the equipment. "Only you got to look at the bright side of your brother finding a woman. If Big could find one, maybe you got a chance."

Border nodded. "I'm thinking of getting my next tattoo to say, *I've had my shots. Take me home.*"

Beau saw his partner's arms clearly in the parking lot light. A full sleeve of tats covered them from wrist to shoulder. "You know, Border, I don't understand it. I think you're downright beautiful."

"I know it," Border agreed. "I'm surprised someone doesn't try to shoot me, skin me, and frame me on a wall."

A car backfired half a block away, and both boys hit the dirt, then laughed. Neither had much in the way of family but they had each other.

They'd driven over to the highway and ordered steaks to celebrate the raise they'd gotten last week. Neither mentioned Beau's father's screaming. Maybe Border thought the lecture was nothing compared to how his stepdad used to beat him and his big brother. Maybe he thought Preacher Yates was simply warming up for the next sermon. Either way, Beau was glad he'd had Border beside him that night just as he was glad his partner was behind him tonight and every night.

Harley, the bar's owner, tapped on the cage door with the corner of the tray he carried.

"Food." Border set down his bass guitar. As he opened the door to what Harley called the stage, he asked, "Any chance we could get a beer to go with our burgers, Harley? I think it might improve my playing."

"It probably would, Border, but it ain't happening." The owner swore. "You boys are lucky the sheriff lets you play in this place. I swear if she caught me giving you beer we'd be locked up until you both turn twenty-one."

Beau took his hamburger and leaned back in his chair as he watched the crowd. In the months they'd been playing here he didn't know Harley Moreland any better than he had when he'd walked in the bar and asked for a chance to play. Harley was a hard man interested mostly in the bottom line of his business. He was fair, but rarely offered a compliment. In fact, his vocabulary consisted mostly of swear words held together by a noun now and then.

Border was half finished with his burger before Beau got his unwrapped.

"You know," Border said as he chewed, "I think there

shouldn't be a drinking age. I think it should go by weight. Anyone over two hundred pounds can drink. You ask me, those skinny girls who drink half a beer and make fools of themselves do a lot more damage than I ever would."

"You got a point," Beau played along. "Then instead of carding people, there could just be a scale at the door. I'm guessing the women wouldn't mind that one bit."

A beer bottle hit the chicken wire of the cage, making Beau jump. "It's going to be a wild night, partner. Not even ten o'clock and the natives are already restless."

Border finished off his dinner. "I don't care, for two hundred dollars a night they can yell and fight all they like."

While Border tested the sound on his bass, Beau looked out at the people crammed into the bar. In the twinkling lights he usually just saw bodies, not faces, but tonight he tried to find anyone in the crowd he recognized.

He barely remembered the people he'd gone to high school with two years ago. The folks from the church where his daddy preached weren't likely to be in the bar. Ronny Logan, who lived next door to Border and his brother, had said she would come in if she could. She was ten years older than him, but Beau called the shy woman a friend. All she did was study and cook, but now, between semesters, she needed to have a little fun.

"You see Ronny?" he asked Border.

"No, she's not coming. She was just being nice by saying she might. Why should she come? She hears us practicing every day."

Beau continued to look. "I'm making a New Year's resolution."

"You're a month late," Border reminded him.

"I don't care. This year I'm going to find a girlfriend. A real one."

"Yeah, I'm getting a little tired of the imaginary one I got too."

Beau glanced at him, trying to figure out what Border was talking about. As usual, he gave up. "I mean a girl who likes me. The women who come in here are all older than us and have been around the dance floor too many times. I want someone my age. Someone smart that I can talk to. Someone pretty without being all made up."

"Well you shouldn't have much problem with the age or finding someone smarter. Only trouble I see you having is talking to her long enough to ask her out. Every time a pretty girl comes within ten feet of this cage you start stuttering."

"I plan to work on that. I think I would be all right if we could just start at the third or fourth date. It's the first one or two that make me nervous."

"How about I put a sack over each of your heads? Then you won't know she's pretty and she won't know she's on a date." Another beer bottle hit the cage. "Third time I put you two together, I'll take the sacks off, and bingo, you're on your third date."

"It's time to go to work," Beau said as he began playing a fast piece that he knew Border would eventually remember and join in on. Under his breath he said to himself, "I'm going to get out there and live so I'll have something to sing about."

Couples moved to the dance floor. It was time for the boot-scooting to begin.